the perfect

murder

(a jessie hunt psychological suspense—book 21)

blake pierce

Blake Pierce

Blake Pierce is the USA Today bestselling author of the RILEY PAGE mystery series, which includes seventeen books. Blake Pierce is also the author of the MACKENZIE WHITE mystery series, comprising fourteen books; of the AVERY BLACK mystery series, comprising six books; of the KERI LOCKE mystery series, comprising five books; of the MAKING OF RILEY PAIGE mystery series, comprising six books; of the KATE WISE mystery series, comprising seven books; of the CHLOE FINE psychological suspense mystery, comprising six books; of the JESSE HUNT psychological suspense thriller series, comprising twenty four books; of the AU PAIR psychological suspense thriller series, comprising three books; of the ZOE PRIME mystery series, comprising six books; of the ADELE SHARP mystery series, comprising fifteen books, of the EUROPEAN VOYAGE cozy mystery series, comprising four books; of the new LAURA FROST FBI suspense thriller, comprising nine books (and counting); of the new ELLA DARK FBI suspense thriller, comprising eleven books (and counting); of the A YEAR IN EUROPE cozy mystery series, comprising nine books, of the AVA GOLD mystery series, comprising six books (and counting); of the RACHEL GIFT mystery series, comprising six books (and counting); of the VALERIE LAW mystery series, comprising nine books (and counting); of the PAIGE KING mystery series, comprising six books (and counting); and of the MAY MOORE suspense thriller series, comprising six books (and counting).

An avid reader and lifelong fan of the mystery and thriller genres, Blake loves to hear from you, so please feel free to visit www.blakepierceauthor.com to learn more and stay in touch.

BOOKS BY BLAKE PIERCE

MAY MOORE SUSPENSE THRILLER
NEVER RUN (Book #1)
NEVER TELL (Book #2)
NEVER LIVE (Book #3)
NEVER HIDE (Book #4)
NEVER FORGIVE (Book #5)
NEVER AGAIN (Book #6)

PAIGE KING MYSTERY SERIES
THE GIRL HE PINED (Book #1)
THE GIRL HE CHOSE (Book #2)
THE GIRL HE TOOK (Book #3)
THE GIRL HE WISHED (Book #4)
THE GIRL HE CROWNED (Book #5)
THE GIRL HE WATCHED (Book #6)

VALERIE LAW MYSTERY SERIES
NO MERCY (Book #1)
NO PITY (Book #2)
NO FEAR (Book #3
NO SLEEP (Book #4)
NO QUARTER (Book #5)
NO CHANCE (Book #6)
NO REFUGE (Book #7)
NO GRACE (Book #8)
NO ESCAPE (Book #9)

RACHEL GIFT MYSTERY SERIES
HER LAST WISH (Book #1)
HER LAST CHANCE (Book #2)
HER LAST HOPE (Book #3)
HER LAST FEAR (Book #4)
HER LAST CHOICE (Book #5)
HER LAST BREATH (Book #6)

AVA GOLD MYSTERY SERIES

CITY OF PREY (Book #1)
CITY OF FEAR (Book #2)
CITY OF BONES (Book #3)
CITY OF GHOSTS (Book #4)
CITY OF DEATH (Book #5)
CITY OF VICE (Book #6)

A YEAR IN EUROPE
A MURDER IN PARIS (Book #1)
DEATH IN FLORENCE (Book #2)
VENGEANCE IN VIENNA (Book #3)
A FATALITY IN SPAIN (Book #4)

ELLA DARK FBI SUSPENSE THRILLER
GIRL, ALONE (Book #1)
GIRL, TAKEN (Book #2)
GIRL, HUNTED (Book #3)
GIRL, SILENCED (Book #4)
GIRL, VANISHED (Book 5)
GIRL ERASED (Book #6)
GIRL, FORSAKEN (Book #7)
GIRL, TRAPPED (Book #8)
GIRL, EXPENDABLE (Book #9)
GIRL, ESCAPED (Book #10)
GIRL, HIS (Book #11)

LAURA FROST FBI SUSPENSE THRILLER
ALREADY GONE (Book #1)
ALREADY SEEN (Book #2)
ALREADY TRAPPED (Book #3)
ALREADY MISSING (Book #4)
ALREADY DEAD (Book #5)
ALREADY TAKEN (Book #6)
ALREADY CHOSEN (Book #7)
ALREADY LOST (Book #8)
ALREADY HIS (Book #9)

EUROPEAN VOYAGE COZY MYSTERY SERIES
MURDER (AND BAKLAVA) (Book #1)
DEATH (AND APPLE STRUDEL) (Book #2)

CRIME (AND LAGER) (Book #3)
MISFORTUNE (AND GOUDA) (Book #4)
CALAMITY (AND A DANISH) (Book #5)
MAYHEM (AND HERRING) (Book #6)

ADELE SHARP MYSTERY SERIES
LEFT TO DIE (Book #1)
LEFT TO RUN (Book #2)
LEFT TO HIDE (Book #3)
LEFT TO KILL (Book #4)
LEFT TO MURDER (Book #5)
LEFT TO ENVY (Book #6)
LEFT TO LAPSE (Book #7)
LEFT TO VANISH (Book #8)
LEFT TO HUNT (Book #9)
LEFT TO FEAR (Book #10)
LEFT TO PREY (Book #11)
LEFT TO LURE (Book #12)
LEFT TO CRAVE (Book #13)
LEFT TO LOATHE (Book #14)
LEFT TO HARM (Book #15)

THE AU PAIR SERIES
ALMOST GONE (Book#1)
ALMOST LOST (Book #2)
ALMOST DEAD (Book #3)

ZOE PRIME MYSTERY SERIES
FACE OF DEATH (Book#1)
FACE OF MURDER (Book #2)
FACE OF FEAR (Book #3)
FACE OF MADNESS (Book #4)
FACE OF FURY (Book #5)
FACE OF DARKNESS (Book #6)

A JESSIE HUNT PSYCHOLOGICAL SUSPENSE SERIES
THE PERFECT WIFE (Book #1)
THE PERFECT BLOCK (Book #2)
THE PERFECT HOUSE (Book #3)
THE PERFECT SMILE (Book #4)

THE PERFECT LIE (Book #5)
THE PERFECT LOOK (Book #6)
THE PERFECT AFFAIR (Book #7)
THE PERFECT ALIBI (Book #8)
THE PERFECT NEIGHBOR (Book #9)
THE PERFECT DISGUISE (Book #10)
THE PERFECT SECRET (Book #11)
THE PERFECT FAÇADE (Book #12)
THE PERFECT IMPRESSION (Book #13)
THE PERFECT DECEIT (Book #14)
THE PERFECT MISTRESS (Book #15)
THE PERFECT IMAGE (Book #16)
THE PERFECT VEIL (Book #17)
THE PERFECT INDISCRETION (Book #18)
THE PERFECT RUMOR (Book #19)
THE PERFECT COUPLE (Book #20)
THE PERFECT MURDER (Book #21)
THE PERFECT HUSBAND (Book #22)
THE PERFECT SCANDAL (Book #23)
THE PERFECT MASK (Book #24)

CHLOE FINE PSYCHOLOGICAL SUSPENSE SERIES
NEXT DOOR (Book #1)
A NEIGHBOR'S LIE (Book #2)
CUL DE SAC (Book #3)
SILENT NEIGHBOR (Book #4)
HOMECOMING (Book #5)
TINTED WINDOWS (Book #6)

KATE WISE MYSTERY SERIES
IF SHE KNEW (Book #1)
IF SHE SAW (Book #2)
IF SHE RAN (Book #3)
IF SHE HID (Book #4)
IF SHE FLED (Book #5)
IF SHE FEARED (Book #6)
IF SHE HEARD (Book #7)

THE MAKING OF RILEY PAIGE SERIES

WATCHING (Book #1)
WAITING (Book #2)
LURING (Book #3)
TAKING (Book #4)
STALKING (Book #5)
KILLING (Book #6)

RILEY PAIGE MYSTERY SERIES
ONCE GONE (Book #1)
ONCE TAKEN (Book #2)
ONCE CRAVED (Book #3)
ONCE LURED (Book #4)
ONCE HUNTED (Book #5)
ONCE PINED (Book #6)
ONCE FORSAKEN (Book #7)
ONCE COLD (Book #8)
ONCE STALKED (Book #9)
ONCE LOST (Book #10)
ONCE BURIED (Book #11)
ONCE BOUND (Book #12)
ONCE TRAPPED (Book #13)
ONCE DORMANT (Book #14)
ONCE SHUNNED (Book #15)
ONCE MISSED (Book #16)
ONCE CHOSEN (Book #17)

MACKENZIE WHITE MYSTERY SERIES
BEFORE HE KILLS (Book #1)
BEFORE HE SEES (Book #2)
BEFORE HE COVETS (Book #3)
BEFORE HE TAKES (Book #4)
BEFORE HE NEEDS (Book #5)
BEFORE HE FEELS (Book #6)
BEFORE HE SINS (Book #7)
BEFORE HE HUNTS (Book #8)
BEFORE HE PREYS (Book #9)
BEFORE HE LONGS (Book #10)
BEFORE HE LAPSES (Book #11)
BEFORE HE ENVIES (Book #12)
BEFORE HE STALKS (Book #13)

BEFORE HE HARMS (Book #14)

AVERY BLACK MYSTERY SERIES
CAUSE TO KILL (Book #1)
CAUSE TO RUN (Book #2)
CAUSE TO HIDE (Book #3)
CAUSE TO FEAR (Book #4)
CAUSE TO SAVE (Book #5)
CAUSE TO DREAD (Book #6)

KERI LOCKE MYSTERY SERIES
A TRACE OF DEATH (Book #1)
A TRACE OF MURDER (Book #2)
A TRACE OF VICE (Book #3)
A TRACE OF CRIME (Book #4)
A TRACE OF HOPE (Book #5)

PROLOGUE

Phoebe walked down the long hallway, listening to the sound of her shoes echoing on the linoleum floor. It was a little unsettling.

She wasn't used to being in Haines Hall at this hour. Professor Tobias's class was in the afternoon and until today, she'd never had cause to come here mid-morning. It was 10:30 and most of the doors to the classrooms and lecture halls in the building were shut, as they were in the middle of class.

She took the stairs to Professor Roman Tobias's third floor office, trying to keep her nerves at bay. She'd never had a one-on-one meeting with the man that *USA Today* had recently dubbed "America's Foremost Celebrity Academic," a title that normal people might find silly. But for an American history major like herself, personally interacting with Professor Tobias was like an unheralded college football player getting to meet with Tom Brady.

The walls of the first and second floors were covered with posters and flyers announcing upcoming UCLA events. But the third floor, where several professors' offices were, was much more subdued. If not for the professor names, room numbers, and departments displayed, it might be mistaken for a standard private sector hallway.

Tobias's office was at the end of the hall and she picked up the pace, realizing that she was now a minute late for their meeting. Phoebe hadn't seen a single person since she entered Haines Hall and she glanced back down the long hallway to make sure she was still alone. With the slick, dusty floor, shoes didn't squeak much. Someone might be walking right behind her and she'd never hear them. But she saw no one.

When she reached Tobias's corner office door, she allowed herself a moment to catch her breath. Then, when she felt ready, she knocked. The door hadn't been fully shut and the force of her hand opened it slightly.

"Professor Tobias," she called out hesitantly. "It's Phoebe Lewis. I'm here for our 10:30 appointment. I'm sorry I'm a little late."

There was no reply. She debated what to do next. Should she just go in? What if he had ear buds in and hadn't heard her? What if he'd gone to the restroom?

After several seconds of indecision, she got annoyed with herself and knocked again, this time much louder. The door opened halfway.

"Professor?"

The lights were out in the room and she suddenly had the terrible feeling that she had gotten the day of their meeting wrong. She pulled out her phone and double-checked. No—the appointment was for Thursday, March 17th at 10:30 a.m. He had insisted on the date and time.

She remembered being glad that he'd picked today and not tomorrow. She planned to do some St. Patrick's Day partying tonight and didn't want to be hungover for a meeting with the most famous professor on campus.

She heard a sound at the other end of the hall and turned around quickly but saw no one. Someone had probably just closed an office door, but she was getting seriously creeped out. Even though it felt impertinent, she stepped inside Professor Tobias's office and closed the door.

She turned around and, from this new angle, she saw that the professor was laying on the sofa near the bay windows at the back of the large office. His back was to her and she couldn't see his face, hidden by his longish black hair.

He must be taking a nap.

She coughed loudly to announce her presence but he didn't stir. As she looked at him more closely, she thought it odd that he would go to sleep while wearing both his sports coat and loafers. Then she noticed what looked like still-wet coffee stains on the carpet, leading all the way from the sofa to right in front of his desk. For some reason she couldn't quite explain—some odd sense that something was off—she turned on the lights.

In the now bright office, she saw that the stains were too thick and red to be coffee. They looked more like blood. She rushed over to Tobias.

"Professor?" she said urgently. "Are you okay, sir?"

He didn't respond. Phoebe wasn't sure if she was overreacting, but in that moment she decided it was better to risk being yelled at for waking up a groggy professor than to just leave his office when the situation seemed so wrong.

She tapped him on the shoulder. When he didn't move, she delicately rolled him over onto his back. At first she was too stunned to scream. His forehead had a cavernous indentation in it, like a watermelon that had been smashed in with a hammer. Blood was dripping down his face, pooling into his wide open eyes.

Only after she had fully accepted the horror of what she was seeing did she start to scream.

CHAPTER ONE

Jessie moved with impressive speed.

She was supposed to be somewhere at 10:45 and it was going to be a challenge to make it. For what was supposed to be a quiet end to the week, things had gotten hectic.

She still had to do a final review of her lesson plan for next week's seminar at UCLA. She and Ryan had agreed that they would prioritize nailing down a wedding date before the end of the week. She still hoped to check in with her sister, Hannah, at the rehab and recovery center where she was currently a resident. And to top it all off, she had to worry about what would happen at the parole hearing for Andy Robinson, the woman who tried to murder her less than two years ago. It was a lot.

She tried to prioritize. The lesson plan could wait a little longer. The truth was that since she was leaving UCLA at the end of the quarter, she could stall a little on seminar prep. They were just happy that they still had her around for a few more weeks.

Jessie had agreed to return to the LAPD's Homicide Special Section Unit full-time at the quarter's end. It had been a tough decision, but when Captain Decker offered her a big raise in addition to letting her remain a consulting criminal profiler rather than an employee, she found it hard to say no.

HSS was where the action was. It was a small, dedicated unit of the LAPD which investigated cases that had high profiles or intense media scrutiny, often involving multiple victims and serial killers. Her fiancé, Ryan Hernandez, was the lead detective for the unit. Jessie had determined that, at least for the time being, she could do more good solving cases in the field than training the next generation of investigators.

The wedding planning could also take a temporary backseat. After several communication hiccups along the way, she and Ryan had agreed to have a smaller wedding. It made sense considering that this was the second time around for both of them. The fact that Jessie's first wedding wasto a man she later learned was a sociopathic killer, made her all the more intent on ensuring that this

4

event was as different as possible. They just had to pick a date and location now.

Her sister's situation was more complicated. Until last year, Jessie hadn't even known that she had a half-sister. Both of them were the daughters of infamous serial killer Xander Thurman. Once he returned to town and killed Hannah's adoptive parents, Jessie had become her guardian.

That official designation would only last until next month, when Hannah would turn eighteen. But until then, Jessie was officially responsible for the girl, who not shockingly, was pretty damaged. It was only recently that Hannah had conceded that she could only really feel emotions in heightened situations and sought those out, even at risk to her own safety.

That revelation seemed tame when Hannah finally revealed an even bigger secret: that when she shot and killed a man who was intent on murdering her, Jessie, and Ryan, she'd felt a massive rush. Worse, she'd been longing to recapture that feeling ever since.

That was why, at the urging of Jessie and her therapist, Dr. Janice Lemmon, Hannah had reluctantly agreed to admit herself to the Seasons Wellness Center in Malibu, where Lemmon served both on the advisory board and as a visiting psychiatrist. The facility specialized in treating mood disorders, loss and grief issues, PTSD, suicidal ideation, and addictions that many other centers steered clear of, like hardcore cutting and life-threatening eating disorders. But they'd never knowingly had a patient like Hannah, who seemed addicted to the high that came from killing a person.

Of course, no one at Seasons other than Hannah and Dr. Lemmon was aware of the real reason for her admission. When she had sessions with other doctors, she was only to discuss her need to put herself at risk to feel emotion. She would discuss the "murder high" issue with Dr. Lemmon exclusively. The problem was that Dr. Lemmon had been laid up in the hospital all week after suffering a herniated disk, so Hannah wasn't getting the chance to make any progress on her more serious area of concern.

Add to that the fact that another patient at Seasons had apparently killed herself less than a week ago. Hannah seemed particularly fixated on the girl, even though she claimed not to have known her well. Whatever the truth was, now wasn't the ideal time for her primary therapist to be unavailable.

That was why Jessie planned to call Seasons to check in on her sister ASAP. But first she grabbed her handbag off the breakfast table and did a quick check in the mirror to make sure she didn't have any food in her hair or teeth. She thought she looked presentable, especially considering that she was fast approaching her thirty-first birthday.

Her brown, shoulder-length hair was food-free, as were her teeth. There were no shadows under her bright green eyes. As she stood straight, reaching her full five-foot-ten height, she thought she looked healthy and strong. That was partly a result of regaining her stamina and strength. Her athletic build felt sturdy, in part due to her five mile morning runs, as well as getting consecutive nights of decent sleep.

As she headed out the door to the garage of her mid-city home, she dialed the number for Seasons. She was just pulling out into the street when someone answered.

"Seasons in Malibu," a friendly female voice said. "How may I help?"

"Yes, hi, this is Jessie Hunt. I'm Hannah Dorsey's legal guardian. I'd like to speak with her please."

"Just a moment, ma'am," the voice said. After a brief pause, she resumed. "I'm sorry but Hannah is in a group session until the top of the hour. Unless it's an emergency, we don't like to interrupt. Can I relay a message?"

Jessie thought about it, but then decided not to leave one. She couldn't say anything of significance to the receptionist and keeping it vague would only stimulate Hannah's tendency to jump to conclusions.

"That's all right," she said. "I'll try again later."

"Yes, ma'am."

"One more question," Jessie added quickly. "Do you know if Dr. Lemmon will be back on site today?"

"I'm sorry, ma'am," the voice said unsurprisingly. "I'm not allowed to divulge that information."

"Okay, thank you," Jessie said, though the woman hadn't been much help at all. She resolved to check back later.

For now, she decided to focus on the fourth action item on her morning agenda: preventing a woman from being released from a psychiatric prison—a woman who had killed her lover's wife, then tried to murder Jessie when she figured it out.

Andrea "Andy" Robinson, had spent the last year in the Female Forensic In-Patient Psychiatric Unit of the Twin Towers Correctional Facility in downtown Los Angeles. But just weeks ago, Jessie had reluctantly agreed to support her transfer to a less odious facility.

That was the price Andy had demanded after she'd provided information which helped catch a former fellow prisoner. Now, after assisting in the capture of a second former prisoner behind Jessie's back, she was on the cusp of being freed entirely.

Preventing that was at the top of Jessie's priority list for the day. That's why she was currently en route to a coffee meet-up with the one person she could count on to stop it from happening.

CHAPTER TWO

Jessie saw that Kat was already waiting for her when she arrived.

The downtown coffeehouse was mostly empty at this hour. The pre-work crowd had long since left and the only people inside were moms with babies in strollers having their second cups of the day and aspiring screenwriters who had taken over their preferred tables as if they were their personal offices.

Katherine Gentry had secured a small table in the corner, apparently sensing that Jessie would want privacy for their conversation. As Jessie wended her way among the tables to reach Kat, her best friend stood up to greet her. She looked good.

She was dressed in her standard outfit of blue jeans paired with a plain shirt under a brown leather jacket, and as usual, her dirty blonde hair was tied back in a workmanlike ponytail. She looked like she could be anything from a contractor to a cab driver. In truth, she was a private investigator, and a good one.

Unfortunately, her skills were often criminally under-utilized. Most of her cases involved surveilling potentially unfaithful husbands or wives, and then reporting her findings back to the spouse that had hired her. It often meant combing through boring financials and sitting in her car outside homes and hotels, waiting to snap surreptitious photos.

But if someone were to look more closely at her, they'd start to notice subtle hints that Kat Gentry was capable of far more than just busting cheaters. At five-foot-seven, her 140 pound body was comprised almost entirely of muscle. Her calm, gray eyes meticulously took in everything she saw, immediately determining if it was a threat.

That ability to quickly assess a situation came from her time serving two tours as an Army Ranger in Afghanistan. In addition to her razor-sharp instincts, there were more obvious reminders of her time in the military: a face pockmarked from shrapnel burns and a long scar that started just below her left eye and ran vertically down the side of her cheek, all the result of an IED explosion.

But at this moment, she seemed untroubled by any of that. She wore a broad smile and her body language was unusually relaxed.

"How's it going?" Jessie asked as she gave her a hug. "You look like a happy lady. Let me guess—Mitch was in town for the last few days."

Mitch Connor was Kat's long distance boyfriend, a sheriff's deputy up in the mountain town of Lake Arrowhead, about two hours northeast of Los Angeles. They'd met when she assisted Jessie on a case last year and visited the town while following a lead. He helped her out; they hit it off and had been going back and forth to see each other every few weeks for months now.

"How'd you guess?" Kat asked, blushing slightly. "Never mind—I forgot who I was dealing with."

"You don't have to be a profiler to figure this one out," Jessie told her. "You look like you're in love."

"Let's just say things are going well," Kat replied, beaming. "But Mitch is headed to a training conference that starts in Bakersfield this afternoon. So I'm solo for the next little bit, which sounds like it might work out, considering your call."

"Clever segue away from your personal life into my problem, Gentry," Jessie marveled. "I guess we're done talking boys then?"

"Unless you care to tell me how the wedding planning is going," Kat teased. "I know how you love that topic."

"So business it is," Jessie announced loudly, impressed at her friend's ability to turn the tables. There was no way she was getting into wedding minutiae right now if she could avoid it. A barista brought over a coffee and put it on the table in front of her.

"I took the liberty of ordering for you," Kat said. "You always get the same thing so I figured I could chance it."

"Thanks, Kat. Who would have thought back when we were butting heads while you ran security at a prison for the mentally ill and I was trying to interview a serial killer there, that we'd end up in our own little coffee klatch?"

"You're stalling," Kat noted.

"Actually, I'm transitioning," Jessie corrected. "The matter I wanted to discuss with you involves a different mentally unstable killer housed in a psychiatric prison facility."

"Andy Robinson," Kat surmised.

"Right," Jessie confirmed. "Do you know the current situation with her?"

9

"You'll need to give me the most recent updates," Kat admitted. "Between my last stakeout and having Mitch around, I haven't been keeping up that much on the local news."

"Okay, I assume I don't need to remind you why she was convicted in the first place."

Kat shook her head.

"I remember," she said. "She killed the wife of the man she was having an affair with and framed the maid, who he was also sleeping with, for the crime. Then, when you figured out what she'd done, she tried to poison you."

"Exactly," Jessie confirmed. "It was my first case for LAPD after getting my masters and I was pretty green. Andy, who was filthy rich, belonged to the same country club as the victim, and offered to help me navigate that world. She was charming and self-deprecating and I was too inexperienced to realize that she was playing me the whole time."

"One thing I never understood was why she wasn't just sent to a regular prison," Kat wondered. "How did she end up in the psychiatric unit?"

"It's a good question," Jessie said. "I think part of it was her thinking ahead and working the system, knowing that if she got siloed into the regular prison system, it would be hard to ever get out, so she amped up the crazy for the jury. At least in a psychiatric setting, if she could show progress, there was a chance she'd eventually get out. But I also think she really belongs there. She's a true sociopath. She never felt guilt for any of her crimes. Plus, she seems to genuinely believe that we could still be friends after she tried to kill me. Sometimes I think that's more important to her than getting out, which I fear may happen."

"Why?" Kat asked.

"Well, do you remember the case that Ryan and Susannah Valentine had a few weeks ago, when a law student was macheted to death in a YWCA shower stall?"

"Of course," Kat said. "You discovered the identity of the killer but she killed herself before they could arrest her."

As Kat spoke, out of the corner of Jessie's eye, she noticed an older guy with a long beard, sun-seared skin, and no shoes walk into the coffeehouse. He wandered over to a nearby table and stood behind a perky, young mom. The woman was scrolling through her phone while rocking a stroller with her sleeping baby inside and seemed oblivious to the man.

"True," Jessie said, her attention split between Kat and the scene a few tables over. "But I got that lead from Andy. She remembered that someone she knew from Twin Towers had talked about her father gifting her a machete. Then, a few days after the prisoner was released from the facility, some poor girl gets hacked to death. So Andy offered me a deal. If I put in a good word at her upcoming status review, suggesting she be switched to a less rundown facility, she'd give me the name of the woman. I agreed. She provided the name: Livia Bucco. I passed it on to Ryan and Susannah, who tracked her down. But Bucco killed herself before they could arrest her. Still, Andy did what she said so I wrote a letter on her behalf and she was subsequently moved."

"That's all vaguely familiar," Kat said. Her back was to the other table but she followed Jessie's gaze. Now her attention was also on the man hovering over the mother and her baby. She adjusted her chair slightly so that she was facing that direction more directly. But when she continued the conversation, her tone was unperturbed. "So what has got you so worried?"

"Something that you might have missed with your stakeout and love nest situation," Jessie continued, trying to keep things light despite the uncomfortable situation fifteen feet from them. "I'm sure you know all about the chemical attack in California Plaza on Monday."

"Of course. Five people killed. Ten more injured. Some woman wiped a liquid on people as she walked by them. She was caught in some seedy apartment before she could attack again. Weren't you in on that too?"

"I was," Jessie said.

Before she could continue, the shoeless man leaned over the young mom's shoulder and muttered something in her ear. The woman gave a surprised yelp and her expression quickly changed from bored to afraid. Whatever he'd said had really upset her.

"Maybe we press pause on this discussion," Jessie suggested and Kat silently nodded.

They both stood up. Jessie approached the man directly and Kat casually moved in behind him. He was still leaning in near the woman, muttering under his breath. Jessie couldn't hear what he said but whatever it was, it had the mom leaning as far away as she could. It was obvious that she wanted to leave but he was blocking her ability to maneuver the stroller away. She was stuck.

"Hi," Jessie said sunnily, keeping her eyes on the woman, ignoring the man entirely. "I'm so sorry I'm late. I hope you weren't waiting too long."

She sat down in the empty chair across from the mom, whose expression went from confused to tentatively relieved.

"That's okay," she said meekly.

Jessie tried to give the guy a chance to leave without a confrontation, hoping that he'd just slink away once he realized his target wasn't alone. She didn't look up at him but could feel his eyes boring into her.

"So I see the little one is as adorable as ever," she went on. "Mind if I get a closer look?"

The woman shook her head and Jessie immediately moved the small table out of the way so she could pull the stroller closer to her. The move had the added benefit of unblocking the stroller from its trapped position and getting the baby farther away from the man. Despite all her efforts, the guy was still hovering over them. She didn't have much choice but to engage.

"Those cheeks are so cute and chubby," she noted before finally looking up at the guy. He was unaware of Kat, two steps behind him, looking somehow relaxed and alert at the same time. Jessie spoke to him for the first time. "Can I help you, sir?"

"I was talking to the lady there," he grunted, the smell of alcohol wafting through the air between them. "You interrupted us."

Jessie turned back to her new tablemate.

"Did you want to continue your conversation with this gentleman?" she asked innocently but with a firmness she hoped to instill in the other woman. "Or do you consider it over now?"

The woman gulped hard before replying.

"I think we're done now," she said quietly.

Jessie looked up at the man and spoke slowly and with conviction.

"She says that you're done now. And we have a lot to talk about. So it's time that you move along."

"What if I don't want to go?" he said belligerently.

"That would be a poor decision," Jessie said, standing up. She was taller than him and she wanted him to know it. "The lady doesn't want to talk to you. You've been asked to leave. Not doing that would turn this into a situation. You don't want a situation. The best move for you right now would be to leave here and find some other way to spend your morning."

The man seemed unsure how to proceed. He was clearly drunk but not so far gone that he couldn't communicate. He seemed to sense that whatever scenario he'd played out in his head wasn't going to happen. He glanced around and saw that all conversation in the coffeehouse had stopped. Everyone was staring at him.

"Maybe you and I should keep talking outside," he growled at her.

"No," Jessie replied. "I'm staying here with my friend. You're leaving now. Any other decision ends very badly for you."

She kept her expression impassive, but inside her everything was tingling as she waited to see how he'd react.

CHAPTER THREE

The man stared at her for several seconds. His right hand moved to his jeans and rested on the outside of his pocket, which clearly had something in it. Kat saw it too and apparently decided now that was the time to join the fray. She slid in beside him. He glanced over at her. She leaned in close.

"You don't want to do what you're thinking of doing," she said quietly, coldly. "That is, unless you're hoping for a broken arm and some time in jail. But I don't think you want to be stuck in jail with your right arm in a cast."

The man stared at her with a mix of resentment and bewilderment.

"Who are you?" he demanded.

"I'm friends with those two," Kat said, nodding at Jessie and the mom. "I'm also the person who's on the verge of making your morning really ugly. You can still walk out of here with your bones unbroken and your pride mostly intact. But time is running short. Like the lady said, you need to leave right now—last chance."

The man seemed to finally take the hint. He eased his hand away from his pocket and, after a beat to show he wasn't being forced, started for the door. When he reached it, he turned around and yelled "bitches!" Then he yanked the door open and ran down the sidewalk.

The coffeehouse remained quiet for several more seconds, then a chorus of applause broke out from customers and staff alike.

"Thank you both so much," the mom said once he was out of sight.

"No worries," Jessie said as she and Kat returned to their table. "And you really do have a gorgeous baby."

"Thanks," the woman said, glancing at the child and seeing that he was now awake. He started to whimper and she picked him up, her attention now fully on him.

"Where were we?" Jessie asked as if there had been no interruption at all. Both of them had been through enough of these situations not to dwell on them.

14

"You were telling me about your involvement in catching the woman who killed all those people in California Plaza."

"Right," Jessie remembered, picking up where she left off. "So I figured out who she was and I was there when we found her. But I wasn't the only one. I was working on another case when the attack went down. Andy tried to contact me, apparently to let me know that she had a suspect in mind. But I didn't realize that. She ended up reaching out to Susannah."

"Your favorite person," Kat noted sarcastically, fully aware of Jessie's distaste for HSS's newest detective.

Detective Susannah Valentine was a smart, fearless cop who worked her way up through the ranks, despite caring for a sick mother and dealing with the disrespect she got because she looked more like a Victoria's Secret model than a police detective. But she was also brash, overconfident, and ceaselessly competitive. She had conceded to Jessie that part of that was an attempt to impress her, but it was still grating. To top it all off, she had a bad habit of flirting with Ryan, which stuck in Jessie's craw.

"Half of me thinks that's why Andy went to her," Jessie muttered, "that she somehow knew I don't love her. Anyway, Andy gave Susannah the name. Unfortunately, the deal they made involved more than just a transfer to a better facility. Susannah went over Captain Decker's head to Chief Laird, who apparently talked to his good buddy, the governor."

"And he's granting parole?" Kat asked, aghast.

"Not quite," Jessie explained. "I don't think he wants the potential blowback that could come from ordering the release of a woman who killed another woman, tried to kill a police profiler, has never shown any remorse, and has served less than two years. So he's passing the buck."

"What does that mean?"

"It turns out that in California, the governor has the authority to affirm, reject, or modify a parole board's decision," Jessie explained. "But he can also simply ask the board to consider reviewing theirs. That's what he's done. Of course, the board knows that he can reverse them, so when he asks them to review a case, they know the writing is on the wall. Unless there's a powerful reason to reject his request, they'll likely do what they know he wants and grant her parole. So she gets out but his hands stay clean."

"I'm assuming that's where I come in," Kat guessed. "What do you need me to do?"

"I want you to find a powerful reason for the parole board to reject his request. Clearly the fact that she's an unrepentant killer isn't enough."

"So I'm looking for dirt on her?" Kat confirmed.

"Look," Jessie replied, lowering her voice, "maybe I'm just too close to this. I suppose it's possible that she really is rehabilitated. If that's what you find, so be it."

"But you don't buy it," Kat pressed.

"Not for a second," Jessie answered emphatically. "Everything I know about Andy Robinson suggests that she's the same charismatic, brilliant manipulator she's always been. The women who committed these crimes were both emotionally vulnerable, easy prey for someone as cunning as Andy. And the language they used when they were caught made it sound like they were doing these things at someone else's behest. I believe she may have actually brainwashed them to do her bidding. I can't prove it, but I think it's entirely possible that she cultivated these women for months, and then sent them out to create mayhem that she could subsequently swoop in and help stop."

"That would be quite the psychotic long con," Kat noted.

"Listen," Jessie said. "Review her case objectively. See if her help was legitimate or if there's anything fishy there. Whatever you find, I'll go with. I trust you."

Kat sat with that for a moment before responding.

"Why me instead of someone from HSS?"

"I can't go to anyone in the department," Jessie said. "Chief Laird made this deal. He wants it to happen. Susannah obviously benefits if it proceeds. I can't ask any rank and file members of the team to do it. It wouldn't be fair. Looking for a reason to scuttle the deal in opposition to the chief of police could get back to him. Everyone else, other than Captain Decker and Ryan, would probably get fired for trying. Decker already tried to push back and got nowhere. He's stuck. And if Ryan tried, it would look like a conflict of interest. That leaves you, the free agent, the independent investigator not beholden to the powers that be at the LAPD."

"That may be true but I don't need to make an enemy of the department."

"I get that," Jessie assured her. "That's why I just want you to bring your findings to me. I'll take it from there. Laird already resents me because I'm a more well-known public figure in this city than he is. He'd have gotten rid of me by now if he could. Alienating him even more isn't an issue for me. So what do you say? I'll pay you for your time with that sweet UCLA part-time instructor money."

Kat laughed.

"Of course I'll do it, Jessie," she promised without hesitation. "And I'm not taking payment, the instructor kind or any other. But I can't guarantee I'll find anything."

"I understand. But if you do find something, it has to happen fast. The parole board meets tomorrow."

Kat's eyes opened wide but before she could respond, Jessie's phone rang. She held it up. It was Decker.

"I've got to take it," she said as she accepted the call. "What's up, Captain?"

"Hello, Hunt," he said gruffly. "If you're not too busy up in that academic ivory tower of yours, I could use your help with a murder case."

Jessie noted his salty tone but decided not to comment on in it. Sometimes it was hard to tell if Decker was actually pissed off or just teasing.

"What happened?" she asked.

"I'll fill you in once you get to the station. Hernandez is waiting for you. For now I'll just say that you're a perfect fit for it."

"Why is that?"

"Because it happened at UCLA."

"I'll be there in ten minutes," she said. After hanging up, she turned to Kat. "I'm sorry to rush off but I have to go."

"Don't worry about it," Kat said. "Do what you have to do. I'm just going to finish up here and maybe make sure that mom and her baby don't run into anyone unpleasant on their way home."

"It looks like you're everyone's guardian angel these days," Jessie said as she got up and headed out.

"I try."

Jessie would have liked to stick around and help out, but she had a murder to solve in her own backyard.

CHAPTER FOUR

When Jessie entered Decker's office, the captain wasn't there, but Ryan was.

He looked up from the file he'd been studying. As always, she marveled at how someone so attractive could be so unassuming about it.

"Hey, my betrothed," he said with a smile. "How was coffee with Kat? Did she say yes?"

"She did. Fingers crossed that she finds something," Jessie said before cutting to the chase. "What's the deal here?"

"I'll let Decker give you the picture when he gets back," he said. "You know how he loves to frame the case. But this is a big one."

"You're not going to tell me anything?" Jessie pressed.

Her fiancé silently flashed his high wattage smile at her. Jessie felt a flicker of butterflies in her stomach. He still had that effect on her. Admittedly, part of it was his sheer handsomeness. His square jaw, dark hair, and muscled frame didn't hurt. But it was those warm, brown eyes staring back at her that did her in. For a super-hot, badass detective, he was shockingly modest and kind.

Ryan looked almost himself again. He'd regained almost all of the weight that he'd lost when he ended up in a coma after being stabbed in the chest last summer. Physically he was back to 95% of his previous physical strength. Jessie worried that. emotionally, he still had a ways to go. But she knew he was sensitive about it and kept her concerns to herself for now.

Just then, Captain Roy Decker walked in. It was barely after 11 a.m. but he looked like he'd already put in a full day's work. He was sixty years old but the deep creases in his face made him appear a decade older. He was tall and rail-thin, with only a few wisps of gray hair preventing him from being totally bald. But his air of perpetual exhaustion couldn't mask his intensity. With his sharp nose and beady, penetrating eyes, he reminded Jessie of an eagle hunting its prey.

His office matched his demeanor. Everything in it, from his dented desk to the metal folding chairs placed opposite it for guests

18

to the ratty couch in the back indicated that Decker wasn't a man who cared about appearances.

"Good morning, Captain," Jessie said sweetly, fully aware that he hated bland pleasantries. It was subtle payback for his ivory tower crack on the phone.

"Glad you could fit us into your busy schedule, Hunt," he muttered as he moved to his desk. Jessie wondered if this case happening at UCLA was what had him on edge. Maybe it reminded him that she wasn't yet working full-time for him. Or maybe he feared that this would somehow make her want to bail on HSS and stay at the school.

"My pleasure," she replied, deciding to let him make himself plain rather try to guess at his motives.

"Here's the situation," he said, launching in. "A little over a half hour ago Professor Roman Tobias was found dead in his office by a student. His forehead was bashed in. The crime scene unit is already en route."

Decker allowed Jessie a moment to process the news, apparently knowing that she'd need it. Roman Tobias wasn't just a professor at UCLA; he was a legend. Despite working in an ivory tower of his own, his outsized personality had made him a celebrity of sorts.

Barely a week went by without his participation in a highly touted on-campus event. He was a regular talking head on television. His books on the American Presidency had sold millions and the PBS series he hosted, ranking the top ten and bottom ten presidents of all time, had broken ratings records for public television. He was quite possibly the most famous professor in America.

"I would want you and Hernandez on this regardless," Decker continued, "but obviously your familiarity with the university offers an extra advantage. You can dive right in without needing to be brought up to speed on how the school operates."

Jessie nodded. It was true. She was more familiar with the world of the school than anyone else he could assign. But personally, it was a double-edged sword. There was something more unsettling than usual about a murder taking place there.

Part of the reason she'd accepted the instructor job there in the first place was because it was a kind of safe harbor, a respite from the brutality of the outside world. Yes, in her seminars, she discussed horrible acts of cruelty, but there was a scholarly

19

remoteness. Now that was gone. Her safe space had been invaded by the very violence she'd gone there to escape.

"What's UCPD's involvement?" she asked, referring to the UCLA Police Department.

"They called us," Decker answered. "They're usually pretty proprietary when it comes to on-campus cases but this is a different animal. They don't have the resources to handle a murder case, much less one of this magnitude. And I got the sense that they were worried about conflict of interest. They don't want to be accused of covering something up in a case that could get national attention."

"Smart," Jessie noted.

"They have a point person overseeing security of the scene but he'll defer to you," Decker told them. "Look for Lt. Larry Schrader. You two should get going. Once this gets out, the campus will be a madhouse."

*

Ryan drove while Jessie familiarized them both with Roman Tobias's record.

"He was a professor of American history, as we already know," she said, skimming through his university bio. "His area of expertise is 'Presidential Rhetoric and Political Argument,' which is why we always see him on TV around inaugurations and State of the Union speeches. The guy's a bit of a wunderkind. He was granted tenure *before* joining the faculty, and he wasn't even forty when he was killed."

"Did you know him at all?" Ryan asked as they tore down the freeway, with lights flashing and siren blaring. Cars moved to right to clear a path for them.

"I was aware of him, like everyone else," she said. "I saw him when I walked around campus. I think he may have even come to one of my seminars. But I don't think I ever met him, not even in passing. I don't really know any more about him than anyone else."

"That's too bad," Ryan said. "I was hoping you might have some inside knowledge."

"I've reached out to Jamil," she said, referring to HSS's researcher extraordinaire, Jamil Winslow. "I asked him to put together a packet on the guy: personal life, financials, that sort of thing. But I'm flying as blind as you on this one. I did find some clips when I was Googling him. You want to hear one?"

"Sure."

"Okay, this is from a debate he had on some cable show a few weeks ago," she told him as she hit "play."

Tobias was seated at one end of a long desk. The show's anchor, a blandly handsome man with a plastic smile, was in the middle. An agitated-looking, middle-aged woman Jessie didn't recognize sat at the other end. She and the anchor were dressed formally. Tobias had a t-shirt on under his sports coat. His longish black hair was slightly mussed and his cheeks were ruddy, as if he'd just come from tossing a ball around with some students.

"You have to admit, Professor," the agitated woman pressed, "that the current political climate makes what you do largely obsolete these days. No one cares what presidents say. It doesn't move the needle anymore. Twitter and Facebook drown all that out. You're clinging to an outdated mode of communication. Any politician who believes otherwise is a dinosaur, just like you."

Her face was a twisted combination of nastiness and self-regard. She thought she'd nailed him.

"What say you to that, Professor Tobias?" the bland anchor asked.

"Well, first of all," Tobias replied in a warm, soothing burr that suggested he wasn't nearly as offended by his opponent's argument as she hoped he'd be. "This is the first time that I've ever been accused of being a dinosaur, but I am pushing forty so I guess it was inevitable. As to Ms. Chambers's larger point, I think that the attitude she espouses can often be a self-fulfilling prophesy. If folks are invested in making sure that what a leader says holds no weight, they'll invariably come to that conclusion, whether the facts bear that out or not—"

"The facts do bear that out, Professor," Ms. Chambers interrupted.

"Come on now, Phyllis," Tobias said with a smile, his voice like molasses. "Has there never been a time when you were moved by what a public speaker said? Maybe it wasn't a politician. Maybe it was a celebrity. Maybe it was a teacher, a pastor, or a coach. We attach value and meaning to public statements when they feel genuine to us, when they speak to something we know to be true both in our hearts and in our heads. The fact that few politicians

21

evoke that reaction in most of us these days isn't a result of our current social media landscape. And it most certainly isn't an indictment of a powerful message. Rather, it's an indictment of today's messengers. We simply need better ones. Don't you think, Phyllis?"

He added that last bit with a flirty wink in his voice that made Phyllis Chambers visibly melt on camera.

"Perhaps," she said reluctantly, blushing slightly.

"It looks like we've seen an example of the power of rhetoric right here on our set," the anchor said self-congratulatorily. "We'll be right back after this."

"Quite the charmer," Ryan noted after the clip ended.

"And you only heard it," Jessie added. "It was doubly effective with the visual. That woman was putty by the time he finished."

"Well, apparently that charm didn't work on everyone," Ryan noted as he pulled off the freeway at Wilshire and headed north to Westwood. "Otherwise he wouldn't be lying in his office with a hole in his forehead."

It was a good point. As they headed to campus, Jessie tried not to let negativity settle in. Just because the UCLA community included over 82,000 people didn't mean they wouldn't find the culprit. It just meant there were a lot of suspects to choose from. It was time to start the search.

CHAPTER FIVE

The madhouse Decker had warned them about hadn't started yet.

As they walked across campus to Haines Hall, where Tobias's office was, it seemed just like a normal Thursday. It was nice day, about seventy degrees, and people milled about everywhere. Many students lay on towels on huge expanses of green lawn, studying while they tanned themselves. One student in a bikini typed away at her laptop. Someone else had set up a hammock in a shady spot between two trees and was highlighting a thick paperback. Two guys in tie-dyed shirts tossed a Frisbee back and forth. Another one sat on a bench, plucking at what looked like a mandolin.

Jessie, who had gone to UCLA's local rival, USC, almost a decade ago, had a powerful flashback to her undergraduate days. But as they neared the east entrance to Haines Hall, her nostalgia quickly dissipated.

While the area was still relatively placid, there were several police cars near the building and it was completely taped off. Small pockets of curious students stood a short distance away, not approaching but not leaving either. Jessie and Ryan walked up to the police tape and he flashed his badge to the officer securing the area.

"We're looking for Lieutenant Schrader," he said.

"Third floor, corner office, number 320," the young campus cop said.

They entered the building and followed the trail of occasional officers upstairs. When they go to the third floor, it was obvious which office was Tobias's. There were two officers at the end of the hall, standing guard alongside a gurney that was currently unoccupied. Jessie and Ryan headed over and showed their IDs to the older of the two officers, who nodded and stepped aside.

"Lieutenant Schrader has been expecting you," he said, pointing at a barrel-chested, bald man by the professor's desk, talking on his phone.

"Thanks," Ryan said. They ducked under the tape and started over to the lieutenant, who saw them coming, hung up, and rushed to meet them. Behind him, on a couch below some bay windows, was what appeared to be Professor Tobias's body. It was hard to get a clear view with all the people around him.

"Detective Hernandez and criminal profiler Hunt, I presume?" Schrader said, extending his meaty hand. His entire body was thick but his eyes were sharp. Jessie got the sense that Schrader was no oaf. "I'm Investigations Division Lieutenant Larry Schrader."

"Thanks for having us, Lieutenant," Ryan said, shaking it. Jessie did the same.

"Your crime scene team is hard at work," Schrader said without needing to be asked for an update. "They've been here for about fifteen minutes. We searched the building on the off chance that there was someone hiding in an office with blood all over them, but came up empty. Then we evacuated everyone and secured this floor. There are still folks on the lower two but they can't access this level."

"What about the student who found him?" Jessie asked.

"Her name is Phoebe Lewis," Schrader said, handing her a few sheets of paper. "She's a history major who had a 10:30 meeting with him. That's when she found him and called it in. She was understandably in shock when we arrived. She's been transported to the Ashe Center for evaluation."

"What's the Ashe Center?" Ryan asked.

"Sorry, I'm used to using shorthand," Shrader said, handing over a business card with some notes on the back. "She's at the Arthur Ashe Student Health and Wellness Center. There's an officer with her. The card includes the contact info for the center, as well as cell numbers for my officer and the student. I told her to expect to hear from you soon and not to speak to anyone else about the incident until then. I've also included a printout of Professor Tobias's schedule for the day, if that helps."

"Thank you, Lieutenant," Jessie said impressed, taking it. "It does."

"No problem," he replied. "We're also pulling camera footage from the area but it may not be hugely helpful."

"Why is that?" Ryan asked.

"Because Haines Hall is one of the oldest buildings on campus, built in the 1920s. We have exterior cameras in the area. But it's been a challenge incorporating interior ones. They have to connect smoothly to our campus watch configuration and the systems in these ancient halls aren't always up to the task. Plus, some students

24

and faculty object to interior cameras in these more historic structures. They say it undermines the 'fragile architectural ecosystem' of the university. They also say it smacks of Big Brother. It's an ongoing issue. The funny thing is that if Professor Tobias's office was in Bunche Hall with the rest of the history department, this wouldn't have been an issue."

"Why not?" Ryan pressed.

"That building is newer, built in the 1960s and more modern looking. There were no complaints when we added interior cameras. Plus, Bunche has a security guard on the first level. You have to check in. All the offices have swipe cards too. But here in Haines, everything is old school."

"Why is Professor Tobias's office here instead of with the rest of the department?" Jessie asked.

"Because that's what he wanted," Schrader answered with a hint of annoyance at the professor's decision. "Bunche Hall doesn't have that conventional, scholarly look. He insisted that his office had to be in an older, more traditional academic-looking setting. He wasn't shy about making that clear. If he was doing interviews, he preferred that the environment reinforce the vibe he was after."

"He told you that personally?" Ryan confirmed.

"Yes. I reminded him repeatedly that with his high profile, it would be more advisable to work somewhere that had at least a modicum of security, but he wasn't interested. We even brought it to the dean's attention, but he couldn't sway Professor Tobias either."

"Were there threats against him that made his decision an issue?" Jessie wanted to know.

"There were comments," Schrader acknowledged, "but nothing that ever rose to the level where we were seriously concerned. It was mostly vague stuff about how he should be fired or imprisoned for his views. We're compiling everything we have for you right now. But I can't recall a single, overt threat of violence. We would have definitely pursued any. Still, his profile was high enough that it was an ongoing issue."

"We'll definitely review the material," Ryan suggested, before glancing over at the couch. "Shall we take a look at the body now?"

Schrader nodded and led them to the sofa, taking care to avoid the trail of blood leading to it from the desk.

"Your crime scene people already took samples from the carpet," he told them. "I guess it's too much to hope that some of the blood is from the attacker."

"You never know," Ryan replied, though Jessie could tell from his tone that he wasn't optimistic.

When they got to the couch, the CSU folks moved out of the way, and they saw the victim for the first time. Jessie allowed herself a moment to let her anger at the brutality of the crime pass through her. Once that dissipated, she took in the details.

Lying in front of them was a man who, apart from the massive, bloody, indentation in his forehead, looked quite dashing. He had a day's worth of stubble and his long, black hair fell into his eyes, where blood had pooled. He didn't wear a wedding ring.

Jessie studied him. They'd need to wait for the medical examiner's take, but based on his coloring and the still-damp blood on the carpet, she estimated that he'd died less than three hours ago.

What wasn't apparent in the TV appearance that Jessie watched was just how tall he was. His long legs dangled over the arm of the couch. There was blood on the bottom of his white sneakers. Jessie glanced back at the carpet and noticed two long impressions in it with hints of blood in them.

"It looks like he was dragged backwards to the couch after he was attacked," she noted, pointing at the lines. "Whoever did it was either really strong or had lots of adrenaline pumping through their system."

"They probably wouldn't need to have had super strength for the actual killing," Schrader said, pointing at a bagged item on a bookshelf. "We think we found the murder weapon and it probably did most of the work all on its own."

Jessie and Ryan walked over to get a closer look. The bagged item was a large award of some sort. The top portion was a metal sculpture, with the design of an unfurled scroll, like the Declaration of Independence or something similar. The base had an inscription indicating that Roman Tobias was a winner of the Jeffersonian Award, which honors "excellence in the field of Revolutionary American History Scholarship."

The base also had what appeared to be blood, skin, and possibly some hair on it. Jessie couldn't be sure without picking it up, but the thing looked like it easily weighed fifteen pounds. The force of it coming down hard into someone's forehead would be more than enough to have killed Tobias.

"Any prints on it?" Ryan asked.

"Wiped clean," Schrader answered, "which is unfortunate since the indentation in the professor's skull matches the corner of the base perfectly."

"Any luck with prints elsewhere in the office?" Jessie wondered.

"The forensic folks aren't done yet but I heard them talking earlier and it didn't sound good," Schrader replied. "Apparently there are so many prints to choose from that it's going to be hard to draw any conclusions. But Gallagher, your deputy medical examiner, is down in the van right now. Maybe she's come up with something we don't know about."

Jessie nodded and walked back over to the door of the office. Ryan joined her and said what she was thinking.

"No obvious signs of forced entry. That suggests that either the door was unlocked or the professor let his killer in."

"So maybe they had an appointment?" Schrader suggested. "That might indicate pre-meditation."

"Possibly," Jessie mused, "especially since the killer got awfully lucky in not being identified coming in or out of the building, so lucky that it might not be luck at all if the timing was pre-planned. Then again, the sheer brutality of the blow suggests there was some passion involved and maybe remorse afterward as well. After all, why drag the body over to the couch instead of just leaving him on the floor? That cost valuable time. The truth is that it's just too early to draw firm conclusions at this point."

Jessie kept one thought to herself for now. Based on her admittedly limited personal experience as an instructor with a high public profile, there were lots of folks who weren't afraid to share their displeasure up close and personal. After her seminars, she'd been accosted on more than one occasion by overly enthusiastic, and occasionally irate, audience members. Nothing ever got physical but it felt possible.

If that happened to her, she could only imagine the passion, and possible vitriol, someone like Tobias might get. He seemed to get enormous pleasure out of tweaking people's dearly held beliefs on national television. That didn't go over well with everyone. Might someone kill over it? Or could this be something more mundane: an unhinged student upset over a bad grade or a jealous colleague whose frustration boiled over? Any of those seemed credible.

Jessie decided the best hope of getting to the bottom of this was starting with unassailable facts. And those wouldn't come from tossing around theories in the professor's office. They would come from talking to someone who could give them some solid answers. She looked over at Ryan.

"We need to talk to an expert," she said. "And I think we both know the perfect person for the job."

CHAPTER SIX

As Hannah Dorsey walked to the main courtyard, she tried to clear her head.

For the last day and a half she'd been turning over the same thoughts in her mind, without coming any closer to solid answers.

"Please wait here," one of the psychiatric aides requested, holding up a hand to indicate people should stop moving forward.

Hannah tried to peer past him to see what was going on in the courtyard beyond. Like all the other patients at Seasons Wellness Center, the Malibu psychiatric rehabilitation facility where she currently resided, all she knew was what had been announced over the P.A. system five minutes ago.

"Staff and residents," the animated, booming voice of the center's administrative director, Marshall Goodman, had announced. "We have exciting news to share with the entire Seasons community. Please come to Tranquility Courtyard for a brief assembly."

Hannah had no idea what the news was but she was happy to have something else to think about. For the last thirty-six hours, almost all her waking thoughts had centered on Dr. Ken Tam, and how he might be a murderer.

It was less than a week ago that she'd found her fellow resident and almost-friend, Meredith Bartlett, dead in her room. Though the death was ruled a suicide, Hannah had serious doubts. Meredith, who went by Merry, was holding a jagged piece of glass and her throat was slashed violently.

It was hard to imagine someone doing that to herself. It was one thing for her to slit her own throat. But this was different, messier. The gash was so large that Hannah could see Merry's windpipe.

For another thing, because of her history of cutting herself, Merry wasn't allowed to have anything sharp in her room, which was searched regularly. They wouldn't even give her a mirror. How had she gotten access to that large chunk of glass? But neither the center, nor the local authorities, seemed to share Hannah's concerns.

So Hannah had begun her own investigation. And after several false starts, she'd come across a notebook locked in the desk drawer of Dr. Tam, one of the staff psychiatrists. But unlike formal patient records, this notebook included personal notes on his sessions with a variety of patients. They also included notations referencing sessions with Merry. But other than dates and times, those pages were blank. There wasn't a single word about the content of their sessions together.

Why no details about their sessions when he wrote in such detail about other patients? Why keep his personal notes locked away? Why have personal notes at all, rather than simply putting everything in the patient's official file?

Hannah wondered if something had gone on in those sessions, something that Dr. Tam wanted hidden, something he would never write down, even in a personal, locked-up notebook. And did whatever occurred in those sessions lead to Merry's "suicide?" Was it possible that there was no suicide at all, that Merry had objected to the nature of the sessions, and that Tam had killed her and staged it to look like a suicide to cover up whatever happened in them?

As a doctor at the center, he could walk freely in the patient dormitory without drawing attention to himself. He had access to the schedule of meals, and even when aides took their breaks. He could easily have snuck in and out without being noticed. He was in a position to guide the investigation of Merry's death.

What if he claimed that she had mentioned taking her life? Who could say otherwise? With Dr. Lemmon away all week, there was no one around experienced enough to call him on it. The current doctor in charge, Dr. Rose Perry, was unlikely to challenge Dr. Tam's conclusions.

Hannah's theory was credible and made logical sense. There was just one problem with it. She didn't have a shred of evidence to back it up. A locked-up notebook that didn't include details of inappropriate behavior was ultimately just a notebook. *Not* including notes about the details of their sessions wasn't proof of what might have happened during them.

Plus, in their few conversations, Merry had never mentioned anything to Hannah about inappropriate behavior on the part of Dr. Tam. Nor, as Hannah recently learned, had she mentioned it to Silvio Castorini, another Seasons patient that Merry had befriended. In her own sessions with Dr. Tam, Hannah had found the guy to be condescending and arrogant, but he'd never said or done anything that could have been reasonably construed as predatory.

Maybe that was the problem. He wouldn't have risked making a move on Hannah, who was still a minor, if only for a few more weeks. But Merry, in her early twenties, was an adult. Manipulating her into an improper relationship was disgusting, unprofessional, and immoral, but was it criminal?

Hannah needed something more to go on. And that meant doing something she feared might come back to bite her. She needed to reach out to other female patients of Dr. Tam to see if the behavior she suspected was part of a pattern.

"I said you can enter now the courtyard now," an aide said to her in an irritated voice, making Hannah realize that he must have told her the same thing more than once.

"Sorry, thanks," she said as she shuffled past him into the crowded space. It was less of a tranquility courtyard than it was a large, cement-covered square with a few sad, isolated trees next to the occasional wooden bench. Smooth jazz played over the loudspeakers, apparently intended to soothe the masses. Hannah found it more grating than calming.

Feeling anxious at the sheer number of emotionally vulnerable individuals nearby, she made her way to the edge of the courtyard, away from the crush of people who were all inching toward a podium at the far end. It took several more minutes for everyone to file in. When they did, the music shut off and several people stepped out of a nearby doorway and walked toward the podium.

The first was the very object of her suspicion, Dr. Tam. In his mid-thirties, he had a haughty air at odds with his squat, dumpy, frame, thinning brown hair, and sad mustache. He was followed by Dr. Perry and another staff psychiatrist, Dr. Cyrus White.

After them came Marshall Goodman, the facility administrator. In his late forties, with graying, perfectly parted hair, wire-rimmed glasses, and a suit which hinted that his paycheck didn't match his title, the man nonetheless had a triumphant expression on his face, suggesting that whatever he intended to announce was a big deal.

The last person to step into the courtyard took Hannah by surprise. It was none other than Dr. Janice Lemmon, who was both Hannah and Jessie's therapist and the woman who had convinced her to admit herself here and finally take on her demons.

In most respects she looked as she always did. She still had her aggressively unstylish perm, comprised of tight little blonde ringlets that bounced like Slinkys when they touched her shoulders. Though she was tiny, barely over five feet tall, she looked wiry strong for a sixty-something woman, likely due to her thrice-a-week Pilates sessions. Her eyes retained their owl-like sharpness, even behind her thick glasses.

As Dr. Lemmon walked out, she had a smile on her face, but Hannah could tell it was forced and she suspected why. The woman was walking gingerly and using a cane for support. Jessie had told her that Lemmon had a slipped disk but she hadn't understood until now just how limited her therapist's mobility would be.

The doctors all stood still as Goodman stepped up to the podium and turned on the microphone. His attention seemed to be focused on something beyond the crowd and Hannah turned to follow his gaze. That's when she saw the video camera on an adjoining roof. Apparently whatever the announcement was, Goodman wanted it recorded for posterity.

"Thank you all for joining us here in Tranquility Courtyard," he said, barely able to contain his exhilaration. "I know this assembly was called on short notice and that for some of you, this is lunchtime. Let me assure you that you won't miss out. We are extending lunch for an extra hour today. But we wanted to share some grand news that will help each and every one of you."

He seemed to expect some applause but when none came, he pressed on, undaunted.

"I am proud to announce, that with a generous contribution from the Alliance for a New Tomorrow Everyday, we are starting a new program called Seasons at Sea. A beach house less than a quarter mile from here is currently being transformed into a grand, water-based, rehabilitative satellite center. There, activities like surfing, kayaking, and scuba diving will be used to build confidence, discipline and team-building, all skills you will need to reintegrate yourselves into lives beyond these walls. We anticipate having the program up and fully operational by the end of the month. How does that sound, Seasoners?"

A surprising number of cheers erupted from the crowd, which made Goodman's face border on cracking, his smile was so wide. While Hannah thought the program sounded reasonable and she would never object to a chance to go surfing, she wondered if

Goodman might be overselling it for the camera. Eventually the applause settled down.

"One more bit of good news," he said, his voice echoing loudly throughout the courtyard. "Some of you may have noticed the recent absence of our senior advisory adjunct psychiatrist, Dr. Janice Lemmon. As you can see, she has rejoined us. She tweaked her back a little bit, which is why she's moving a little slower than usual and using a cane. I know you're all excited to welcome her back, but please, do so gently. She's still on the mend."

There was another round of cheers for Dr. Lemmon, even louder than for the beach house.

"One last surprise, we're doing something special tonight. You all know that we always start a new month with Billy Bob's Barbecue. Well, we are doing a special, unscheduled, mid-month Triple B dinner in honor of Dr. Lemmon and the Seasons at Sea program. So when you come to eat tonight, bring your appetites and we'll bring the bibs!"

A third cheer erupted as the assembly ended. Dr. Lemmon was immediately swarmed. Hannah would have loved to join them but her conversation would require a little more privacy.

She wanted to tell the doctor about the progress she was making. She wanted to share how she was not seeking out dangerous situations or confrontations just for the sake of the emotional high they gave her; she had actually reined in the urge to verbally crush several people who had deserved it in the last few days. She wanted to describe the moment when she actually empathized with Silvio, something she didn't think herself capable of, and tried to ease his emotional his pain by sharing a painful moment of her own. She wanted to brag—if one could brag about such a thing—that she hadn't felt the desire to recreate the thrill she got from killing a man at all this week.

But most of all, she wanted to talk to Dr. Lemmon about Merry, to tell her about her suspicions regarding Dr. Tam and find out if someone she respected thought they had merit. But Dr. Lemmon looked like she would be busy with well-wishers for quite a while, so any discussion of personal growth or murderous psychiatrists would have to wait.

Hannah continued toward the courtyard exit, waiting for the crowd to thin out so she could shimmy through the narrow outlet. Just in front of her was a painfully skinny, young woman with long, red hair and a small backpack purse with "Robin" sewn into the back.

Seeing the name piqued Hannah's interest. One of the names mentioned in Dr. Tam's notebook was Robin Carmell. Though Hannah had never met her, she recalled Tam's description of her as a twenty-four-year-old battling an eating disorder. Could this be her? And if so, might she have some useful information to share?

"Are you Robin Carmell?" she asked before she could stop herself.

When the woman turned to face her, she knew she had the right Robin before a word was spoken. Her face was gaunt and her eye sockets swallowed up her eyes. The pointy ends of her collarbones just below her neck jutted out forcefully. And most disturbingly, her teeth were jagged and discolored, likely the result of years of purged stomach acids.

"What do you want?" she asked defensively.

"Sorry," Hannah said, attempting to dial back the intensity from her first, out-of-the-blue question. "I just saw the name on your backpack and wondered if you were the same Robin who sees Dr. Tam regularly?"

"Why?" she demanded, still on guard.

"I had to switch to him recently, since Dr. Lemmon has been away, and when I signed up for my first session I saw that name on the schedule too. I thought if you were that Robin, you might be able to give me a preview of what to expect? Is he good? Should I switch to Dr. Perry?"

"He's fine," Robin said curtly.

The girl's eyes darted around as if she feared someone might be listening in. Hannah didn't know whether she was hiding something or if the response was just a nervous tic.

"For real?" she pressed, adopting a conspiratorial tone. "I just don't want to end up with some dude who doesn't get my issues."

'What are your issues?" Robin asked bluntly, apparently not finding the question inappropriate. In fact, social niceties didn't seem to be in her bag of tricks at all. But Hannah decided to use that to her advantage.

"Actually, I'm working through some trust issues related to past sexual abuse," she lied. "An older man took advantage of me and made me feel responsible for it. Do you think Dr. Tam would be sensitive to that in our sessions?"

She watched for any reaction from Robin that suggested it might not be advisable to let Dr. Tam address matters of sexual transgression in a therapeutic setting with a young woman. But Robin remained blank-faced.

"I don't know," she replied flatly. "I see him because I throw up every meal I eat and freak out if I weigh more than seventy-nine pounds. I don't have a lot of older guys trying to get with me."

Hannah pretended not to be shocked at the plainspoken nature of Robin's comments or the deep illness it revealed. The two of them were about the same height, five foot nine, and Hannah considered herself a little on the skinny side at 125 pounds. This girl weighed forty-five less than that. Rather than lingering on that horror, she honed in on Robin's last statement.

"Is that something you've addressed with Dr. Tam, not getting interest from older guys?" she asked, hoping to get some hint as to whether the young woman might have been manipulated by the doctor.

But Robin apparently didn't interpret the question as it had been intended.

"Listen whoever you are," she said sharply, through the gritted, pointed nubs that served as her teeth, "not all of us can be blonde, green-eyed model types like you. I'm sure older guys are throwing themselves at you left and right. But you don't have to rub it in."

"That's not what I meant—," Hannah started to insist before Robin cut her off.

"Whatever. Save it for your fashion week friends," she retorted before pushing her way through the crowd and out of sight.

Well, that went well.

Not only did she potentially send an already vulnerable person into an even more precarious psychological state, something she felt unexpectedly bad about, she had made zero progress in determining if Dr. Tam had behaved improperly with Robin. The effort had been an almost total failure—almost.

The one good thing she could take from the awkward encounter was the idea that precipitated it. There were multiple other women listed in Dr. Tam's notebook, along with their ages. Because she'd only gotten to skim the pages, Hannah could remember just a few of those names, but she did recall that several were of legal age.

Maybe she'd have more success talking to them about their experiences with Dr. Tam. It wasn't much of a lead, but it was all she had, so she intended to follow it wherever it took her.

CHAPTER SEVEN

Jessie and Ryan didn't have to go far to find the expert they were looking for.

As soon as they stepped out the back entrance of Haines Hall, Jessie saw her near a familiar black van and waved. But Cheryl Gallagher, the deputy medical examiner assigned to the case, wasn't looking her way. Her attention was focused on something in the back of the medical examiner's van.

"Shall we go say 'hi?'" Jessie asked Ryan, who nodded absent-mindedly. She noticed that his interest was centered on the crowd behind the police tape, which had grown larger since they first entered the building. She knew what he looking for: folks who seemed overly interested in what was going on or who averted their eyes when he stared at them. She stayed quiet as they walked, not wanting to interrupt his concentration.

"Find anything?" she asked as they neared the van.

"No one obvious," he answered quietly and shifted his focus to the woman in front of them.

"How's it going, Cheryl?" he asked, startling the M.E., who jumped slightly. She turned around and Jessie noted that she looked the same as always. She wore black pants and a blue top, both of which were partially hidden under a lab coat. Her blonde hair was pulled back in a tight ponytail which matched her perpetually tight face. She wasn't the warmest person Jessie had ever met but she was good at her job.

"Not great," she admitted. "No usable prints so far. No defensive wounds or other obvious signs of struggle either, which is unfortunate. The physical evidence isn't panning out as I'd hoped."

"Actually, that does help us in one regard," Jessie pointed out." "Between the lack of both defensive wounds and any evidence of a break-in, it seems increasingly likely that Tobias knew his killer and didn't view them as a threat."

"Either that," Ryan offered, "or the killer simply moved too fast and got in the death blow before Tobias could react."

"Well I'm glad to offer some constructive information," Gallagher said. "At least it's more useful than my preliminary time of death, which isn't much more specific than what you could get by just looking at the guy and taking a guess."

"Which is exactly what I did," Jessie told her. "I estimated it was in the last three hours. How'd I do?"

Gallagher looked at her watch.

"Not too bad," she replied. "It's just after 12 noon now. I'd peg it closer to one and a half to two hours ago, but like I said, that's preliminary."

"But assuming that's correct, we're looking at a window of 10 a.m. to 10:30," Ryan confirmed.

"Don't lock those times in," Gallagher warned. "I'd maybe extend it a half hour on either end, but you're in the correct universe."

"Well, we know that he was discovered by his student, Phoebe Lewis, at 10:30," Ryan said. "Assuming we find her credible when we speak with her, that shortens the window of death from about 9:30 to 10:30."

"I wouldn't sign my name to it yet," Gallagher warned, "but that sounds about right."

"That's still a tight stretch of time," Jessie noted as she pulled out the daily schedule for Roman Tobias that Schrader had provided them with. "In fact, if his schedule is to be believed, there shouldn't have been much of a window at all."

"What do you mean?" Ryan asked.

"According to what I see here," she explained. "He was supposed to be at some major lecture held in the concert hall at Royce Hall that ran from 9:45 to 11. Why would he schedule a meeting with a student at the same time he intended to attend a lecture?"

"Maybe he just decided to bail on the lecture entirely and forgot to update his schedule?" Ryan suggested.

"Maybe," Jessie conceded, "but I doubt it. The thing was being held in the concert hall, which is huge. And it says here that he was supposed to offer brief introductory remarks prior to the lecture. He had to know that might run long. Why risk a time conflict?"

"What if he left right after his remarks?" Gallagher suggested. "How far is Royce Hall from this building?"

"They're close to each other, actually," Jessie admitted, "From the main Royce Hall exit to this entrance, it's just a few minutes' walk. But it strikes me as pretty rude, even for a celebrity professor like him, to just walk out after introducing someone. Also, his schedule says his office hours are typically Mondays and Wednesdays from 3 to 4 p.m. Why see Phoebe Lewis at 10:30 on Thursday morning?"

"Maybe it was some kind of academic emergency," Ryan suggested. "That's definitely something we should ask her about."

"Agreed," Jessie said. "In fact, unless you have something more to share at the moment, Cheryl, I think that's something we should look into right now."

"Not right now," Cheryl replied.

"Then let's get going," Ryan said.

Jessie didn't say it out loud, but as they headed out, something felt off to her. All the possible explanations that Ryan and Gallagher had offered for the inconsistencies in Roman Tobias's schedule were perfectly reasonable. But unlike her, neither of them had worked in an academic setting with lectures that regularly ran late or long-winded students who could turn brief chats into hour-long affairs.

Tobias was intimately familiar with those challenges and yet he seemed to court conflicts with his scheduling. Maybe he was just disorganized, absent-minded, or lazy, but Jessie couldn't shake the feeling that he'd planned the conflicts intentionally. Before she could ask herself why, Ryan got a call on his cell phone.

"It's Schrader," he said, then answered, putting the call on speakerphone. "What's up, Lieutenant?"

"I'm sorry to interrupt you in the middle of your work, but I just got a call from the university chancellor, Martin Elliott. He'd like to speak with you in person."

"Okay," Ryan said. "We were just going over to talk to Phoebe Lewis. Can you text me his location and let him know we'll see him as soon as we're able?"

"I'm sorry, Detective Hernandez," Schrader said, sounding genuinely embarrassed. "I hate to push but Chancellor Elliot made it clear he wanted to talk with you now. He specifically mentioned wanting to meet Ms. Hunt. I think he's a fan."

"Seriously?" Jessie said, immediately put off.

"Seriously," Schrader told them. "Of course, I could stall for you—maybe say you're in the middle of a crucial interview—but I recommend we avoid that. Having the chancellor's backing would be a tremendous asset to making your investigation run smoothly. Making him feel as if he's *not* a priority could have…the opposite effect. I know it shouldn't be that way. But speaking from experience, you might be better served by meeting with him and putting on the charm. It could be the difference between having doors opened for you or slammed in your face."

Ryan looked borderline pissed but Jessie was already resigned to the inevitability.

"Thanks for the heads up, Lieutenant," she said with a sigh. "Let him know we'll be right there."

"Let's get this over with fast," Ryan muttered after hanging up.

"Agreed," Jessie said. "But don't make it look like we're rushing him. We don't need to make an enemy of the most powerful person on campus, especially with a killer on the loose. We may end up needing the guy. We have to handle this just right."

CHAPTER EIGHT

Jessie was surprised to hear the chancellor was a fan.

Despite having taught at UCLA for close to a year, she'd never met him, nor had cause to visit his office, located on the second floor of Murphy Hall. After they arrived, his assistant asked them to take seats in the waiting area. But once she alerted him to their presence, they only had to wait for a few seconds before they were ushered into his office. The place was cavernous, with wood paneling alternating between the giant windows and thick carpeting that swallowed the base of his desk. A separate dining area had an oak table and six chairs.

Jessie had barely managed to take it all in before the chancellor bounded toward them with his hand extended in greeting. A squat, powerfully built man in his sixties with a bald pate, ruddy skin, and a broad smile, he looked like he'd already had three cups of coffee today.

"Thanks so much for coming by," he said, shaking Jessie's hand vigorously before doing the same to Ryan. "I'm Marty Elliot. It's so great to meet you both, even if it is under these circumstances."

"Thank you for having us, Chancellor," Jessie said, waiting for her fingers to fully regain the circulation that had briefly stopped when he squeezed them.

"Please call me Marty," he said, his voice dipping dramatically into an apologetic tone as he motioned for them to sit on two leather chairs opposite the one he settled into. "I'm ashamed that this is the first opportunity I've had to speak with you in particular, Ms. Hunt. You've graced us with your presence for months now and despite my best efforts, I still haven't had the opportunity to sit in on one of your seminars."

"I understand, Marty. You're a very busy man."

"Nonetheless, it's unacceptable," he insisted, suddenly sounding angry with himself. "And now I understand you're leaving us at the end of this quarter?"

"Yes," she replied. "As much as I've loved teaching the students here, I feel like it's time to dedicate more to case work. Homicide

Special Section has been without a full-time profiler for nearly a year now."

"Yes, I know," the chancellor said, again adopting a more tempered manner, "ever since the untimely passing of your mentor, Garland Moses. What a loss. And I certainly understand your desire to pick up his mantle. Your work in recent months has been invaluable to the city. I was especially impressed with how you took down the leader of that Eleventh Realm cult, Sterling Shepherd, although I have heard that some of his followers have reconstituted a new group called ANTI or ANTE—something like that. I hope they don't prove equally troublesome."

"I hadn't heard about that," Jessie said, glancing over at Ryan, who looked equally mystified, before adding, "We'll have to look into it."

"Indeed," the chancellor replied, now once again breaking out the megawatt grin, "But I do hope that you'll consider returning to us at some point. As I think you know, you have an open invitation to come back whenever you like. I shouldn't say this, but your seminars have gotten higher student ratings than those of most of our full-time professors, even our now departed friend, Roman."

"Speaking of Professor Tobias," Ryan said, using the mention to get them back on track. "We understand that you wanted to discuss the matter with us."

The chancellor frowned slightly.

"Not so much 'discuss' as to just let you know that all our university resources are at your disposal," he told them. "While my hearty greeting may have given a different impression, I must assure you that I, along with the whole UCLA family, am in a state of shock and mourning. I'm sure I don't have to tell you what a titanic figure Roman was, not just here on campus, but in the broader academic and cultural community. So if there's anything you need or questions you have, please don't hesitate to reach out to me directly. The more you keep me looped in to the progress of your investigation, the more I can be of service to you. My hope is that we can create a partnership that gets to the bottom of this horrible deed while preventing any further rupture to the fabric of this school and those who love it."

"Thank you, Marty," Jessie said, deflecting the polite "you scratch my back and I'll scratch yours" suggestion and focusing on the comment she could actually do something with. "And since you

42

mentioned it, we would like to ask you a few questions about Professor Tobias, if you have an extra minute or two."

"Of course," he said, "Whatever I can do to help."

"Just generally," Jessie asked, "are you aware of any enemies the professor may have made? I'm not talking media or political figures who opposed his views, but people closer to home—maybe a dispute with another professor involving jealousy over tenure or department funds? Perhaps a human resources issue of some kind? Or possibly even a student stalker? Was there an angry alum or booster?"

"Wouldn't that be a question better addressed to campus police?" Chancellor Elliot asked.

"We've asked them," Ryan volunteered, "and they don't have any record of anything like that. But Marty, you know as well as we do that sometimes these kinds of issues are handled through unofficial channels. At Professor Tobias's level of distinction, we might expect some involvement from you to smooth things over. Did that ever happen?"

"Not that I can recall," Chancellor Elliot said carefully. "To the best of my knowledge, Roman was adored by everyone he came into contact with. Even those who disagreed with him couldn't help but be charmed by his charisma. I guarantee you that once news of his death becomes public, we'll be overwhelmed with expressions of sympathy and praise. Already, I know that word has started to leak out on the web. I've been getting texts, calls, and e-mails asking me if it's true, praying that it's not. Once we put out our press release, I expect to be inundated with heartfelt words of tribute to him."

"The longer you can hold off on that, the more effective our investigation will be," Ryan pressed. "When we question people, we'll be better served if those we speak to don't know that the professor has died, much less been murdered."

"That's the other reason I wanted to meet with both of you, Detective," he replied, his tone very grave. "I suspected that you might feel that way. And I didn't want to blindside you by releasing a statement without your knowledge or approval. But it's already written and I'm afraid I can't hold off much longer on sending it out. Sooner than any of us would like, what's on the internet will be on the news. I don't want our students, faculty, and staff to learn about Roman Tobias's death via tweet or on some gossip site. The university needs to be the one to share this tragic news."

Jessie sighed. As frustrating as it was, the chancellor wasn't being unreasonable. Now it was just a matter of time.

"Give us an hour," she requested.

The chancellor's brow furrowed.

"That's an eternity in this media landscape," he said.

"Please, Marty," she pleaded. "We need a little bit of time to talk to his colleagues and staffers. It could be the difference between solving this case and you having a killer wandering free on campus. I know you don't want that."

Now it was Marty's turn to sigh.

"Fine," he said. "But one hour. I can't wait a minute more than that or else I'll be facing my own interrogation by the Board of Regents. The clock starts now."

Even as Jessie glanced at the clock on his wall and saw that it was 12:23 p.m., she was pushing herself out of the chair. Ryan was already ahead of her, yanking the door open so they could dart out. Neither of them bothered to close it behind them.

CHAPTER NINE

"Who else can we talk to?" Ryan asked when they reconvened.

It was 1:16 p.m. and they were standing in the administrative office of the UCLA history department on the sixth floor of Bunche Hall. They'd split up to save time during their questioning, running up and down the halls to conduct breathless interviews with other professors and department staffers. They would have spoken to Tobias's personal assistant too, but she was on vacation in the Bahamas, and had been all week. At least that eliminated her as a suspect.

"Let's review where we're at so far," Jessie suggested, pulling out the list of people they'd decided to speak to. "Did anyone you spoke to have an axe to grind?"

"No one volunteered anything," Ryan said. "Everyone I spoke to was shocked—bereft even—at the news of his death. No one had any idea who would kill him or why. There wasn't a single mention of jealousy. No word of rivalries. No hints at secrets. Everyone kept calling him a wonderful man, an incredible scholar, and an admirable representative of the university. It got tiresome after a while."

"That's funny," Jessie said. "Now that I think about it, I kept hearing the same thing, sometimes word for word."

"What do you mean?" Ryan asked.

"Several people called him a wonderful man," she said flipping through her notes. "I didn't think much of that. But one professor used the phrase 'estimable scholar' and another described him as a 'worthy representative of the school.' It's almost like they were all coached to say these things."

"Maybe they were," Ryan replied. "Could Chancellor Elliot have sent out talking points?"

"After promising to keep a lid on things for an hour?" Jessie asked skeptically. "That would be a pretty bold move, and counterproductive for him if we found out. I doubt it. Besides, everyone I talked with appeared genuinely stunned when I mentioned Tobias's death, which makes me think these talking

45

points were in place well before he was killed. And if they were, the question is why—why did the powers that be feel the need to train the entirety of the history department in reciting bland praise of one of their own? That's something you'd expect when an organization is in damage control mode."

Ryan nodded in agreement.

"It's starting to feel a lot like there's more under the surface with Professor Roman Tobias than we've been led to believe."

"Well, we have about four minutes to see what we can unearth before that press release goes out," Jessie noted. "And there are three people left on this list we haven't spoken with. Mark Rawls, the dean of the department, is at an event across campus so we'll have to hold off on him. But the other two both work here in the administrative office. Who do you want?"

"I'll take Carla Taylor," he said.

"Okay, that leaves me with Constance Espinoza," Jessie replied, noting where her office was. "See you back here in a few."

Ryan nodded as he jogged down the hall away from her, clearly worried that he was going to get to Carla after she heard the news. It seemed like a smart move and Jessie did the same, walking briskly down the hall in the opposite direction until she found a small office marked "Constance Espinoza: Administrative Coordinator."

Sitting at her desk with her attention focused on her computer screen was a pleasant looking woman in her forties. She wore bifocals and her blackish-gray hair was tied in a bun. Jessie briefly debated how to approach the woman, but with time running short, she decided to do away with the niceties and just dive in.

"Constance Espinoza?" she asked, stepping into the doorway.

"Yes," the woman said, reluctantly tearing her eyes away from the screen. Something in her expression told Jessie that Constance already knew the news. Glancing at the clock on the wall, she saw that it was 1:21. Marty Elliot had jumped the gun by two minutes. In light of the pressure he was under, she was impressed that he'd held out that long.

"My name is Jessie Hunt," she said, holding up her ID. "I'm a criminal profiler with the Los Angeles Police Department and I'm here to talk to you about what you just read."

The woman's expression went from confused to terrified.

"Why? What do I have to do with this?"

"Probably nothing, Ms. Espinoza," she assured her. "What I need from you is information. How does that press release say Professor Tobias died?"

"It doesn't—just that he passed away earlier today. There are no details."

Jessie was at least glad for that bit of restraint on the chancellor's part. It might allow them a little more time before the media frenzy got totally out of control.

"I'm sorry to be so blunt with you but he was murdered," Jessie told her. "And we're trying to find out who did it. Now are you aware of anyone in the department who held a grudge against the professor? Anyone he had a conflict with?"

Constance Espinoza looked stunned. Jessie sympathized. Two minutes ago the woman was doing administrative coordination. Now she was being questioned in a murder investigation.

"I can't think of anything like that," she said after swallowing hard.

"What about any controversies involving him that might have been a source of upset. Anything the general public didn't know about but were open secrets here in the department? Was he abusive? Did he hit on his students? Plagiarize others' work?"

The woman took a second to work through the enormity of the question being asked of her. Even before she responded, Jessie knew this answer would be different.

"He could sometimes be demeaning to his students," she said quietly. "I fielded several complaints that talked about him being unnecessarily cruel when he called people out in class."

As she answered, she averted Jessie's gaze, as if ashamed that she hadn't taken action.

"Do have the names of any of the students who filed those complaints?"

Espinoza shook her head.

"No," she said. "They were always anonymous. But there were enough of them over the years that I know they weren't isolated incidents here and there. It wouldn't shock me if he said the wrong thing to the wrong student and this was the outcome."

Jessie thanked the woman and returned down the hall to the administrative office, where Ryan was already waiting, sitting in a chair with a sour look on his face.

"What's wrong?" she asked.

"Carla Taylor was a bust," he said, dispirited. "The most she could offer was that Tobias was occasionally mean to students."

Jessie felt a prickle at the back of her neck as a thought entered her head.

"My person said the same thing," she told him, formulating her idea as she spoke. "Isn't it odd that when we finally get some folks to reveal something uncomfortable about Roman Tobias, that it's the same detail?"

"Is it that odd?" Ryan wondered. "If it's true, then I'm not shocked that it came up more than once. It might be the sort of thing administrative staff would pay more attention to than fellow professors."

"Fair point," Jessie conceded. "But it also has that 'coached' feel to me. What if this was the default answer they were told to give if questioned aggressively about Tobias, the bone they were told to throw."

"What are you implying?"

"I'm just wondering if this revelation was by design," she mused, recalling how Constance Espinoza had seemed ashamed and wondering if that hadn't been a ruse. "What if these women were told that if they had to give something up about Tobias, to make it this. How would most people react? I'm betting they'd think that while being unkind to students is not ideal, it's not worthy of more than a slap on the wrist. But what if the allegation is a misdirect? What if folks asking questions, like us, are given this claim so we don't go looking for something bigger, messier?"

"What's the bigger, messier thing that you suspect?"

"I don't know," Jessie conceded. "But if we spend our time on a wild goose chase, trying to track down anonymous students who accused Tobias of being a jerk to them in class, that's time not spent on his personal life. It's almost as if we were given bread crumbs intended to focus our attention on these students and draw it away from Tobias."

"Okay," Ryan said, though Jessie could hear the skepticism in his voice. "Assuming that's what's going on, what do you propose we do next?"

"Probably what we would have done at some point anyway—a deep dive into the life of Professor Roman Tobias," she replied. "We already have Jamil looking into his personal financials. Let's have him and Beth expand the circle. They can check for past lawsuits, accusations of personal or academic misconduct, leaving prior schools under a cloud—the works. We can set up shop in one of the main library's study rooms. That's what I do sometimes when I'm prepping a seminar. We'll be away from prying eyes."

"That all sounds good," Ryan said as they took the elevator down to the lobby of Bunche Hall. "But while Jamil and Beth are gathering that stuff, I think we should go see Phoebe Lewis. We've already waited too long."

"Sure," Jessie agreed. "Do you want to call the officer with her to let her know we're on our way?"

Ryan nodded and pulled out his phone as the elevator doors opened. By the time they were outside, the call had connected.

"Hello," he said. "This is Detective Ryan Hernandez. I just wanted to give you a heads up that we're on our way over to interview Phoebe Lewis."

Jessie watched Ryan's face as he listened to the officer on the other end of the line. She could tell something was wrong.

"How long will that take?" Ryan asked.

There was another brief silence as he listened to the officer. She wished he had put the call on speaker.

"Okay, thank you," he finally said. "Please let me know as soon as that happens."

"What is it?" Jessie asked worriedly as soon as he hung up. "Did something happen to her?"

"She's okay," he assured her, just now realizing how concerned she was. "Apparently she was still incredibly upset when they took her to the wellness center. The officer said it was a full-blown panic attack and no one could calm her down. So the doctor ultimately gave her a sedative by injection. It knocked her right out. She's been asleep for the last two hours. They say she should wake up in another hour or so. They're going to call me the second she does."

Jessie was relieved. Her imagination had envisioned much worse scenarios.

"I was worried that something happened to her," she said.

"Sorry," he said. "I didn't mean to freak you out."

"You know what I could use?" she told him, choosing to turn a negative into a positive.

"What's that?" he asked.

"A good old-fashioned study session. Let's get to the library and start cramming. I have a feeling that our final exam is coming up soon."

CHAPTER TEN

Kat's eyes were starting to blur.

She'd been at this for two hours now and there was no end in sight. Jessie had asked HSS's junior researcher, Beth Ryerson, to quietly send her everything on the two cases that murderer-turned-hero Andy Robinson had helped with, and it was a *lot*.

In addition to those extensive files, Kat had secured records from the Female Forensic In-Patient Psychiatric Unit at the Twin Towers Correctional Facility. That was where Andy had been incarcerated along with Livia Bucco, the perpetrator of the first attack, and Eden Roth, who'd committed the second one earlier this week.

They had copious notes on both women: what got each of them placed at Twin Towers in the first place, their behavioral records while inside, and the reason for their eventual release. The only information not available to her was the notes from their medical and psychiatric sessions, which were protected under HIPAA.

As she read through the documents, Kat did her best to maintain a clinical perspective and not jump to any conclusions. Her job was to determine if Andy really was genuinely helping to solve cases involving the mentally unstable patients she had interacted with, or if, as Jessie suspected, Andy was actually the mastermind behind them, somehow manipulating these women into crimes.

Livia Bucco certainly seemed easy to manipulate. She'd been bullied for much of her youth, partly because of her large size and partly because she had rosacea. Kids called her the Red Hulk. Eventually she ended up on the street, consumed by alcohol and drugs. It seemed that hardly anybody had been kind to her in her entire life. Kat suspected that if Andy had shown even a smidgen of decency towards her, Livia would have devotedly lapped it up.

Unfortunately there was no hard evidence that the two women hung out regularly at Twin Towers, other than what Andy had already told Jessie. Specifically, she revealed that Livia once mentioned that her father gave her a machete as a present and that she had a fantasy about cutting up the first innocent-looking person she saw when she got out of the facility. When Andy saw on the news that someone had chopped up a law student volunteering at a local Y.W.C.A., she remembered Livia's comments and that she'd just been released from Twin Towers. It was her tip that led Ryan to Livia Bucco.

The Eden Roth case had similarities. Her time at Twin Towers overlapped with Andy's but there was no record of regular interaction between them either. Unlike Livia, Eden didn't commence her attack—wiping poison on passers-by in a busy downtown plaza—until eight months after her release. Ultimately five people died.

In that case, Andy said she remembered that Eden had been put in Twin Towers in the first place for slicing open her palms and wiping her own blood on unsuspecting people in public places. Once again, she saw the story about the attack on the news and made the connection. Only this time, when Jessie didn't return her call, she gave her information to Detective Susannah Valentine instead. But she didn't do it until she secured the Board of Parole hearing that Jessie worried would lead to her release.

And she might be right to worry. Nowhere in the files of either Bucco or Roth was there any mention of Andy Robinson and there were no references to either of them in Andy's even thicker file. If they spent time together, it either wasn't enough to get noticed by guards or doctors, or they did it surreptitiously. Either way, there was no paper trail to suggest that she was their leader and they were her acolytes.

But there was something else. Just before Livia Bucco—trapped and about to be arrested—plunged her machete into her own forehead and fell off a roof to her death, she said something unusual to Ryan. She told him that explaining her actions to him would be "a violation of the Principles" and that "my work here is done."

Similarly, just before smearing the poison that she developed onto her own body, Eden Roth told Jessie, Ryan, and the other detectives who found her that "I have followed the Principles and protected the Principal. My work here is done." She had so far survived her self-inflicted poisoning but was still at the hospital in critical condition and not in a position to explain herself.

It was clear to Kat that Jessie had felt certain about three things: that Andy Robinson was "The Principal," that the "Principles" both women followed were hers, and that it was actually *her* "work" that they were doing. Kat had to admit that there was a real cult-y, Jim

Jones vibe to their language, their crimes, and their willingness to die. But vibes weren't evidence.

Jessie had also noted how convenient it was that Andy just happened to know the very details that could help catch these women. Was she that lucky? Or did she intentionally incorporate those details into the very attacks she helped plan?

Kat couldn't say for sure. When stuck in a prison for people with mental disorders, who knew what kinds of stories people shared with each other? Just a few years ago, Kat had been the security chief at a lockdown facility housing the criminally insane. The things those guys casually said still made her queasy.

Jessie also questioned how likely Andy would be to remember details shared with her months earlier. But the problem with that argument was that Jessie herself had remembered the same details. According to Andy, she remembered Eden telling her about smearing blood on people. Jessie had only read the same story when skimming Eden Roth's file several weeks prior to her attack. If she remembered it just from reading a reference to it in a prison file, was it that hard to believe that Andy Robinson would remember the story, told to her by the person who committed the act?

And if Kat was questioning her best friend's reasoning on those points, she doubted the parole board would be more receptive to it. No—the best bet to determining whether Andy was a Good Samaritan or a Machiavellian manipulator was to focus on this "Principal/Principles" thing. Both women, just prior to their imminent capture, used nearly identical language. It didn't automatically implicate Andy but there was no way it was just a coincidence.

If any lead could help keep the woman behind bars, it was that one. And Jessie was counting on Kat to make sure she stayed there. If someone as dangerous as Andy Robinson, who had already tried to kill Jessie once, was released, there was no telling what she might do.

But with the parole board hearing tomorrow, time and options were running short. Kat could only think of one idea that, under such constraints, might shake things up. The only way to determine the truth and protect her friend was to go directly to the source.

She needed to talk to Andy Robinson in person.

CHAPTER ELEVEN

As it turned out, Jessie's good, old-fashioned study session wasn't all it was cracked up to be.

The location was fine. They found a well-situated study room hidden in a secluded corner behind rows of books. The internet connection was solid and they were able to conference in Jamil and Beth so they could all communicate in real time.

The problem was that, at least in the hour that they'd been investigating Roman Tobias's life, they'd come up empty. Jessie could tell that Jamil Winslow, the unit's head of research, was getting frustrated. That wouldn't seem to be a big deal. But Jamil—only twenty-five, with a scrawny frame and a shy disposition—was a legitimate genius, and when his formidable skills didn't provide answers, he tended to get testy. Jessie could tell that he was on the verge right now.

"His financials are a mess," he said irritably, "But not in a suspicious way. He's just incredibly sloppy with how he conducts himself. But because he's doing so well, what with his books and public appearances on top of his university salary, he doesn't really have to worry about making it all add up."

"Are you sure the sloppiness isn't a clever way of hiding impropriety?" Jessie asked.

"Not that I can tell," Jamil answered. "It's been this way his whole career, other than the brief four-year stretch when he was married. His wife made a valiant attempt to clean things up. But once they broke up, so did his financial clarity."

"Speaking of the divorce," Ryan said, "did you guys find anything in the filing?"

"No," Beth Ryerson, the junior researcher told him. "It never gets more specific than 'irreconcilable differences.' There are no details on the cause of the breakup. And Tobias gave his wife everything she wanted in the settlement, most of it in one lump sum. Since then, there's been virtually no communication between them."

"Out of curiosity, where was she today?" Ryan asked.

"On a yacht in the Greek Islands, with her European tech billionaire boyfriend," Beth answered. "The way things turned out for her, she doesn't seem to hold a grudge."

Beth sounded as relaxed as Jamil was tense. At six feet tall, the understatedly attractive former beach volleyball player never seemed to let the stress of a situation get to her. Jessie noticed that sometimes her chill demeanor could settle Jamil down. But not today.

"So financials are a dead end," he grumbled. "The divorce turned up nothing. He's never had a formal complaint filed against him—personal or professional—by a student or faculty member, either at UCLA or at American University, where he worked for six years before coming west. He's never had an allegation of plagiarism or any other academic impropriety. His books, all three of them, are bestsellers. Hell, he barely even got any bad reviews."

"What about social media?" Ryan wondered.

"That's clean too," Beth said. "He almost never posts anything genuinely personal. It's always information on upcoming speaking engagements or TV appearances, links to articles he likes, or brief mentions of why a given date is important in history—safe to the point of boring, time and time again. It actually surprised me because his public persona is so outsized."

"Apparently we've found the one legitimately squeaky clean public figure in America," Jamil said, sounding personally offended by the notion.

Hearing him say that out loud almost made Jessie laugh; it was so patently ridiculous.

"No we haven't," she said.

"What do you mean?" Jamil demanded, his tone bordering on something he never was—rude.

"Settle down," Beth whispered to him, though not quietly enough that Jessie couldn't hear her over the phone line. Though she couldn't see it, she smiled at the thought of the Amazonian trying to gently calm her tiny but excitable supervisor.

"I mean that the very fact that we can't find dirt on this guy assures me that it exists," Jessie. "No one with Roman Tobias's personal profile is this squeaky clean."

"How can you be so sure?" Beth asked.

"Look, we already suspect that people in the history department here were coached to offer the most blandly positive descriptions of him, descriptions that don't match his public persona at all. The worst anyone could come up with was that he was sometimes mean to students, but we don't have a single named complainant to follow up with. Somehow this brilliant, wealthy, attractive, uber-charming academic celebrity, who enjoys poking his opponents in televised debates, maintains a straight-arrow social media presence and has never alienated anyone for crimes beyond poor office security measures and lazy financial record-keeping. Does that sound believable to you?"

There was a brief moment in which Ryan smiled and those on the phone were stunned into silence.

"Not when you put it that way," Beth finally answered.

"Exactly," Jessie said approvingly. "We may not be able to prove it yet but there's no way a guy like that has led such a pristine life. The very fact that he doesn't seem to have anything to hide makes me sure that he's hiding something. And let's be honest, he's been doing a great job of it. But we're pretty damn good at our jobs too. That's why we're going to find his secret. And when we do, I have a feeling it's going to break this case wide open."

Before anyone could respond, Ryan's phone rang.

"Yeah?" he said and after listening briefly, added, "We'll be right there."

He hung up and looked at Jessie with a smile.

"That was the officer with Phoebe Lewis," he said. "She just woke up."

CHAPTER TWELVE

Jessie thought the girl could use another injection.

When they arrived at the Ashe Center, Phoebe Lewis didn't have the appearance of someone who'd been recently sedated. Jessie and Ryan watched her through the glass window of the door to her room and noted that she was agitated and jumpy, turning her head at every sound she heard, no matter how small.

"How would you feel about me talking to her alone?" Jessie asked him. "She's already so tense that I worry that both of us questioning her at the same time might overwhelm her."

"That's fine," Ryan said, before acidly adding, "I'll check back in with Jamil and Beth. Maybe they discovered something in the ten minutes that we've been gone."

Jessie didn't comment on his pessimism as she entered the tiny room and looked over Phoebe Lewis, who was dressed in jeans and an oversized sweater. Under normal circumstances, the girl who was seated upright in the hospital-style bed would have been cute in a mousy, bookish way. Her features were delicate and she had short, brown hair cut in a pixie style. She wore glasses with funky, paisley frames. But right now, that was all undermined by the fact that she looked petrified. Jessie pulled up the lone chair in the room, sat down next to Phoebe, and offered a half-smile.

"Hi Phoebe," she said quietly. "I'm Jessie Hunt. I work with the Los Angeles Police Department. I was hoping to talk to you about what happened this morning. Would that be okay?"

"Am I in trouble?" Phoebe asked anxiously. "I didn't do anything. Are you going to arrest me?"

"No, no," Jessie assured her. "You're not in trouble and I'm not even a detective. I help them solve crimes. That's why I'm here. Since you're the one who found Professor Tobias, I want to ask you some questions about it. We need your help. You could make a big difference in our ability to find whoever did this. But it's important that we talk while it's still fresh in your mind."

"To be straight with you, I don't *want* it in my mind," Phoebe said, squeezing her eyes shut tight.

"I get that," Jessie said, "which is why I'll try to make this as quick and painless as I can. And you know what? A lot of people have told me that sharing their experience actually helped them. Once they turned the images in their heads into words, those images didn't hold such power over them. I'm hoping that can be the case for you too."

"Okay," Phoebe said softly.

'Great," Jessie said, pulling out her phone. "I'm just going to record our discussion so I can refer back to it and make notes later on. Is that okay?"

Phoebe nodded. Jessie turned on the recorder, placed the phone on the small bedside table, and began.

"This is LAPD criminal profiling consultant Jessie Hunt speaking to Phoebe Lewis at 2:34 p.m. on Thursday, March 17th about the death of Professor Roman Tobias."

She worked her way quickly through the obligatory questions about Phoebe's birthdate, address, major and the like. After that, she walked the young woman through what she saw when she got to Tobias's office. Then she got to the meat of it.

"Where were you just prior to seeing Professor Tobias?"

"I was hanging out with my friends, having coffee and a snack in Dickson Court," she explained. "It was close to Haines Hall so I didn't leave until just a couple of minutes before the meeting."

"And why were you meeting with the professor this morning?" she asked.

"We were going to discuss a paper I was working on."

The way Phoebe said it sounded more like a question than an answer. Jessie decided to push ever so slightly.

"You know, I was a little surprised that you were meeting with him at that time," she mentioned casually. "When we were reviewing his office hours, we saw that they're on Mondays and Wednesdays from 3 to 4 p.m. How come you were meeting with him at 10:30 today?"

Phoebe looked a little flustered but pushed through.

"I don't know," she said. "He said that time was better for him and I didn't question it. When someone like Professor Tobias sets aside time for you in his schedule, you accommodate him."

"Got it," Jessie replied as if the matter was resolved, then added, "but it is a little strange, because his schedule said he was supposed to be attending a lecture from 9:45 until 11 a.m. that morning. In

58

fact, he was supposed to give introductory remarks. It seems odd that he would double book the time. Did he mention anything about that lecture to you beforehand, maybe warn you that he might be a little late getting to the office?"

Phoebe shook her head uncertainly.

"Okay," Jessie said, shrugging. "It is weird though, don't you think, that he insisted on meeting you at a time when he had something else going on, especially when his office hours were on the day before and after?"

Phoebe started to shake slightly.

"What's wrong?" Jessie asked.

"Are you going to arrest me if I said something that wasn't totally true earlier?"

Jessie kept her voice even as she responded, not wanting to betray her growing excitement. She felt sure that what Phoebe said next might be the break they'd been after.

"That's not my plan," she reassured her. "If you misspoke earlier and you want to correct the record, that's okay. Just make sure that what you tell me now is an accurate reflection of events."

"Okay," Phoebe whispered, looking pained as she got the words out. "I didn't really need Professor Tobias's help with a paper. He asked to meet with *me*. He chose the date and time."

"Did he say why he wanted to meet with you?" Jessie asked with as little emotion as possible.

"Not really," Phoebe said, looking away as her face turned bright red. "All he said was that he needed help with a special project that was very hush-hush and that because I showed great promise, he thought of me. I wasn't to mention it to anyone because the project was still in the early stages."

Jessie could feel embarrassment radiating off the girl. It was clear that even if she didn't know for sure, Phoebe had her own suspicions that this "special project" might not be exactly what Tobias suggested.

"Did he say how long your meeting would be ahead of time?" she asked, careful not to sound accusatory, "Or give any hint as to its parameters?"

"Uh-uh," Phoebe said, briefly making eye contact before looking down again. "He was really vague about it."

"Can you think of any reason why he would schedule the meeting at the same time that he had another event?"

"Maybe he just forgot about the lecture?" Phoebe suggested unconvincingly.

"I suppose that's possible," Jessie conceded before offering her own theory. She was curious to see how the student reacted to it. "Do you think there's any chance that he wanted to have the lecture on his schedule so that if he snuck out early at some point, no one would realize that he was doing something else?"

Phoebe squirmed in her hospital bed and Jessie knew that the girl was wondering the same thing. She also knew that Phoebe would now be prepared for the next question that she had to ask.

"That's okay," she said. "What about this: Do you think it's possible that Professor Tobias wanted to meet with you for some other reason, unrelated to a project, and that he didn't want anyone to know about it?"

Phoebe shrugged.

"I don't know," she answered meekly.

"When I asked you earlier why he wanted to meet with you, you blushed," Jessie reminded her. "To me, that suggests that you had at least a suspicion that his motives might not have been what he claimed. What might give you that kind of suspicion?"

She waited for Phoebe to vehemently insist that she never had any such suspicion, but she didn't. After briefly hesitating, she answered.

"I'm not accusing him of anything," she said instead, unintentionally acknowledging that she had her doubts. "It's just that when he told me that I showed great promise, he stared into my eyes and got really close. It was probably nothing."

"And yet it felt off to you," Jessie prodded.

"He never tried anything," Phoebe said. "But I just got this…feeling. So when I went to meet him this morning, I was a little nervous, wondering if I had misread it. I just don't know. Like I said, it could have been totally innocent. I just wasn't sure, you know?"

"I do," Jessie replied. "Listen, Phoebe, I really appreciate you being straight with me. I know it wasn't easy, but your information could be very valuable to solving this case. You should be incredibly proud of yourself."

"What do I do now?" the girl asked, forlorn.

"First off, you might want to talk to one of the mental health counselors here," Jessie suggested. "You don't have to get into details, but take advantage of the resources available to you. Just talk about how you're feeling. Don't hold it all in. If they suggest additional medication, take it."

"Okay."

"But one caution," Jessie added, "I wouldn't be too quick to mention your involvement in the case to anyone else yet. The press is going to have a field day with this. I recommend you take the rest of the day off, maybe the whole weekend. I know that might mean skipping your classes tomorrow, but you've got a pretty good excuse."

"I won't get in trouble?" Phoebe asked.

"I'm sure the counselor will write you a note, and if they don't, I will," Jessie promised. "Don't leave the state but maybe go on a weekend camping trip with your friends or rent a cabin in the mountains. Just get away from the frenzy that's coming. And here's my card. If you have any questions or remember anything else, don't hesitate to call. Even if you just need to talk, that's okay. I can't promise I'll answer right away because, you know, I'm working a murder investigation, but I will get back to you. Okay?"

Phoebe nodded and reached out, grabbing Jessie's hand and giving it a tight squeeze.

"Thank you," she whispered.

Jessie smiled as she got up. It wasn't until she left the room that she turned her full focus to the question that had been nagging at the back of her mind ever since Phoebe made her admission. If Roman Tobias had asked her to meet him to work on a "special project," who else had he made the same request of? And just as important, who else knew about it?

CHAPTER THIRTEEN

Jessie took a mental break from fixating on one concern to focus on another.

As she and Ryan headed back to the library, she called Seasons again, in the hopes of getting hold of Hannah.

"I'm afraid she's taking a tour of our new Seasons at Sea facility," the receptionist said after putting her on hold for a minute. "All of our residents are taking a bus to the site for tours throughout the day. I can give her a message when she returns."

Jessie was briefly tempted to ask what the hell Seasons at Sea was, but decided it wasn't important right now.

"Actually, can you please connect me to Dr. Janice Lemmon?"

"I'll see if she's available," the receptionist replied.

"Tell her it's Jessie Hunt."

It only took ten seconds for her to come back on the line.

"Hold for Dr. Lemmon," she said.

"Jessie?" asked a familiar voice moments later.

"Hi, Dr. Lemmon. It's so great to hear your voice," she said. "How are you doing?"

"Oh you know, not so bad for a decrepit old lady," she joked.

"Are you kidding?" Jessie said. "You're in better shape than most people half your age. And I say that as someone who *is* half your age."

"That's very sweet of you," Dr. Lemmon replied. "My back might have a different opinion however. How are you?"

"I'm okay. We're in the middle of a murder investigation at UCLA, which is weird considering that I teach here too. But that's not why I'm calling. Have you had a chance to talk to Hannah since you got back?"

"I'm afraid not," Dr. Lemmon said. "I've been trapped in paperwork and meeting hell all day. Plus, they approved this Seasons at Sea thing while I was in the hospital and they're rolling it out today."

"What is that anyway?"

"It's actually a quality idea for a program," she said."They use water activities like surfing, scuba diving, and kayaking to build residents' self-esteem and teamwork. My issue is with the funding source. It's some foundation with questionable financing called the Alliance for a new something or other. That's why I hadn't signed off on it. But while I was gone, the center director leapt at the chance to finalize it. He's—how can I put this diplomatically?— very enthused about the publicity it's bringing the center and himself. Anyway, that's not your concern. Is something wrong in regard to Hannah?"

"Not that I know of," Jessie told her. "I just haven't been able to get in touch with her today and I was a little worried."

"About what?"

Jessie proceeded to fill Dr. Lemmon in on the conversation she'd had with Hannah earlier in the week, specifically how she had found Meredith Bartlett's body and seemed to be having trouble processing it.

"I'm worried that she might feel responsible in some way," she added, "that she thinks she could have saved this girl's life if she'd noticed the signs."

"I'll make sure to check in with her," Dr. Lemmon promised. "It's been over a week since we had a one-on-one session anyway and I want to see how she's progressing on the issue that brought her here in the first place."

Jessie admired how delicately the doctor referred to the "issue," which happened to be an intense desire to recapture the thrill that Hannah got from killing a man. But neither of them needed to get that specific.

"That would be great," Jessie said, her attention pulled away by Ryan, who was holding up his ringing phone. The caller ID showed Captain Decker. She wrapped up quickly. "I have to go, but please keep me updated."

"Of course," Dr. Lemmon said just before Jessie hung up.

Ryan had already answered his call and put it on speaker.

"Hello, Captain," he said. "I'm here with Jessie."

"It seems that you two are seriously ruffling some feathers," Decker said without preamble.

"What do you mean?" Jessie asked.

"I just got a call from Mark Rawls, the dean of the history department. He was complaining that you were harassing people in the department."

Ryan looked angry but Jessie couldn't stifle a laugh.

"I think by 'harassing,' he's referring to what we might call 'questioning,' Captain."

"I figured as much," Decker sighed. "He had some particularly choice words for you, Hunt. He claimed that your involvement in the case was a conflict of interest, that since you work at both the school and with LAPD, you should be removed immediately."

Now it was Jessie's turn to be annoyed.

"That's ridiculous," she said. "I've never met Roman Tobias or even set foot in the history department until today."

"Plus," Ryan added, "In our face-to-face meeting with the university chancellor, he welcomed us and offered us any help we needed. And didn't the university police request that we take over the case?"

"All points I made to Rawls," Decker told him. "I explained that HSS was there by invitation and that I had no intention of pulling anyone off the case. But I wanted to make you both aware because he didn't sound too happy about it. I wouldn't be surprised if he tries something else."

"Thanks, Captain," Ryan said as they arrived at the front steps of the library.

Once they hung up, Jessie turned to Ryan and added something she'd held back from saying to Decker because she knew he'd consider it speculative.

"You'd think the dean of the department would want to get the bottom of this as quickly as possible rather than booting the profiler working the case," she noted. "It's almost enough to make someone suspicious that Rawls is worried I'll unearth some bit of dirty laundry which could be worse than the school's prized professor getting murdered."

"Almost," Ryan replied drily.

They were just starting up the steps to the library entrance when they got another call. This time it was Jamil.

"What's up?" Ryan asked after picking up.

"I don't know if this is enough to dirty up the professor's squeaky clean image," he said, "but I think I found something."

Jessie could tell from Jamil's excited tone that he believed it was more than just "something."

"Tell us," she said.

"I found a grievance filed against him," he said. "The reason that we didn't discover it initially was that it was retracted the very next day. As a result, it was purged completely from the history department records, as if it had never been filed at all."

"But..." Jessie prodded, starting to understand why Jamil sounded so amped.

"But we—," he started to say.

"Not *we*," Beth corrected, "You."

"Okay, I," Jamil continued, his blushing almost audible through the phone, "was doing a search of the entire university database, looking for anything. Unlike the history department, they keep digital records of all grievances filed, whether retracted or not. They have a separate, hard-to-find file for retracted ones, which are purged two years after the original complaint, kind of like a statute of limitations. But since this grievance was filed twenty-two months ago, it's still in the system."

"What was the nature of the grievance?" Ryan asked.

"That's redacted," Jamil said. "But the name of the filing complainant isn't. Would you like it?"

"If you don't mind," Jessie said, letting him extend his moment in the sun a little longer.

"It's Monica Littleton. She a professor in the— wait for it...history department."

"That's awesome!" Jessie exclaimed, startling a student just walking out of the library. "Great work, Jamil. We're going to head back over there now. Please send us everything you have on her."

"Will do," Jamil promised, sounding as giddy about the praise as about what he'd found.

Jessie and Ryan had stopped at the top of the stairs when they got the news. Now they simultaneously turned back around in the direction of Bunche Hall.

"I guess I know where we're headed," Ryan said.

"If I didn't think it would draw attention," Jessie replied. "I'd already be sprinting there."

65

CHAPTER FOURTEEN

Ryan was glad they didn't end up running, as it would have taken longer than expected.

They started down their normal route to the history department, which would have taken them right past Haines Hall. But when they rounded the corner, they saw a massive swarm of media encircling the building. In order to avoid being seen, they had to go the long way around, adding several wasted minutes to the trip.

Just as they finally entered Bunche Hall, Ryan felt his phone buzz. He saw that Jessie got a message at the same time and knew it must be from Jamil, providing the requested information on Monica Littleton.

"Can you check that while I sign us in?' he asked.

Jessie nodded and started scrolling through the data as he checked in with the security guard. It wasn't the same guy from before, when they'd been in such a rush to interview people just before Chancellor Elliot sent out the press release announcing Tobias's death. That guy had simply waved them through right after they signed in. This guard apparently hadn't gotten the memo.

"Include your driver's license number and make a note of who you're going to see," he said brusquely, wearing a sour expression.

"How about I use my badge number?" Ryan offered, pulling it out and thumping it down on the counter harder than was necessary.

"That would be fine," the guard said, his tone suddenly meeker.

"Great," Ryan replied, writing it. "We're seeing Professor Littleton. Which office is hers?"

"She's in 617, Detective," the guard answered quickly.

"Thanks," Ryan said gruffly, grabbing his badge back and turning around without another word. He wanted to leave guard to stew in his newfound humility.

"That was a little harsh," Jessie whispered as they headed for the elevator.

"He pissed me off," Ryan told her. "You shouldn't have to be a cop to get a polite greeting."

"I didn't know I was engaged to Miss Manners over here," she teased.

He couldn't help but crack a smile at the dig.

"Point taken," he said. "So what did Jamil find?"

"It looks like Monica Littleton is an associate professor of Renaissance-era Italian history," Jessie said, reading from her phone. "She's thirty-three and has been here for three years now after a stint at Boston University. She's single, has an apartment in Silverlake, and has almost paid off her 2015 Hyundai Elantra. Never been arrested. No lawsuits. No financial red flags."

"She's sounds a lot like Tobias in that way," Ryan noted as they got in the elevator, "squeaky clean. Why didn't we interview her during the mad dash earlier?"

"She was teaching a class while we were running around here, so we missed her," Jessie explained.

Once they exited at the sixth floor, they moved quickly down the hall until they got to her office. The door was open but the room was empty. Ryan knocked lightly just in case she was behind a cabinet or something but there was no response. They both took a half step over the threshold to get a peek inside.

Unlike Roman Tobias's expansive office, Littleton's quarters were cramped. There was enough room for her desk, one chair opposite it, and two filing cabinets. It was a good thing that there were built-in bookshelves or she wouldn't have had anywhere to put her massive collection. Ryan guessed that there were over two hundred books crammed on the shelves. A quick scan showed that the bulk were on her area of expertise.

"Can I help you?" someone said from the hallway behind them.

Ryan and Jessie turned around to see a diminutive woman in a loose-fitting, black dress, with extremely long, dark hair staring suspiciously back at them. She was attractive in a severe way—pale with dark eye makeup. She reminded him of a woman who knew she was too old to keep up the Goth look she had in college but couldn't completely let it go yet.

"We hope so," Jessie said warmly in what Ryan knew was an attempt to lower the hostile energy they could both feel coming from her. "We're with the LAPD. This is Detective Hernandez. I'm Jessie Hunt. We're investigating the death of Roman Tobias."

"Of course you are," Littleton said emotionlessly, sliding past them into her office and taking a seat at her desk. "I keep hearing from all my colleagues that they'd been questioned. I was borderline offended that you hadn't sought me out yet."

"I assure you, we tried," Jessie replied. "You were apparently in class when we were here before. But we're glad to have the opportunity to talk now. Do you have a couple of minutes?"

"Sure," Littleton said with a shrug, before sarcastically adding, "I'm honored to be in the presence of perhaps the second most famous instructor on campus. But I don't know how much help I'll be. It's not like Roman and I crossed paths much. I know it's not nice to say under the circumstances, but I wasn't really a fan. I don't really go in for cult of personality professors. And I gather you know my academic focus. It's not like there's much cause for overlap between professors of American history and the Italian Renaissance."

"But you must have had some interaction," Ryan said. "Otherwise why file that grievance two years ago?"

Littleton looked genuinely surprised for the first time. Her jaw dropped open briefly before she recovered.

"That was retracted," she said defensively.

"Sure," Ryan replied. "But you filed it. What was the complaint about?"

Littleton looked reluctant to answer but seemed to realize that not doing so would reflect poorly on her. She sighed.

"He was misusing department resources. He commandeered materials, had other instructors bumped from lecture halls he wanted to use with little to no notice, and was relentlessly condescending about all of it."

Ryan was about to follow up but Jessie jumped in first.

"With all due respect, Professor Littleton, that sounds like the behavior of lots of big-time professors. It hardly seems like the sort of thing that would normally be handled through a formal grievance. I have to wonder what was really going on."

Littleton looked put out by the comment and her already gloomy disposition turned darker.

"Nothing was going on," she snapped angrily. "And all of a sudden, I think I'm tired of answering these questions."

Ryan knew better than to get in front of what was coming next. As Jessie Hunt's partner and fiancé, he learned long ago that few things riled her up more than arrogant power plays.

"Monica," Jessie said, dropping the honorific, as well as her deferential tone, "you seem to be under a misimpression. We are questioning you, not having a little chat. And if you aren't forthcoming to our satisfaction, this conversation can turn into a formal interrogation real fast. Whether you were a fan or not, Roman Tobias is dead, murdered by someone on this campus. So you better stop being 'tired' of our questioning and find your second wind."

Ryan locked a scowl in his face for fear that he might break into a grin. Watching Jessie dress down someone who deserved it was one of the greatest pleasures he got in life, not to mention a major turn-on. Monica Littleton looked less enthused. She still had a disagreeable air about her, but now it was tinged with fear.

"Fine," she muttered petulantly, doing her best to hide her apprehension. "About two years ago, after a department symposium, a few of us went out to a bar for drinks. This was before I had formed my opinion of Roman. We flirted. One thing led to another and we ended up in bed back at his place. But the next day he gave me the cold shoulder. He didn't just act like that night was no big deal, which it wasn't; he barely conceded that anything happened. He made me feel like a stupid, needy schoolgirl for just wanting him to acknowledge it."

She stopped to see if either of them was going to say anything but both knew not to interrupt when someone was getting something off their chest.

"It pissed me off," she admitted. "I was fuming all day and by that evening, I'd worked myself up into a lather. So that night, after a few glasses of wine, I accessed the department portal to file the grievance. Since there wasn't an option in the drop-down menu for being an asshole after a one night stand, I went with 'misuse of department resources.'"

"But you retracted it," Jessie reminded her.

"Yeah—when I woke up the next morning, I wasn't as worked up. In retrospect, I guess I should have slept on it. More importantly, I realized that it wasn't a good look for some junior professor to file a complaint against the most prominent academic name on campus unless I had a major issue. It was sure to backfire and make me look petty. So I retracted it. No one ever reached out to me. I have no idea if he ever even knew about it. He never said anything, not that there was much opportunity. We barely spoke after that."

"You said that unless you had a major issue, it wasn't a good move to file a grievance," Jessie noted. "Are you saying you never had reason to complain about anything else? No other concerns in your time here?"

"No," she said, "Why?"

Ryan saw Littleton perk up at the leading nature of Jessie's question and jumped in to tamp down her curiosity.

"Just being thorough," he said sharply.

Ryan knew Jessie was trying to uncover other secrets Tobias might have, ones that seemed to have the whole history department in "circle the wagons" mode, but he was focused on something else. Bitterness over the fallout from a sexual encounter gone south was a pretty strong motive for murder, though he would have expected Littleton to act on it back at the time when it was most raw. Maybe something happened recently to re-open the wound.

"Did you have any run-ins with him of late?" he followed up before the professor could ask anything else about Jessie's line of questioning.

"No. I can't remember the last time we exchanged more than perfunctory greetings. And even that might have been as long ago as the holiday party in December."

"When did you last see him?" Ryan pressed. After all, just because they didn't talk, that didn't mean that she couldn't be set off by something she observed him say or do.

"Actually, I saw him this morning. I was attending a lecture at Royce Hall. He gave some introductory remarks. Then he took a seat at the back. When the lights went down for the associated video presentation, he waited about five minutes and snuck out. It wasn't even 10 a.m. I considered it incredibly rude."

"And you stayed the whole time?" he asked.

"Yes," she said, before adding, "well almost. I had to leave before the Q&A was over because I was teaching an 11 a.m. class. But I was there for the entire lecture."

Ryan looked at Jessie and saw that she was thinking the same thing he was.

"Was anyone with you at the lecture?" she asked.

"Sure," the professor answered blithely. "I went with two colleagues. We got there about ten minutes early to get good seats. "

"And how far was the lecture from your class?" Jessie followed up.

"Maybe a three minute walk—why? Wait, are you checking my alibi?" she wanted to know, before pressing ahead excitedly. "If that's the case, I have about fifty students who can vouch for me."

Ryan's heart sank. If Monica Littleton really was at the lecture nearly the whole time and then went directly to teach a class, their timeline was shot. If what Littleton said was true, Roman Tobias was murdered between 10:00 and 10:30. Pending witness confirmation, it appeared that Littleton was in a different building that whole time.

She wasn't their killer. They were back to square one.

CHAPTER FIFTEEN

Jessie tried to cheer Ryan up, to no avail.

He'd committed the cardinal sin, one he'd often warned her against: getting too excited about a lead. Inevitably, if it fell apart, it could mess with your mindset going forward.

When she returned to where he was waiting for her in the library study room that was their makeshift headquarters, she pulled out a protein bar she'd bought at a vending machine.

"Sugar always makes it feel better," she said playfully, tossing it at his downcast face.

He caught it just in time, ripped it open, and took a bite.

"Don't think I can be soothed so cheaply," he muttered as he chewed, though he did seem to be slightly buoyed by the snack.

"Maybe I can find some other way to lift your spirits later this evening," she suggested with an arched eyebrow, "but for now let's set aside your failed theory and try mine on for size."

"I'll happily take you up on that offer," Ryan replied, "and I know your theory: that if Tobias made Phoebe Lewis feel awkward, maybe he acted even more inappropriately with other girls."

"You agree that it's possible," Jessie said.

"Sure, but if that was going on, don't you think Monica Littleton would have leapt at the chance to take Tobias down for something legit? When you asked if there was anything else about him that concerned her, she said no."

"Right," Jessie agreed, "but it's for that very reason—because of their messy history together—that Tobias would be super careful not to let her see anything untoward. He'd have to know that after being spurned by him, she was unlikely to let his fame stop her from raising the alarm if she knew about any misbehavior on his part. Hell, maybe he *did* know about the grievance she filed and kept his nose clean around her for that very reason."

"That's a lot of speculation without any evidence to back it up, Jessie," he said.

"I acknowledge that, but we have to think outside the box here. We're not getting anything useful from anyone in a position to help, which is sketchy in itself. You have to admit that almost everyone associated with the history department has been in lockstep. No one even mentioned the stuff about co-opting lecture halls and materials. You're telling me no one else was bothered by that stuff?"

"I'm sure they were," he allowed. "But for them, what was the point in bringing that up with us? Before anyone we interviewed knew he was dead, they were too intimidated by him to say anything. And once they learned, it probably seemed petty to complain about a dead man being kind of a jerk."

Jessie wasn't convinced. People in the department weren't just reluctant to speak ill of Roman Tobias; they all regurgitated the same rote praise of him. That wasn't evidence but it felt important. She saw Ryan's expression soften slightly and wondered if he was reconsidering his position or worrying that she might retract her offer to lift his spirits later.

"So what do you want to do next?" he finally asked, his resolve fading in the face of her certitude. The question was so direct that it caught her off guard.

What do I want to do next?

"Give me a second," she said, closing her eyes and trying to concentrate.

She knew what she wanted to do: determine if the uncomfortable vibe that Phoebe Lewis got from Tobias was just an innocent misunderstanding, an isolated instance, or something more. She felt certain that was the key to solving this case. The problem was finding a way to answer that question when the professor was dead and no one was talking.

But that isn't entirely true. One person has talked about this: Phoebe. And we know a lot about her.

Jessie opened her eyes.

"I need you to humor me here," she said.

"Story of my life," Ryan quipped.

But her mind was racing too fast to react.

"So let's assume for the moment that Phoebe Lewis's concerns about Tobias were well-founded," she said, "that he *was* coming on to her and that he intended to take it farther when they had their meeting this morning."

"That's a big assumption."

"I know," she admitted, "but it's not crazy. He asks her to meet outside normal office hours for a vague 'special project' that she wasn't supposed to mention to anyone. Then he sneaks out of that lecture, potentially so that he could claim to have an alibi if Phoebe balked or said anything later. He could say that he was at the lecture, even gave the introductory remarks. Hundreds of people would have remembered seeing him. If Monica Littleton hadn't noticed him sneak out in the dark, he would have had clear sailing. No one would know he was alone in his office with a student."

"Okay, assume all that's true," Ryan said. "How does it get us any closer to finding out who killed him?"

"Because if he did all that, it shows what kind of deceitful trickery he was capable of," she replied. "And if he was capable of that with Phoebe, he was capable of it with other students too."

"And you think that's why everyone in the department gave bland commendations for him?" Ryan asked.

"Exactly," Jessie said. "That's the kind of behavior that might make his enablers offer all those stock compliments when asked questions about him. And if it's true, then it opens up a whole new pool of suspects: the students he manipulated, their angry boyfriends, maybe a disgusted fellow professor who'd just had enough of it."

"So how do you propose we determine if it's true?"

"By using the one lead we have: Phoebe," Jessie answered. "We know what kind of person she is: smart but very quiet and shy, cute but almost embarrassed by it. She wears glasses that distract attention away from her face. She has a short, unpretentious haircut. She dresses in jeans and a sweater way too big for her. She's self-conscious and full of uncertainty about everything but her academic prowess."

"Okay," Ryan said, obviously waiting for her to connect the dots.

"What if *that* was Tobias's type?"

"Shy girls?"

"Yes, but not just that—shy girls who look the part. The university has an online directory of every student, including photos. Obviously that's a massive data set. But what if we get Jamil and Beth to help us? Give them the names of every female student in Tobias's classes in the last two years. Then match that with photos of girls who look like Phoebe—short hair, glasses, body-hiding clothes. Filter the list more by eliminating the ones in sororities or other heavily social clubs. Make sure to include anyone who dropped his class before the semester ended. That will give us a pool to work with."

"That's good," Ryan said and she could tell that he meant it. But then he frowned and she knew she'd lost him again. "But it's still just guesswork. What are we going to do after we get the names—call them up and ask if they're shy?"

"We won't need to," Jessie assured him. "We've got someone else for that. All Tobias's classes are upper level. If these women were in them, they were almost certainly history majors, with an emphasis on American history, just like Phoebe. It's a pretty decent bet that she knows a lot of them or has at least taken classes with them. She can tell us which ones fit the profile, personality-wise."

Ryan sat with that for a moment, silently trying to poke holes in the idea. Then he looked straight at her.

"Let's call Jamil," he said.

CHAPTER SIXTEEN

Even Jessie was amazed when it took them less than an hour.

Working together, Jamil and Beth came up with a list of female students who took Tobias's courses in the last two years, then culled through university photos to find ones who met the physical criteria Jessie had given them. After that, they eliminated members of socially extroverted, non-academic, or political clubs. That left them with seven names.

"What if we're eliminating potential victims?" Beth asked.

"That's a risk," Jessie acknowledged. "But we've got to start somewhere."

She reviewed the list to see if she recognized any of the names. Two of them were familiar.

"We can eliminate Heather Langley and Greta Culp," she said. "Both of them are in my profiling seminar and neither is a shrinking violet. They don't fit the profile."

"That leaves five for us to check with Phoebe," Ryan noted. "Shall we make the call?"

Jessie was already looking up her number.

"I'm going to conference everyone in after I get her permission," she said as she dialed, "but please let me do the talking. I want to make sure she's doing okay. She's pretty fragile right now and I don't want to freak her out by introducing new people for her to deal with."

Moments later, Phoebe picked up.

"Ms. Hunt?" she said hesitantly.

"Hi Phoebe, it's me. You can call me Jessie. How are you doing? Did you get out of town?"

"Not yet," Phoebe said. "But a friend of mine's grandparents live in Palm Springs. They have a guest room and they said we could stay there for a few days. So we're leaving town after traffic dies down tonight."

"That's a great idea, especially since the campus is overrun with media types," Jessie told her. "You'll be off the beaten path, far enough away for some privacy but close enough to get back if you need to. And I'm assuming your friend's grandparents don't refresh TMZ hourly so hopefully they won't be peppering you with questions about what happened?"

"She didn't get into the details of why we're coming. She just said she needed a break and asked to bring a friend. I explained what you said to her—that I shouldn't broadcast my involvement and she totally understood. She actually started tearing up when I told her that she was the only one I was trusting with this. I haven't even told my folks yet. They would stress me out more than I already am."

"It sounds like you're handling this as well as you possibly can," Jessie reassured her.

"Thanks. Is that why you called?"

"Partly," Jessie said. "I wanted to check up on you, but I also need your help. Would that be okay? It's just a matter of a few questions."

"Okay," Phoebe said apprehensively.

"Thanks. I'm actually going to conference in some other people I work with—a detective and two police researchers. They'll just be listening in but I want everyone to hear what you have to share in real time. It could really help with the case. Is that all right?"

"I guess," Phoebe said. "You're not going to record it for a trial or something, are you?"

"Definitely not," Jessie promised. "It's informational only."

"Okay."

Jessie conferenced the others in and continued.

"Guys, I'm on the line with Phoebe. Is everyone there?" she asked. After a chorus of affirmatives, she proceeded. "So Phoebe, I just want to find out if you know any of the students whose names I'm about to mention. Are you ready?"

"Uh-huh."

"Okay, I have Bettina Ashrani, Kaitlyn Roy, Vivien Crump, Annie Boyd, and Teri Rosner."

"I know all their names," Phoebe said. "I think they're all history majors. But I've never met two of them. I wouldn't even know what they look like."

"Who are they?" Jessie asked.

"I don't know Kaitlyn or Vivien."

"But you're familiar with the other three?"

"Yes," Phoebe said. "I've had multiple classes with each of them."

"Can you describe them?"

"What do you mean?" Phoebe asked, confused. "Like what they look like?"

"No, their personalities—are they outgoing or more reserved?"

"Oh," Phoebe said, and then paused briefly before answering. "Teri is definitely more on the outgoing side. She's a real chatterbox, sometimes too much. And though she doesn't look like it, I know she likes to party. I wouldn't call Bettina outgoing, but she's not reserved either. She answers questions in class without prompting. She's friendly. I think she's in a band too."

"And Annie?"

"She's more on the shy side," Phoebe said. "She likes to sit in the very back in class and blushes whenever a professor calls on her."

"Did Professor Tobias call on her?" Jessie pressed.

"He used to, but he stopped lately. I think that after a while he got tired of having to drag answers out of her."

Jessie wanted to hang up and call Annie Boyd right now but restrained herself.

"Thanks so much, Phoebe," she said with an air of finality.

"Was that helpful?" the girl asked. "I don't know if I answered right."

"You were great," Jessie pledged. "I'm hoping this will make a big difference. Now don't worry about that anymore. Just enjoy getting away for a few days."

"Thanks, I will."

Jessie had barely hung up when Jamil started speaking.

"It's just after 4 p.m. so all of Annie Boyd's classes are done for the day. She's not officially registered as part of any clubs that meet this afternoon. In fact, she's not part of any clubs at all. She lives in a dorm that's within walking distance of you. If she's really the wallflower that Phoebe described, she might be there now. I'm sending you her address, phone number, and a few other photos beyond the one in the student directory."

"Wow, that was fast," Ryan marveled. "But I am a little disappointed that you didn't include her astrological sign too."

"She's a Gemini," Beth volunteered. "She turns twenty in June."

Ryan rolled his eyes at Jessie, the only person who could see it.

"Serves you right for being snarky," Jessie scolded him. "Let's go see what Annie has to say."

78

CHAPTER SEVENTEEN

Jessie decided not to call.

They could always do that if Annie wasn't in her dorm room, but her preference was for their first interaction to be in person.

They walked to the student housing section of campus called The Hill, and arrived at Annie's dorm, a visually uninspiring red and white brick five-story building. After following an oblivious student through the main door, they checked in with the on-site security guard, who gave them temporary swipe cards to access other areas. As they waited for the cards, they received a text from Jamil, helpfully pointing out that Annie had classes at 9 a.m. and 10 a.m., making her an unlikely suspect in the murder.

Annie's room was on the third floor. They took the stairs and wended their way through the hallway, dodging students, all of whom looked at them curiously. They reached the door to room 312, which had a whiteboard and black pen hanging from a plastic hook. The board was blank. Jessie looked over at Ryan.

"I think you should knock," he suggested. "If what you think happened did happen, I'd rather she see your face first."

Jessie agreed and rapped gently on the door. She could hear a rustling inside as someone came close.

"Who is it?" asked someone with a young, female voice.

Jessie realized that the door didn't have a peephole so there was no way the person could see out. She didn't love that.

"My name is Jessie Hunt. I work with the Los Angeles Police Department. I'm looking for Annie Boyd."

She could almost hear the person processing what she'd said and expected more questions. Instead the door opened to reveal someone who looked even more timid in person than her pictures suggested. She was like the blonde twin of Phoebe. Small, with short, flaxen hair, porcelain skin, and black-framed glasses; she was wearing sweatpants and a heavy hoodie. She wore no cosmetics at all.

Like, Phoebe, she was indistinctly cute, unlikely to draw the attention of the boys on campus who were constantly in search of model types. But all it would take was a few fashion tweaks and a bit of makeup for them to take notice. Jessie suspected that someone else already had.

"I'm Annie," she said softly. "Is this about Professor Tobias?"

For one of the few times in recent memory, Jessie's jaw dropped.

"Yes," she said once she'd recovered. "We were hoping you could answer some questions for us. I'm here with Detective Hernandez. May we come in? If you'd rather it just be me, he can wait outside."

Ryan stepped into sight and gave her his best "I won't be offended" smile.

"That would be good," she said, before whispering, "If it's okay?"

"Of course," he said warmly, using the same tone he employed when soothing traumatized victims of violence. "I'll be out here if you need me."

They stepped inside and Jessie closed the door. She looked around the tiny space, which was smaller than some prison cells she'd encountered. There was a twin bed pushed up against the back wall, under the lone window. A Spartan desk was built into one wall, along with a wooden chair. There were two shelves attached to the wall above the desk, comprised mostly of books on the American Revolution and the Civil War. To the left of the door was a narrow closet, half of which was taken up by a rickety-looking chest of drawers, with a mirror affixed to the wall right behind it.

"Nice place you've got here," Jessie said, trying to break the tension.

Thankfully, Annie giggled at the crack.

"I once saw a documentary on those coffin apartments in Hong Kong," she said. "When this place starts to close in on me, I try to remind myself that I have it better than those folks."

"Good attitude," Jessie replied, looking at the posters that covered nearly every spare inch of the wall, and nodding at one corner. "I like the Dua Lipa poster."

"Are you a fan?" Annie asked, unable to mask her surprise.

"That might be overstating it, but my little sister is a senior in high school, so I'm well-acquainted with her work."

Annie sat down on her bed and immediately curled her body into a protective ball.

"So I guess we can't stall forever," she said. "What do you want to know?"

"I gather you heard about what happened to Professor Tobias," Jessie replied, pulling over the desk chair and sitting beside the bed.

"I know that he died," Annie confirmed. "The rumor around campus is that someone killed him in his office."

"That's correct," Jessie told her, seeing no reason to hedge. "Let me ask you, Annie, how did you know that I wanted to talk to you about him?"

The girl shrugged.

"I guess I just figured that once the folks investigating his death started digging into his life, you'd start coming across people like me."

Jessie nodded sympathetically and lowered her head, though not for the obvious reason. She was trying to hide the mix of shock and giddiness she felt at the answer. Annie had said "people," as in *plural*. It was like a blinking red light staring her in the face and all she wanted to do was ask a follow-up question. But that might spook Annie, so when she replied, she did her best not to reveal the magnitude of those words.

"What exactly was the nature of your relationship with him?" she asked gently.

"You know what's funny?" Annie wondered, though she wasn't smiling. "Until he died, I never would have considered telling you this. His being gone is like having a gag suddenly yanked out my mouth. So here's the truth. The nature of our 'relationship' was that he turned me into his sexual plaything and somehow made me think it was an honor."

Jessie sighed deeply, allowing herself a moment to process what she'd just heard. Finally, after butting her head against metaphorical walls for hours, her suspicion had been borne out. But her satisfaction was severely tempered by the horrific nature of Annie's revelation. Tobias wasn't just sleeping with her, it sounded like he was toying with her.

Jessie also noticed that, for the first time, there was something in the girl's voice other than self-doubt. She sounded angry. Jessie nodded again, using it as a stalling tactic so that she could best form her next question.

"How did he do that?" she inquired delicately.

Annie closed her eyes and shook her head, as if trying to force the memory out of her brain.

"Well, first he groomed me, complimenting my analysis in the papers he assigned, asking me to stay after class for an extra few minutes to discuss the lecture topic in greater detail. After a while, he invited me to walk him to his office while we talked. He might make a mention of how remarkably gifted I was, and casually throw in a flattering remark about how my jacket brought out the color in my eyes."

She stopped for a second and it looked like she was about to cry. But she swallowed hard, took a deep breath, and continued.

"I don't mean to offend you, Ms. Hunt," she continued, her voice full of pain, "But looking the way you do, it might be hard to understand what I'm about to say. Can you imagine how powerful it would be to have your intellectual hero, the man you've been reading about and watching on TV for years, and maybe nursing a schoolgirl crush on, tell you that you are smart, that you are special, and that you are *pretty*? Other than my dad, no man ever called me pretty in my life, and he left us when I was twelve, so that ended up being a tad emotionally complicated for me."

She laughed bitterly at the thought, but then quickly regained her focus.

"Professor Tobias knew exactly how to work me," she said. "He understood my weak spots. He knew what made me vulnerable and how to build me up and break me down when it suited him. The next thing I knew, I was showing up at his office at all hours to do…whatever he instructed me to do. I let him do things to me that would make my mother cry. He preyed on me, Ms. Hunt, and had me thanking him for it."

Jessie was quiet for a while, wanting to be respectful of what she'd been told but cognizant that she needed more.

"How long did this go on?" she wanted to know.

"About six weeks," she said. "When I finally started to realize what was happening and tried to find a way out, he threatened me. He said that if I breathed a word of this to anyone, it would be reflected in my grades. He told me he could put obstacles in the way of my graduation. And then, when he had me petrified that I'd be kicked out of school and branded a whore, he kicked me to the curb."

Her voice quavered as she finished. Jessie took her hand and squeezed.

"Listen, what happened to you was wrong," she said, looking Annie in the eyes. "It's over now, so allow yourself to breathe, okay?"

Annie nodded silently as she took Jessie's advice and sucked air in through her nose. As she slowly exhaled, Jessie continued.

"As someone who has been through my fair share of trauma, I can tell you, this is going to come back at you, probably when you least expect it. You should take advantage of the school's resources, talk to someone. This happened on their watch and your care will be on their dime. They won't balk but if anybody gives you a hard time, you call me. Got it?"

Annie nodded again. She seemed to be breathing more normally now so Jessie proceeded tentatively.

"Can I ask you a few more questions?"

"Of course," Annie said.

"You said that at some point, Tobias 'kicked you to the curb.' How long ago was that?"

"About two weeks ago," she answered, "which was right around the time I started to pick up on the signs that I wasn't the only one."

"What do you mean?"

"I started thinking about this other girl in the class with me. I remembered that earlier in the year, before he noticed me, he would invite her to stick around for an extra minute. It occurred to me that she was a lot like me: quiet, shy, almost invisible in class, except to him. She even looked like me."

"How so?" Jessie pressed.

"She's tiny with short hair and glasses," Annie explained. "I remembered that at some point he stopped inviting her to stay after class. Later on, she was always the last one to enter the classroom and the first to rush out when it ended, like she didn't want to be stuck alone with him for any reason."

"Do you think she was the only one?"

"I can't say for sure," she admitted, "but I doubt it. He was too polished with his act, like he'd been at it for years. In fact, now that I think about it, there's this one girl in my class who he just started chatting with this week after the lecture was over. Her name is Phoebe something. She's a quiet one too. I hope he died before he started in on her. Hey, maybe one of his playthings decided to turn the tables on him. Wouldn't that be something?"

Jessie didn't comment on that, not wanting to violate Phoebe's privacy or fixate on the understandable vitriol in Annie's words.

"Thanks, I'll look into that," she said. "In the meantime, can you give me the name of the girl that you mentioned, the one you thought might have been your predecessor?"

Annie hesitated.

"I don't want to get anyone in trouble," she said carefully.

"Neither do I," Jessie replied, not entirely truthfully. "But with you, this Phoebe girl, and the one before you, that looks like a pattern. We need to pursue that, not just in case it's relevant to the investigation, but to get these girls help. There may be a lot of you out there."

Annie appeared convinced by that.

"Okay. Her name is Rachel Jones. She actually lives on the fifth floor here."

That name rang a bell. It took a second for Jessie to remember that she was one of the girls eliminated from the database.

"Wait. I've seen photos of Rachel Jones," she said. "She doesn't wear glasses."

"She only wears them in class," Annie said.

Jessie heart rolled over sickeningly in her chest. They had eliminated a possible victim simply because she didn't wear glasses in her directory photo. How many other girls did they remove from the list for the same reason? Or because they had long hair when their photo was taken and subsequently cut it? If Tobias had targeted three girls in a matter of just a few months, how many had he victimized in his half a decade here? Or before that?

Her mind was swimming and she felt slightly ill.

"Thanks for your help," she said quickly to Annie before darting out of the room. "Remember to take advantage of those resources. I'll be in touch with updates."

She closed the door quickly behind her and moved toward Ryan, who was staring at her, confused.

"What is it?" he asked.

"I know who we need to talk to next," she said as she wrapped her arms around him and burrowed her head in his chest, "but first I could really use a hug."

Rachel Jones took longer to open up than Annie.

But once Jessie made it clear that she wasn't in trouble, she came clean too. Her story was remarkably similar. A self-conscious bookworm, unpopular in high school, never confident about anything other than academics, suddenly overwhelmed by the flattering attention of a personal hero.

"He had me strip naked as part of this sick twist on that cruel sorority thing. He would circle parts of my body, but instead of pointing out flaws, he would tell me why they were beautiful. In the moment I thought it was romantic. But looking back, it was just a different kind of sick—a grown man in a position of power over a girl less than half his age, picking apart her body as a way to assert his dominance. I'm glad he's dead."

"I get that," Jessie had told her, "but that's also why I need to know where you were this morning between 9:45 and 10:30."

The question had made Rachel laugh.

"I was in the library, working on a paper for *his* class," she explained. "That place is littered with cameras. You should be able to find me without any problem."

Before Jessie left, Rachel also gave her the name of two other female students she suspected Tobias had been with. Like Annie, she'd never seen anything overt, but she recognized the grooming behavior he used on her being employed with them too.

Jessie and Ryan visited both girls, who each shared their experiences before offering other potential victims to follow up with. It was after getting the same story from the seventh girl, who, like all the others before her, had a solid alibi, that Jessie reached her limit.

"I need a few minutes here," she said after they got a text from Jamil for the address of the eighth potential victim. "It's starting to get late and I'm losing my dispassionate professionalism."

"When have you ever been dispassionate?" Ryan asked, obviously hoping to lighten her mood a little but failing.

"I've felt nauseated for the last two hours, Ryan," she said earnestly, looking at her watch and seeing that was after 6 p.m. now. "This is a man who hunted the most susceptible victims—the introverted girls who stayed home every night in high school, who had body image issues, who always felt like ugly ducklings. And he

85

used their hero worship of him to prey on them. I've pursued serial killers less creepy than this guy. And it's been going on under everyone's noses, with what seems like something bordering on tacit approval."

"I know," he said quietly, aware that there wasn't much more he could add.

"And to make it worse, when Decker calls us for an update, we're going to have to tell him that we're no closer to finding out who killed this bastard. Every one of these girls has an alibi, thank God. I don't know what I would do if one of them did it. Part of me is praying that it was some equally awful professor who bashed his head in during some dispute over which president had the worst State of the Union speech."

"We can dream," Ryan said, giving her hand a squeeze, before looking up at the address on a nearby building. "I think we found the apartment of the next girl. What's her name again?"

"Natasha Myers," Jessie said, looking at her phone.

They entered the vestibule, looked through the unit directory, and buzzed Natasha's apartment.

"Hello," said a frantic-sounding female voice. "Is that you, Natasha?"

Jessie and Ryan exchanged perplexed looks.

"No," he said. "This is the LAPD. We were hoping to speak with Natasha."

"You can't," the young woman told them loudly through the intercom, her voice cracking slightly.

"Why not?" he asked.

"Because I think she's missing."

CHAPTER EIGHTEEN

"Calm down," Jessie pleaded with Natasha's roommate after she let them in.

"I can't," Simone said. "I thought I was doing okay but when I heard 'LAPD,' my brain broke. I think I'm starting to hyperventilate."

"What's your name?" Jessie asked, trying to get her to focus on something simple.

"Simone Howard," she gasped.

"Come lie down on the couch, Simone," Ryan said, guiding her at first, and then, when she seemed incapable of walking, juts picking her up and carrying her over.

As he got her settled, Jessie looked around the apartment. Compared to the tiny dorm rooms she'd seen, this place was a palace. It had a nice kitchen, a roomy living room with a giant television, and a balcony that looked out over the hills to the north. Considering the location and amenities, she suspected that one or both of these girls' parents were rich.

Simone seemed to be settling down. Ryan was coaxing her to breathe slowly through her nose and it appeared to be working. Eventually, she felt well enough to sit up and Jessie was able to get her first good look at her.

Unlike her roommate, Simone Howard definitely didn't look like Tobias's type. She was tall and angular, with sharp cheekbones and long, lustrous back hair. She had on tight yoga pants and a sports bra and hadn't made any attempt to cover up. By any reasonable measure, she was stunning and she clearly knew it.

Not only did she seem physically uninhibited, but she carried herself with a dramatic flair that was the polar opposite of the professor's type. In fact, Jessie wondered how someone like this became roommates with Natasha, who another victim they spoke to tonight had described as "scared of her own shadow" and "the very embodiment of mousy." Considering that the girl who said that was herself a jumpy, fearful type, that was really saying something.

"So why do you think you think Natasha is missing?" she asked once Simone seemed relatively composed.

"I haven't heard from her since this morning," Simone explained. "At first, I didn't think much about it because I had back-to-back classes from 8 a.m. until eleven. But later on, when I tried to reach her, she didn't answer any of my calls or texts. Plus, I checked with some people she had classes with this afternoon and they said she wasn't there."

Jessie made a mental note. She'd half-wondered if Simone might be capable of killing Tobias, but assuming they could confirm that she was in class as she claimed, they had one less suspect.

"Is it that unusual for her to be out of touch?" Ryan asked. "Maybe her phone died. Maybe she skipped a few classes."

"No way, Nat doesn't skip classes. It's not in her to do it. And she always carries two chargers with her every day, just in case. She likes to be prepared," Simone said, picking up speed and intensity with each new word. "Plus, unless she's studying in the library, she always comes right back here after class. And just yesterday, she told me how psyched she was not to have any major assignments due for a week, so there was no reason for her to go to the library today."

"Okay," Jessie said slowly, preparing to broach the issue they needed to address carefully, "but I'm guessing that if this had all happened yesterday, you wouldn't be as upset as you are right now. What makes today different?"

Simone looked at her with a mix of uncertainty and guilt. Any doubt Jessie had disappeared instantly. It was clear that Natasha was one of Tobias's victims and that her roommate knew all about it.

"I'm not sure...it's just that—," she mumbled before trailing off.

"Simone, if you want our help, you have to be straight with us. Why are you so worried about Natasha?"

The girl bit her lip nervously, seeming to weigh how to respond.

"I guess if you're here," she finally said, "you already have a sense of what it might be."

"Probably," Jessie replied, "but we need to hear it from you."

Simone nodded silently and her expression hardened, as if she'd come to a decision.

"Okay," she said, leaning in, "Nat had a fling with Professor Tobias, the one who died today. But she wouldn't call it that. She was madly in love with the man. I told her that he was taking advantage of her, that he was using her as his personal sex toy because he knew that she'd never say anything. I only found out at all because I came across a poem she'd written but never gave him. It fell out of her backpack. When I asked her about it, she swore me to secrecy. She said that if he found out, he would end it, which is what he ended up doing anyway."

"Did she say why he ended things?" Ryan asked. "Did he maybe sense her starting to pull away at some point?"

"Are you kidding?" Simone said, "She never pulled away. She was as devoted to him on the day that he dumped her as the day they started up. No, it was him. According to Nat, he told her he was bored with her. She offered to spice things up, which is really saying something considering some of the stuff she told me they did. But he wasn't interested. He said that it was over and that if she ever breathed a word about them, he'd destroy her academically, say she cheated on a test or something and get her kicked out of school."

Jessie did her best to mask her revulsion at the depths Tobias was capable of.

"Why do you think he dumped her?" she asked evenly, wondering if Simone's answer would match her own theory.

"I never told Nat this, but I think he got spooked," Simone replied. "By the end, she had gotten really intense. I think he was worried that she was going to spill the beans somehow and ruin his career. So he shut it down and threatened her into silence. It was a form of self-protection, even if it destroyed her, which it did."

Jessie suspected the same thing. It fit his M.O. perfectly.

"She really reacted that badly?" Ryan asked.

"That's partly why I'm so worried," Simone explained. "After he dropped her, she was devastated. At one point, she even threatened to kill herself. I wanted to tell her parents but she said they'd be humiliated if they found out what happened. And if you can believe it, she was worried that they'd take legal action against Tobias. She didn't want his reputation harmed. Their affair ended over four months ago and she was still as raw about it yesterday as when it happened. So when I heard that he died, I knew it would gut her. That's why I've been trying to reach out to her. I'm worried that she might do something crazy, maybe hurt herself in some kind of delusional Romeo and Juliet death pact."

Hearing that, Jessie now understood why Simone had been in such a frenzy to find Natasha. If she was still that broken up about being tossed aside months later, learning the man that she thought she loved had died might push her over the edge.

Of course there was an alternative theory. It was just as conceivable that after months of being treated like trash, Natasha's devotion to Tobias had curdled into something closer to venom. If she saw him with Phoebe or one of his other conquests, it could have spurred her to confront him. And if that went poorly, was it that hard to imagine that she might have snapped, decided that if she couldn't have him, no one could, and killed him in a moment of jealous fury? Either way, they needed to find her fast.

CHAPTER NINETEEN

Hannah didn't know which throbbed more, her head or her feet.

She trudged to her room slowly, trying to ignore both of them. To even get a couple of ibuprofen here was a whole production, and not worth the effort. So she tried the breathing techniques that Dr. Lemmon had taught her to use when she felt urges she wasn't supposed to. If they worked for murderous desire, maybe they'd work on body aches too.

She rounded the main hall that connected to hers and noticed that the psychiatric aide on duty at the nurses' station, a tall, skinny, bespectacled twenty-something named Brian, was looking at her oddly. It was unsettling, especially since he rarely seemed to take much interest in the people he cared for.

Her only personal experience with him was when, earlier this week, he threatened to transfer Silvio Castorini to the Assistance Wing when he got too loud in the cafeteria. The Assistance Wing was the official name for the secure wing where people stayed until they were no longer deemed a potential threat to themselves or others. Hannah managed to massage the situation and convince Brian to back down, but it was touch and go there for a while.

As she shuffled to her room, an unpleasant thought popped into her head. What if all the work she'd done today, having "casual" conversations with other young women in Dr. Tam's notebook was a waste? Maybe Brian the aide was the killer. She made a half-serious mental note to shove her chair against the door handle tonight. Considering that they weren't allowed locks, it might be her only protection.

She closed her door and plopped down on her bed. Looking up at the ceiling, she couldn't help but silently chuckle to herself. This was supposed to be a relaxing place where she could focus on the hard work of getting better. But today felt like a different kind of work, one filled with stress.

Trying to shoehorn sensitive discussions with reluctant women in between a way-too-involved tour of the Seasons at Sea beach house was already tough, even before she learned that the tour included a three mile beach hike and a weird, "listening session" with the leaders of ANTE, the organization funding the program.

Then there was the challenge of trying to talk to Dr. Lemmon about her concerns. Hannah had gone to see her earlier today, and was pleasantly surprised to learn that the doctor had been trying to find time to do the same. But with all her meetings and phone calls, along with people constantly walking in and out of her office, there was never more than ten seconds to talk alone. Finally Hannah gave up.

"Can we set a time for a formal session tomorrow?" she asked. "I need to talk to you about something important. But it has to be in private."

"Are you okay?" Dr. Lemmon asked. "I feel terrible that we haven't been able to have a check-in for so long."

"I'm actually doing pretty well," Hannah reassured her, "but this isn't about me. I'll explain when we talk."

"Okay," Dr. Lemmon said with an intrigued expression on her face. "Make an appointment at the desk and we'll hash it out. By the way, your sister was trying to reach you earlier, but every time she called, you were in the middle of something. It's nothing pressing but you should expect her to try again tomorrow."

That conversation was this afternoon and Hannah was still curious what Jessie had wanted. If she'd had the time, she might have tried to call her sister to find out. But she was too busy pursuing new and creative ways to convince the women in Dr. Tam's notebook to reveal if he'd ever behaved unprofessionally with them.

That would have been hard enough in a conventional environment. But this was a center for people with deep psychological trauma and crushing addictions. She couldn't just walk up to them and say "hey, did Dr. Tam ever try to get with you during one of your sessions?" These women were already in precarious emotional positions. She didn't want to be responsible for pushing them over the edge.

As it turned out, it didn't really matter. Of the women whose names she could recall, two of them didn't even understand what she was asking about. Two more got it but vehemently denied anything happened. One of them responded with language that was full of impressively filthy word combinations which Hannah had never heard before.

The last woman, a heavily tattooed blonde in her early thirties named Pam, said that *she'd* come on to Dr. Tam, but he'd rejected her. Then, right there in the courtyard, Pam tried to feel Hannah up. That was how she learned that Pam was a sex addict.

Someone might have been lying about the sessions with Dr. Tam, but it didn't seem that way from their reactions. Maybe Merry had been an isolated incident after all. If so, Hannah had no idea how she could possibly prove it.

Suddenly, her eyes felt heavy and she could feel herself starting to drift. She debated whether to get up to turn the light off. She was still on the fence when she heard a light rap on her door. Her eyes popped open and she immediately regretted not having shoved the chair under the door handle.

"Who is it?" she called out.

"It's Dr. Tam," came the reply.

Before she could respond, the door opened and the doctor had stepped inside without asking for permission. Hannah sat up in her bed and gripped the sheets. This felt very wrong.

"I was about to go to sleep," she protested loudly.

"This won't take long," he said, closing the door behind him.

Hannah stood up, her entire body wired with adrenaline. If this guy thought their encounter was going to end like the one with Merry, he had another thing coming. She'd fought off serial killers, a kidnapper, and her sister's psychotic ex-husband. She wasn't going down without a fight.

"I didn't give you permission to come into my room," she said through gritted teeth, waiting for him to make the first move.

"Center physicians don't need permission," he said calmly, not making any attempt to move closer yet, "and you certainly didn't get permission before sneaking into my office and looking at my personal notes."

Hannah couldn't stop her jaw from dropping.

"That's right," he continued, leaning back confidently against the door, blocking her exit. "You didn't think that a doctor in a facility like this might have cameras in his office for security purposes? I could have you arrested right now for trespassing or worse. Should I do that, Hannah?"

It took her a moment to regroup, but when she did, she made sure her voice was clear and unafraid.

"Do you really believe it's a good idea for you to call the authorities, Dr. Tam?" she challenged.

"I don't know," he replied, unruffled by her veiled threat. "Sneaking into my office, looking at private medical information, approaching my patients to ask grotesquely inappropriate questions about my interactions with them—that seems like a pretty airtight list of charges."

She was about to tell him the charges he might be in danger of facing when he held up his hand.

"Please don't say something you'll regret," he advised condescendingly. "If you want to know what I wrote about you, just ask. But what you *cannot do* is snoop around, invading my privacy. It's unacceptable. Because of the affection that I know Dr. Lemmon has for you, I'm willing to let it go this one time. If it happens again, I won't be nearly as understanding. Have I made myself clear?"

Hannah was confused. Was he dropping the whole thing? Did he really think she cared what he wrote about her in his notebook more than what he *didn't* write about Merry, who he strangely hadn't mentioned at all yet? Was this détente he offered just designed to get her guard down or was it genuine?

"Yes," she said, choosing to figure it out once he was no longer in her room, preventing her from leaving, "you've made yourself clear."

"Good," he replied, then left without another word.

Hannah sat back down on the bed, completely befuddled. He hadn't physically threatened her, so telling someone about his unannounced visit might not be the slam dunk she hoped would bust him. In fact, he'd carefully avoided saying anything that could be construed as overtly aggressive. He could simply claim that he was having a cautionary conversation with a patient who had violated facility rules. Technically it was true.

She had no idea what game Dr. Tam was playing but she did know one thing: she was jamming the door handle with her chair *and* sleeping under her bed tonight. If he came back, she'd be ready.

CHAPTER TWENTY

They were running out of options and Jessie was running short on energy.

For the last two hours, and with the help of Jamil, Beth, and Detective Jim Nettles, coordinating back at the station, the LAPD had canvassed airports, metro stations, as well as local hospitals. So far, there was no sign of Natasha Myers.

Jessie and Ryan had done a more personalized, but equally exhausting search, using information from Simone. They reached out to Natasha's aunt, who lived in Thousand Oaks. They checked at the coffee shop where she worked on most weekends. They drove around to every place she liked to hang out, which mostly meant vintage record stores, used bookstores, and a local café. They were all dead ends.

As Ryan drove them back to campus, Jessie stared at the photo of Natasha that Simone had given them before they left, hoping it might offer some answers. But all that stared back at her was a young woman with a forced smile on her face, trying to hide the perpetual uncertainty lurking behind her eyes. She had short, red hair, pale, freckle-dotted skin, and wire-rimmed glasses that gave her a bookishly off-kilter appeal. Unfortunately, it was masked by her wan, washed-out appearance and uncomfortable bearing.

Jessie remembered Simone's answer when she'd asked her how the two of them ended up friends. considering how radically different they seemed.

"She saw the best in me," Simone had said. "We had a class together freshman year. Everyone thought I was a bitch on wheels, maybe because I speak my mind or because I don't apologize for how I look—probably both. But Nat never made any assumptions about me. When some guy made a crude crack that he thought I didn't hear, I started to tear up."

She had paused briefly at the memory and looked like she was on the verge of tears again. But after a moment, she managed to continue.

"Nat overheard, came over, and gave me a tissue. We started talking, which probably never would have happened otherwise, and I realized that she was just this kind, truly genuine person. I don't know very many of those and I wanted to keep her in my life. She told me I made her laugh. So we became friends, and then roommates."

Jessie thought about what Simone had said and couldn't help but fixate on the irony. The very character trait that had drawn her to Natasha was what made her friend vulnerable to Roman Tobias. Her kindness and willingness to believe the best of people had blinded her to his deceit and manipulations, even after he cast her off.

As she ruminated over that realization, another one came to mind. If Natasha was so loyal to Tobias when he was alive, despite the way he'd treated her, why wouldn't she be equally devoted after his death? She looked over at Ryan, who had been reviewing fruitless updates from officers checking yet more metro stops.

"I think I know where she is," she said.

"Where?" he asked.

"You're driving in the right direction."

*

"Are you sure about this?" Ryan whispered as they quietly approached Haines Hall.

"No, but it makes sense," she replied in hushed tones. "If Natasha was in love with this man and crushed by his loss, where would she want to go most? To the place where his life ended—his office. Whether she killed him in a fit of rage or she had nothing to do with it, I think she'd want to be as close to him as she could get while mourning him. And I can't think of a better place to do that than where they shared all those intimate moments and where he ultimately died."

"But we've had university cops posted in and around the building all day," he pointed out.

"She might be a shrinking violet in other parts of her life, but when it comes to her obsession with Roman Tobias, Natasha Myers doesn't strike me as the kind of woman who would let that get in her way."

They circled around the front of the building, where the lone officer on duty stood guard. The police tape was still up but there wasn't much need for it right now. After a frenzied afternoon in which every local news station—and some national outlets too—had converged on the scene to do live reports, the university had asserted its authority over the property and kicked everyone out until tomorrow. Other than some students wandering down several adjacent paths, the area was disturbingly quiet.

After the officer let them in and gave them a key, they made their way up to Tobias's third floor office. When they arrived at the door, which had also been taped off, Jessie knew right away that her suspicion was right. The "LAPD CSU" sticker that sealed the door and the jamb was split.

Ryan saw it too and silently motioned for Jessie to unlock the door while he removed his gun from its holster. She counted to three, turned the key, and pushed the door open. Ryan stepped quickly through and she followed. Even in the darkened room, they could see a figure curled up on the couch where they'd found Tobias's body. The person stirred at the sound of their footsteps.

"Don't move," Ryan ordered forcefully.

The person froze.

"We're going to turn on the light," he said, nodding at Jessie. "Stay where you are."

Jessie flicked on the light to reveal Natasha Myers, who, despite having a gun pointed at her, was still blinking the sleep away. She looked a mess. Her red hair spiked out in all directions. Her skin was blotchy. She wasn't wearing her glasses so there was no hiding her red, puffy eyes.

"What's going on?" she mumbled.

"We're with the LAPD," Ryan informed her. "Slowly sit up, keeping your hands visible at all times."

Natasha did as instructed. As she sat up, something on couch fell at her feet. Jessie squinted for a second before realizing that it was a long, ornate, gold letter opener. She could only imagine what the girl had in mind for that.

"Kick the letter opener toward us, Natasha," she said as coolly as she could.

Natasha did so without a word. Once the opener was out of her reach, Jessie bent down and grabbed it. Ryan holstered his gun.

"Can I please put on my glasses?" Natasha asked, nodding at the pair resting on the table beside the couch. "I can't see a thing without them."

"Slowly," Ryan warned.

Once they were on, Natasha seemed to relax slightly. Though Jessie felt guilty about it, she needed to shake the girl out of that comfort zone.

"Care to explain why you're sleeping in a sealed crime scene?" she demanded, pretending not to already know the answer. "That's a chargeable offense."

The tactic worked. Natasha's shoulders slumped and the mousy, frail demeanor she'd briefly lost returned.

"I was just..." she started to explain, then paused before continuing. "Professor Tobias was my favorite teacher. I had great admiration for him and I guess I just wanted to say goodbye in my own way. I know I shouldn't have broken in here, but I didn't think it was hurting anyone."

While nothing she said could technically be called a lie, it was clear that she wasn't going to reveal the true nature of their relationship without a push.

"Natasha," Jessie said gently, hoping that lowering the temperature might win the girl's trust. "My name is Jessie. This is Detective Hernandez. We're investigating Professor Tobias's death. But we've also been looking for you."

"Why?" Natasha asked, suddenly agitated.

"Because your roommate, Simone, was worried about you," Jessie told her. "She's been trying to reach you all day and you didn't come home tonight. She thought you might do something rash."

A cloud of shame crossed Natasha's face at what she'd put her friend through, but she quickly fought it off.

"That's ridiculous," she said, arching her back haughtily. "I just wanted to pay respects to a teacher that meant a lot to me, nothing more."

Jessie grabbed one of the chairs near Tobias's desk, pulled it over next to the couch, and sat down close to the girl, who looked to be shaking slightly.

"Natasha," she whispered, "we know."

Those red puffy eyes opened wide.

"Know what?"

"We know about all of it," Jessie told her. "Your involvement with Roman Tobias, his breakup with you and his threats to your academic status if you said anything, your difficulty getting over him—there's no point in denying it."

She watched as an enormous, invisible weight seemed to topple off the girl. The tension in her shoulders melted away and her brittle, forced smile disappeared, replaced by a sigh of giant relief.

"I loved him so much," she said, her voice quavering. "But I couldn't talk about it with anyone other than Simone and I knew she didn't like him. When I heard the news today, I couldn't believe it. I ran right over here. I heard people in the crowd saying he might have been murdered and it was just too much to process. So I just left."

"Where did you go?" Ryan asked.

"I just got in my car and drove north on the Pacific Coast Highway. When I hit Santa Barbara, I pulled over and sat on the beach for a little while. At some point I realized I couldn't just drive away from my feelings, so I turned around and came back. Somehow I felt like he needed me to return."

"And you came here?" Jessie wondered, not commenting on the girl's delusional mindset for now.

Natasha nodded.

"They were letting students and professors back in on the first floor for classes," she explained. "I just had to show my ID. Then I waited in the restroom until there were fewer police around. I snuck up to the third floor and hid in a storage closet that the professor and I used for…well, the point is that I knew the lock didn't work well. When it got late enough, I checked the hallway. There was no one up here so I came to his office. The professor keeps an extra key hidden behind a bust of John Adams right outside the door. He always said no one cared about Adams so it was a safe hiding place. Sure enough, it was still there. So all I had to do was unlock the door, break the seal, and come in. I've been here ever since, communing with his spirit."

Jessie sighed at hearing those depressing last words. She tried to focus on something else that Natasha said: that she knew where Tobias kept the key. That meant she could have easily snuck in this morning and hidden, waiting to attack. She already had a potential motive. Now she was basically admitting that she had the means and possibly the opportunity.

But why would she admit to such a thing when she didn't have to, especially when it could implicate her. The reason appeared obvious. Natasha Myers was guileless, largely incapable of believable deception. That conclusion wasn't based on the evidence but on Jessie's read of the girl's psychological makeup—her profile. She suspected that if Natasha had killed Tobias, she'd already have admitted to it by now. It was for that reason that Jessie felt comfortable saying what came next.

"We can get into this more another time," she said wearily, "but you know he's not worth any of the emotional energy you're pouring into him. Don't get me wrong, we're going to find out who killed Professor Tobias because that's what we do. But he was a bad guy, Natasha. What he did to you, he did to lots of others. I think you know that."

Natasha bit her lip but didn't argue.

"I'm afraid we have to ask this," Ryan said, "but where were you this morning between 10:00 and 10:30?"

"Are you asking me for an alibi?" she asked, truly stunned. "You think I killed him? I would *never*."

"You seem pretty passionate about the man," Ryan noted.

Jessie knew he was just doing his job, getting a potential suspect off balance, but it made her cringe nonetheless. To her surprise, Natasha didn't take the bait.

"Why would I kill him?" she asked sincerely. "I loved him. Besides, if I wanted to make him suffer, to destroy him, it would have been easy. I knew what we were doing wasn't aboveboard, and I knew about the other girls, at least some of them. I even hid in that maintenance closet and watched him bring them here, logged dates when he was with some of them. I know their names. I'm embarrassed to say that, but I did it. I could have reported him to the university or to the media. I could even have blackmailed him. I could have watched his life fall apart at my hands. But I didn't do any of that, did I?"

Neither Jessie nor Ryan had an immediate response to that. It didn't matter because she wasn't done.

"And to answer your question, I had a test in sociology today. The class runs from nine to ten-thirty. There are two dozen students and an instructor who can verify that I was there the whole time."

Jessie looked over at Ryan and read his mind. It was easy because she knew he was thinking the same thing: after all this, they'd hit another dead end.

Captain Decker was going to be pissed.

100

CHAPTER TWENTY ONE

Decker wasn't pissed, but he was disappointed.

"I wanted to give you the space to work the case so I didn't tell either of you this earlier," he said over the phone as Ryan maneuvered through the late evening traffic, "but Chief Laird is worked up over this one. With all the local and national press, he says this is giving L.A. a black eye. I held him off for now by telling him that every student Tobias ever taught is a potential suspect so it'll take time, but he'll want an update tomorrow morning, which means I will too. Start fresh then. For now, you can call it a night."

Jessie had rarely heard a more welcome sentence. As they drove home mostly in comfortable silence, she found herself close to drifting off on several occasions and tried to shake it off. If she was tired, so was Ryan, and she didn't want him to drive into a ditch because they had both fallen asleep. So she did what always kept her awake: think about the case.

She thought about what Natasha had said—that she could have easily destroyed Tobias simply by reporting him, could have blackmailed him if she chose. It was true, but not just for her. Any of the other young women he manipulated, used up, and tossed away could have done the same thing. They all could have obliterated his reputation, his entire career, without actually killing him. That wasn't proof that they hadn't, but without as strong a motive, each of his victims seemed considerably less compelling as suspects.

In fact, it made much more sense that the killer knew nothing about Tobias's affairs. Without that knowledge and the ability it provided to ruin his life without ending it, the killer may have felt that murder was their only option. Of course, that begged the question: what would have motivated someone who wasn't aware of Tobias's myriad secrets—professional jealousy? Some financial factor they'd overlooked? Or could it just have been a student with poor anger management skills who got upset over a bad grade?

The first two options certainly made sense if the crime was premeditated. After all, the body had been dragged across the carpet and carefully placed on the couch. And the school's cameras didn't catch anyone in the area. Then again, the moving of the body could have been a panicked choice and not being caught on camera might have been pure luck. Those factors fit better with the heat-of-the-moment, unhinged student theory.

Ryan pulled into the driveway, which was good because Jessie could feel her brain starting to melt. Before it completely turned to mush, she texted Kat to see how her day on the Andy Robinson "proof of guilt" hunt had gone: *Any updates?*

The brief reply came quick: *Working on it. Will keep you posted.*

Jessie decided not to push. She picked Kat for this job for a reason. Now she just had to trust her judgment. Besides she was too wiped out to do anything else. She and Ryan both lumbered inside. Ryan turned on the kitchen light. Jessie looked at the breakfast table and groaned. Strewn about right where she'd left them this morning were brochures for half a dozen wedding venues.

The sight of them added an extra layer to her exhaustion. She was excited about getting married, but the actual planning part was a constant source of agitation. Even after Ryan had relented on his preference for a big wedding, they still had to pick a date, create a guest list, invitations, and course, select the dreaded venue.

"Don't worry about it," Ryan said, reading her mind. "We'll deal with all that later."

"Bless you, kind sir," she replied, her hands pressed together as if in prayer.

"How about instead of that, we focus on who can fall asleep faster?"

"I thought you were hoping that I'd 'lift your spirits' tonight," she said.

He shrugged.

"I didn't want to assume," he said bashfully. "I figured you'd want a rain check."

The thought had occurred to her, but she didn't want to renege.

"I'll make you a deal," she offered. "If you can promise me that I'll be asleep in fifteen minutes, I'll happily find a way to lift those spirits a lot more than that protein bar from earlier did."

"Sold!" he shouted, darting for bedroom with a goofy grin on his face.

*

102

She could feel him staring at her.

No matter where she moved in the mansion's giant living room, his eyes followed her. She pretended not to notice, walking over to the large fireplace at the far end of the room and stoking the smoldering logs with the poker.

Of course, that was just a ruse. She'd grabbed the poker for a very different reason. She listened for footsteps getting closer, but heard none. She wanted to turn around to see where he was in the room but couldn't. Her legs were locked in place, unresponsive. She was helpless to protect herself like this.

Then she heard them, footsteps echoing throughout the enormous room. They were getting closer. She thought she could hear him breathing. And yet she still couldn't move. She was frozen. As the pace of his steps and his breathing quickened, she used the one thing at her disposal.

She lifted the poker up by her shoulders as if preparing to face a pitcher, then swung it down hard, slamming it into her left shin. The pain was excruciating but it also snapped her out of her paralysis. Her legs were suddenly responsive.

She spun around to find him standing only feet away from her. In the smokiness of the room, it was hard to see him clearly but she knew who it was: her father. Xander Thurman, the man who'd murdered her mother right in front of her when she was six years old, then left her to die in a snowy cabin, looked just as he did when she'd last seen him.

His lean, wolfish body was hunched over. His long, dark hair was dotted with visible gray. His green eyes, the same shade as hers, gleamed maniacally. He was still the same serial killer, who, after two decades spreading mayhem across the country, had come to L.A. to convert or kill her.

But then the smoke cleared and she saw that she was wrong. It wasn't her father in front of her but Bolton Crutchfield, her father's protégé, who escaped from a psychiatric prison, then returned to torment and occasionally assist her. Short and pudgy with brown hair parted neatly to the side, he stared at her unblinkingly with steely brown eyes.

The room was so smoky that the overhead sprinklers turned on. Water poured down from above, mixing with the smoke to make the air dank and thick. In the middle of it, she realized that she'd been mistaken. The man in front of her, tall and blond with cold, blue eyes and broad shoulders, was actually her ex-husband, Kyle Voss, who'd cheated on her, killed his mistress, and then tried to frame her for it. That was before he got out of prison and tried to kill her, Hannah, and Ryan. He'd almost succeeded.

As she held the poker tight, waiting for him to advance on her, she became aware of something that had been tickling the corner of her brain. All of these men were dead, all killed by her in fact, while defending herself. That's when she knew she was dreaming.

But even that knowledge didn't help. The man, whoever he was, advanced on her quickly. She raised the poker higher, waiting. When he was close enough, she swung with all her might. Just before the tip of the poker made contact with his skull, she saw his face clearly. But it wasn't a man at all. It was Andy Robinson. And she was smiling.

Jessie sat straight up in bed, gasping for air, her heart pounding.

The clock read 2:53 a.m. She looked over and saw Ryan to her left, sprawled out, his legs creeping well over onto her side of the bed. Her t-shirt was soaked with sweat, as were the sheets below her. She allowed a few seconds for her body to regulate.

It's been a while since I've had a dream like that.

She slid out of bed and got a big towel from the linen closet, which she laid over the damp part of the sheets. Then she headed to the bathroom for a quick shower and change before returning to bed and hopefully, some semblance of sleep.

It had been months since she'd had a nightmare that vivid. She didn't recall ever having one with all those people in it and tried not to fixate on the fact that the only one of them who was still alive might be set free tomorrow. Instead, she let her mind drift to another equally troubling concern.

Will I ever get past my demons? And if I can't, what hope does Hannah have?

CHAPTER TWENTY TWO

Kat made sure to arrive early.

She'd never been to the Western Regional Women's Psychiatric Detention Center, or PDC, before and wasn't sure what their visitor admission process was. But if she wanted to help Jessie, she didn't have much choice but to find out.

Andy Robinson lived here, at least for the time being, and if Kat was going to keep it that way, she had no choice but to go to the woman herself. It was a long shot, but maybe she could get Andy to let something slip, some detail that could prove her involvement in these crimes and prevent her release.

She had considered telling Jessie what she was doing when they texted last night, but she didn't want to get her friend's hopes up. And knowing Jessie Hunt, she'd tell her not to come at all, because someone on Andy Robinson's radar was someone at risk. She'd be right, but that was Kat's risk to take.

After going through one security check at the entrance to the parking structure (which included a search of her car), and two more upon entering the building, she finally reached the reception desk at 8:24 a.m.

"I'm here to see Andrea Robinson," she said.

"Residents aren't permitted to meet with visitors until 9.a.m. but you can fill out the forms now. Does she know you're coming?"

"No," Kat said, "but when she finds out who it is, she'll want to talk."

"What's your name?"

"Katherine Gentry."

"There's the sign-in list," the receptionist said, already bored for the day. "Return your forms when you're done."

It took Kat nearly a half hour to complete all fourteen pages, including authorization to do a background check on her and a release indemnifying the PDC if something happened to her. By the time she got approval to go back, it was almost 9:30. A brawny, brown-haired man wearing white pants and a white shirt opened the door.

"Katherine Gentry?" he asked, and when she stood up, said, "Follow me."

Once the reception door locked securely behind them, he led her down a long hallway painted a soft yellow. She noticed that attached to his thick waist belt was a can of pepper spray, a baton, and a stun gun.

"I thought that security here wasn't as hardcore as at Twin Towers," she said, pointing at the belt when he gave her a perplexed look.

"No," he said defensively, "we're just as secure. We're just more modern and, in my view, more responsive. The philosophy here is that if we treat the residents with respect, we're more likely to get acceptable behavior."

"How's that working out for you?" Kat asked before she could stop herself.

He looked at her sideways, unsure if she was sincere or messing with him.

"Depends on the day, I guess," he finally answered. "But as long as we're discussing security, let me fill you in on our policies for visitors. Don't be misled by the lack of bars, glass, or restraints in the visitor center. Almost everyone is here because they committed a crime, many of them violent. Only those without outbursts of any kind in the last three months are even allowed visitors other than physicians, lawyers, and law enforcement."

Kat wondered how she'd gotten in at all considering that she was none of those things and Andy Robinson hadn't been here anywhere near three months. She glanced down at her authorization slip and noticed the name of the person who authorized her entry: R. Decker. It seemed that even though he couldn't do anything overtly to countermand Chief Laird's desire to release Andy, Captain Decker was still doing whatever he could to help Jessie, just on the down-low.

"Residents wear ankle bracelets that can deliver a debilitating shock," the burly aide continued, "but sometimes it takes an aide a few moments to push the button. By then, the damage has often been done, so keep your distance. Stay on your side of the table. Don't let any part of your body cross the red line in the middle of it. And especially with this patient, stay alert. We've never had a problem with her, but don't let her appealing personality fool you.

106

This woman murdered one woman and almost killed a second one. Don't get too comfortable."

Kat didn't need any of those warnings. She knew what Andy was capable of, having heard it firsthand from the woman who was almost killed. But she appreciated the fact that not everyone around here seemed to be snowed by her charm offensive.

"Good to know," she said as he led her to the door marked "Visitors."

"After I swipe you in and you enter, this door locks behind you. There are as many psychiatric aides as residents inside so you won't be alone in there. But if you start to feel threatened or need to leave for any reason, just raise your hand high above your head. Someone will immediately escort you out. Understood?"

"Yep," she answered. He was about to swipe her in when a question occurred to her. "Wait, is she already in there?"

"Yes," he said. "She's sitting at table eight. So put your game face on now."

That was smart advice. In fact, it was the very reason she'd asked. She didn't want to walk in there looking clueless. Even though they'd never met, she knew that with someone like Andy Robinson, it was never a good idea to give her any advantage.

The door opened and she stepped in, trying to appear as bored as the receptionist out front had. She let her eyes wander around the visiting room, resisting the urge to immediately look for Andy.

It was less a room than a giant hall, which made sense when she saw the tables the aide had mentioned. They were big and circular, making it nearly impossible for visitors and residents to get close to each other. The tables were also placed far apart from each other, thus the need for the large space. There were only nine tables in total and each one had an aide standing nearby.

Based on the configuration of the tables closest to her, Kat could guess which one was number eight. Finally, after taking what she deemed to be an appropriately annoying amount of time, she looked in the direction of the table. Sure enough, Andy Robinson was leaning back in her chair, staring at her with a half-smile playing at her lips.

Kat walked over, making sure to never break eye contact. Andy, like all the other inmates, wore a long-sleeved, baby blue shirt and gray, loose-fitting pants. Her blonde hair was tied back in a ponytail. Though she wasn't quite pretty, even without makeup, she was striking. That was almost exclusively due to her eyes, which were bright, blazing blue, too intense to be called beautiful but impossible to ignore.

Kat pulled out the seat across the table and sat down. Andy looked content to wait her out and Kat was fine with that. She knew that she had to be the aggressor. This woman wasn't going to volunteer anything incriminating without a push.

"Do you know who I am?' she finally asked.

Andy continued to stare at her for several more seconds and Kat began to wonder if she intended to speak at all. She did.

"Of course," she replied. "You're Katherine Gentry, former Army Ranger, wounded in the service of her country while on a tour of duty in Afghanistan. You're also the former security head of the Norwalk State Hospital's Non-Rehabilitative Division, where you were released from your duties after a serial killer named Bolton Crutchfield killed a gaggle of your guards and escaped. You're currently working as a private detective, spending most of your time taking photos of people in compromising positions, usually for the benefit of their justifiably suspicious spouses. Most importantly, you're Jessie Hunt's bestie, at least for the time being. Is that why you're here? Was she too scared to come see me in person?"

"Wow," Kat said, genuinely impressed. "That was a comprehensive, if loaded, description of my employment history. I didn't think you had access to LinkedIn in places like this. And to answer your question—I came here on my own."

"Now that's exciting," Andy replied, leaning in for the first time. "To what do I owe the pleasure?"

"Well," Kat answered, leaning back in her chair in response, "I hear this may be a big day for you. I thought this might be the only chance I'd get to talk with you before you were feted by the press and the folks down at LAPD headquarters."

Andy smiled back warmly, and despite everything Kat knew about her, she could feel herself soften just a bit. The woman did have charisma.

"That's not up to me, Katherine," she replied. "The vagaries of the justice system are mysterious. I would never presume to predict what will happen."

Kat decided it was time to ever so slightly poke her opponent for the first time.

"Based on everything you've done to help the authorities," she said with faux earnestness, "it seems only fair that you get your due."

Andy continued to smile, but out of the corner of her eye, Kat noticed a tiny twitch of the woman's left pinkie finger. She wondered if that was Andy struggling ever so slightly to control herself. But then it was gone, leaving her unsure if she'd just imagined it.

"You don't sound sincere, Katherine." Her voice wasn't cold exactly but it didn't match the warmth of the smile either.

"To be honest, Andy, I was hoping you could persuade me that I should be. You obviously have a complicated history with my friend, Jessie. Cards on the table here—I'm concerned that if you're released you might try to do her harm. So I'm here to be convinced otherwise. I thought if you could tell me about these cases you were involved in, you might prove that you've been genuine in your efforts to help, and that this isn't just some really, long, elaborate con. I want to walk out of here with a sense of confidence that you really are rehabilitated."

Andy nodded, seemingly glad that they had come to the true purpose of the visit.

"Here's the thing though, Katherine," she said quietly. "I don't *need* to prove anything to you. Whether you believe I'm reformed or not doesn't really matter one iota as to what happens."

Kat smiled back at her. She was starting to get a sense of this woman.

"Are you too scared to tell me, Andy?" she asked, throwing the woman's earlier question right back at her. "Worried you'll slip up and reveal something that might threaten your impending freedom?"

Andy didn't twitch this time. Whatever momentary weakness that had slipped through earlier was gone now.

"You're a bold one, aren't you?" she marveled. "Are you sure it's wise to taunt a convicted murderer?"

"Why should I be worried? You're reformed, right?"

Andy leaned back again and closed those startling, blue eyes. Kat wasn't sure what to make of it. Was this conversation over? Then Andy opened them again.

"Shall we start with Livia Bucco or Eden Roth?"

"That's up to you," Kat said, doing her best to hide her surprise at this turn of events.

"I didn't know her well, just that she'd had a troubled childhood. She once told me that kids use to make fun of her by calling her the Red Hulk simply because of her size and her unfortunate rosacea diagnosis. Can you imagine the cruelty? Somehow, I think you can, Katherine. I suspect that you already know everything I'm telling you."

"Please, continue," Kat said, offering nothing.

Andy smiled. She knew she had the upper hand now.

"What wasn't in her file until I told Jessie about it," she said, "was how, in a passing conversation, Livia mentioned her father gifting her a machete and how she planned to use it upon her release. Now, I must tell you, I heard a lot of things in that facility. One inmate said she was going to steal the nuclear codes and start World War Three. Another said she planned to assassinate John Lennon, who was still alive and secretly living in a barn in Maine. Both of those women were released while I remained incarcerated there, which is a discussion for another time, Katherine. But to the best of my knowledge, no nukes have been fired recently and John Lennon remains dead, so I didn't think much of it. But the machete thing was different. When that poor law student was butchered, I felt it was my obligation to share what I 'd heard with Jessie."

Andy told a similar tale about Eden, all the while emphasizing how it would be irresponsible for her to have access to life-saving information and do nothing. She explained how helping prevent the future deaths of people she would likely never meet gave her a new insight into what kind of person she could be if she really committed herself to putting others before herself.

Kat listened to all of it impassively. But in her bones, from almost the first few words Andy spoke, she knew it was a lie. There were too many lucky coincidences, too many fortuitously shared personal revelations, for everything to have happened as she claimed. But more than that, it was clear that Andy wasn't really trying to convince her at all. She was showboating, enjoying weaving her tale for a new listener. It felt less like a heartfelt explanation than a dress rehearsal for the parole hearing later today.

The problem was that as she recounted her heroics, Andy didn't make any obvious mistakes. Nothing she said was inconsistent with her prior statements. She never shared anything that only a person who was involved in planning the crimes could have known. There was no misstep that might prove she was in league with these women. For that, Kat would need to ask some specific questions.

"Thanks for all that," she replied. "It definitely offers some perspective. Now I'd like to follow up on a few things you said. First, tell me—."

"I'm afraid not," Andy said, cutting her off. "I've told you my truth. I'm not interested in answering any more questions."

"But you didn't actually answer any questions," Kat pointed out. "You just monologued for five minutes. Is there some reason you're reluctant to provide specific responses to a few questions?"

Andy raised her hand above her head. The nearby aide moved toward her.

"It was wonderful to meet you, Katherine," Andy said smiling, pushing back her chair and standing up. "I hope we can do it again sometime."

The aide motioned for Andy to leave. Realizing she was out of time, Kat decided to ask the one question she'd been holding back, the one she hoped would elicit a genuine reaction.

"Are you the Principal, Andy?" she asked simply.

The woman opposite her gave no overt sign that the term meant anything to her. The smile remained affixed to her face. But for the briefest of moments, Kat thought she saw Andy's blue eyes burn with even greater intensity than before.

Then she turned and left without offering a reply. Kat sat there, watching as she walked away, never looking back. Only when Andy had left the room did she allow her frustration to bubble to the surface, gritting her teeth and pressing her palms hard into the table. Finally she got up and headed for the exit.

Each step reminded her that she was leaving with nothing tangible. She'd gotten no accidental revelations, no leads to follow, and no clear way to stop the parole hearing. It was always a long shot but now there was no shot.

She had failed her friend.

*

Andy returned to her room silently, glad that her back was to the aide walking behind her so he couldn't see her face. She was seething.

She knew that Kat was Jessie's best friend and she had made it her business to learn everything about the woman. But meeting her in person for the first time was something different.

Katherine Gentry wasn't what she'd expected. Even aware of her personal history, Andy was surprised at how casual and self-assured the woman was. After all, she was sitting mere feet away from a notorious killer, one who'd almost killed her friend, and she never seemed rattled. In fact, she almost appeared to be enjoying herself.

That was what had briefly thrown Andy. That's why she wasn't prepared to stop her intermittent finger twitch. She was sure Kat had made note of it and it killed her that this confident bitch had gotten a peek into her small reservoir of self-doubt. She'd managed to control it afterward, especially when Kat threw the "Principal" curveball question at her, but that brief slip-up still gnawed at her.

She could see why Jessie was drawn to Kat, who was an ocean of calm. That must have been very comforting to someone whose life was so regularly consumed by chaos. It was infuriating to see the dynamic at work and not be able to undermine it.

Just as bad, Jessie had sent this person in her stead. It was hurtful. Not only had she not come to visit, she sent a proxy, as if she couldn't be bothered to make an appearance. Andy was supposed to be playing the role of the BFF who steps in when the going gets rough. It's the role she was born to play. Instead this understudy, this scarred usurper, was doing it.

When Andy got out of here, and she was certain that she *would* get out, she'd have to do something about that.

CHAPTER TWENTY THREE

Jessie stepped outside.

They'd already been back at Powell Library, going at it for over an hour, when she decided to get some air and call Hannah.

As she opened the library doors to the still-cool morning, she tried to let her frustration go. Despite their best efforts so far, they'd found nothing to support her alternate theory that Tobias's murder was a pre-meditated attack borne out of jealousy or greed.

Jamil and Beth had reviewed Tobias's financials again and came up empty. There were no red flags. And other than the retracted grievance from Monica Littleton, who had an airtight alibi, there was no evidence of conflict with other professors. The lack of paperwork didn't mean animosity didn't exist, just that they couldn't track it, especially with everyone so closed-mouthed.

Jessie took a deep breath, and then exhaled, trying to push all thoughts of the case out of her head. She didn't want to bring any of that anxiety to her call with Hannah, nor did she want her sister to pick up on the exhaustion she was already starting to feel due to her recent nightmares. This time the receptionist put her straight through.

"You're actually there!" she said when her sister came on the line.

"Oh yeah—Dr. Lemmon said you'd been trying to reach me."

"A couple of times," Jessie confirmed, "but you were always busy with a session, or in one case, a tour of some beach house where they've started a new program?"

"Don't get me started," Hannah said. "The place is nice enough, but the people who run it are a little off, weirdly new age-y and doctrinaire at the same time."

"Sounds trying. How are you doing otherwise?"

"Pretty well actually," Hannah said, "I haven't shot anyone for the thrill of it even once in here, and believe me, there are some folks who deserve it."

"That's good to hear," Jessie said carefully, unsure whether to be concerned or heartened by Hannah's playful tone.

"Seriously," her sister continued. "I have a session with Dr. Lemmon later today. I think she'll be impressed with my development. I've been working on techniques to help me redirect my emotions when I start to feel….restless. And you'll be happy to know that I've vastly reduced the number of confrontations I seek out just for the adrenaline high."

"But not eliminated?" Jessie probed.

"I'm a work in progress, sis."

"How are you doing since the girl you know died?" Jessie asked, deciding not to push on the confrontation thing.

There was a brief pause on the other end of the line.

"I'm working through it," Hannah eventually said. "I can't say it's all good but I'm getting there."

For the first time in their conversation, Jessie got the sense that her sister was holding something back. She was debating whether to press the matter when Hannah beat her to it.

"What about you?" she asked. "I haven't watched the news in a few days. Would you be on it?"

"Probably." Jessie answered. "I'm working a case involving the murder of a famous UCLA professor. There's been some press."

"Any good leads?" Hannah asked.

"I thought so but none of them are panning out."

"So what are you going to do?"

"I'm going to have to do what I always do when I hit a dead end on a case: go back to the beginning, where it all started, and see if I missed anything," Jessie said.

"So where's the beginning?"

Jessie didn't want to get into that with her little sister. She didn't want to talk about the possible origins of this crime, and how it might be connected to the victim's exploitation of girls just a few years older than she was. Hannah was about to enter a bigger world and, despite everything she'd suffered through, she was still vulnerable.

There wasn't much Jessie could do about that in the time they had left together. Even with her stay at Seasons, Hannah was on track to graduate this spring. She wouldn't be going to UCLA. In fact, she was more interested in going to culinary school than college. But wherever she went, she'd likely be around older men with an aura of authority and respect. The idea that she could be

114

manipulated by someone like Roman Tobias created a pit in Jessie's stomach.

"I'm still working on finding the beginning," she said evasively. Now she was the one holding back and Hannah seemed to sense it.

"Classified, I guess?" she teased.

"No, just complicated," Jessie replied. "Anyway, I better get back to it. But I was hoping to come by this weekend if that's cool."

"Sure," Hannah said with unexpected warmth. "But who knows if I'll even be here. Maybe Dr. Lemmon will cut me loose after our session today."

"Keep me posted," Jessie said, not wanting to offer false hope or come across as negative.

"Will do, and good luck on your case."

"Thanks."

"I love you," Hannah said, perhaps the first time she'd ever said it first.

"I love you too."

The phone went dead and Jessie stood there, the phone still to her ear, lingering in the moment a little longer. Her little sister, who she didn't even know about until recently, who had been through endless trauma, who was currently living in a residential psychiatric facility, loved her. Whatever else Hannah was keeping from her, she'd told her that, unprompted. And for now, that was enough.

When Jessie returned to the library study room, she immediately knew that something was up. Ryan had the same expression as the time when he came back from the grocery store and realized that he'd forgotten to get the mint chocolate ice cream she'd specifically asked him to buy. It was his "you're not going to like what I have to tell you" look.

"What happened?" she asked.

He didn't try to sugarcoat it.

"I just got off the phone with Captain Decker," he said. "Do want the bad news, the really bad news, or the worst news?"

"How about we go in that order?" Jessie suggested.

"Okay, there's still every indication that Andy Robinson's hearing is going to happen as planned today."

"That sucks," Jessie replied, "but it's not really a surprise."

"That's why it's only the bad news. The really bad news is that Chief Laird is turning the screws extra tight now. He apparently said that if we don't have this wrapped up today, he's making a change."

"What does that mean—that he wants to replace us?"

"Not us," Ryan told her wincing, "just you. He wants Decker to replace you with Susannah Valentine."

Jessie was quiet. Ryan tried to fill the silence.

"I told him that he can't do that—that HSS has full independence and discretionary authority. I reminded him that Susannah's not a profiler, she's a detective, so the move doesn't even make sense. He agreed with all that but said his hands might be tied anyway."

"What's the worst news?" she asked flatly.

Ryan grimaced before replying.

"Mark Rawls, the dean of the history department, is at it again. It seems that he wants you bumped from the case as much as Laird does. He's filed a formal complaint, again asserting that you have a conflict of interest because you lecture here. He's demanding that you either be removed from the case or from your teaching position."

"You know," she said, her downcast spirits suddenly raised. "This Rawls guy really wants me out of here. That was curious even *before* we knew that Tobias was sleeping with multiple students, almost like he didn't want me to find something. Now it's downright suspicious, don't you think?"

"I do," Ryan agreed, his mint chocolate ice cream shame face fading.

"How about we go pay Dean Rawls a little visit and find out what exactly is going on with him."

*

They didn't have to go far but it took a while.

Rawls's office was on the fifth floor of Bunche Hall. Though the crowd of news crews surrounding Haines Hall was slightly smaller than yesterday, they still didn't want to risk being seen, so they again took the long way around. Fifteen minutes after leaving the library, they were approaching Rawls's door. Jessie let Ryan take the lead. She wanted her large, muscular fiancé to stand in the man's doorway and flash his badge. That tended to shake the confidence of most folks, no matter their position of authority.

The door was slightly ajar. When Ryan knocked, it opened halfway. He peered inside.

116

"It doesn't look like he's here," he said.

"Are you sure he's okay?" Jessie asked, her tone hinting at her real intentions, "maybe we should go in to make sure that he's safe and not a victim of this killer too, lying on the floor or stuffed in a closet."

Ryan rolled his eyes, well aware that she was coming up with an excuse to search the man's office that could later be justified as exigent circumstances. But he didn't object.

"Better safe than sorry, I guess," he said, kicking the door open the rest of the way. "Dean Rawls?"

He stepped inside and Jessie followed. The office was large. Had they not been in the university chancellor's just yesterday, it would have felt grandiose. But by comparison, it was merely showy. The bookshelves were lined with doorstop-sized biographies. On the walls, in between his various diplomas, there were dozens of framed photos of the man with an assortment of luminaries in the world of historical celebrity, including Doris Kearns Goodwin, Joseph Ellis, Nikole Hannah-Jones, Jeff Shaara, and even a group picture that included Ken Burns.

While Ryan made a token attempt to justify the search by calling out the dean's name and opening the doors to the closet and the small bathroom, Jessie headed straight to Rawls's desk, which was barely visible under a blanket of paperwork. It was a complete mess and she had no idea how to determine if anything before her was of use. But then she noticed something.

On the right, under the local news section of this morning's paper, was a thick binder that was much better organized than anything else on the desk. It almost looked like Rawls had tossed the paper on top of the binder in a rushed effort to keep it out of sight. She slid the paper to the side and opened the unmarked binder.

As soon as she did, she knew she'd hit pay dirt. The first page was a table of contents with headings that included: incidents, testimonials, photographs, missed obligations, and more. She flipped through the pages and found that Rawls appeared to be building a case against Tobias, though not a great one. The data was inconsistent and the investigation was slipshod, with uncorroborated allegations, hearsay, and pictures that didn't actually catch any illegal behavior.

This was nothing that would hold up in court, but it painted a picture. And it was undeniable proof that for some time, Mark

Rawls had harbored the same concerns that Jessie and Ryan had uncovered. But as she leafed through the binder, it became clear that the dean's focus wasn't so much on amassing evidence to provide the authorities with proof of a crime against his students. Rather, it seemed that it was all geared toward getting Tobias fired without going public. It looked like Rawls was hoping to blackmail him into quietly quitting.

"What did you find?" Ryan asked.

She looked up to see him staring at her with interest and realized that she'd been poring over the binder silently for a while now.

"It looks like Rawls figured out what was going on and was gathering enough dirt to force Tobias out without a fight."

"How'd he do?"

"There's not enough here to convict, but what he's got definitely should have raised alarm bells. In light of what I'm looking at, the fact that Tobias was still interacting with students is a disgrace. It looks like Rawls was sitting on it for—."

A cough in the hall outside the door made her stop. They both glanced in that direction but didn't see anyone. Ryan dashed into the hall and Jessie followed right behind. Halfway down the hall, they saw a door slowly closing. They both ran in that direction.

Someone had been listening in on their conversation, someone who didn't want to be discovered. That only made Jessie run faster.

CHAPTER TWENTY FOUR

Jessie got to the door first.

When she arrived, she saw that it led to the stairwell. She yanked it open and was about to step through when Ryan pulled her back.

"They might have a gun," he whispered loudly, before stepping in front of her with his in his hand.

She let him pass even though she doubted he could navigate the stairs as quickly as her. He was ninety-five percent recovered from his stabbing and coma last summer, but that remaining five percent tended to manifest when he was running full out or navigating stairs.

She tried to keep track of their quarry, which looked to be two flights of stairs below them. She still couldn't see who it was, but based on brief glimpses, the person appeared to be wearing a sports jacket.

After half a minute of circling down the stairs, the footsteps stopped. Ryan was just rounding the stairs from the second floor to the first with Jessie behind him when something caught her eye. It looked like the second floor exit door wasn't quite closed, as if someone didn't want to risk the sound of it clicking shut.

"Hold on," she said. "I think he went out here."

Ryan was already halfway down the next set of steps when he turned around.

"Are you sure?" he asked.

"No. But the door isn't closed and the footsteps stopped earlier than I would have expected if he was going to the first floor."

"Okay," Ryan replied. "You try this level. I'll go down to the lower level in case he did go all the way down. That way, even if he's on the second floor, I can help corner him."

Jessie nodded and opened the second floor exit door. She was greeted by Palm Court, Bunche Hall's interior atrium populated by giant palm trees reaching four stories high. As beautiful as the courtyard was, it also created a challenge. The trees in the middle of it made sight lines difficult. Their target could be right across the courtyard from her but still impossible to see.

She started running to her right, hoping that changing her angle might help. It worked. With several large palm fronds out of the way, she saw an older man in a sports jacket walking around the corner toward the stairwell exit on the other side of the courtyard. She was already suspicious of him because he was moving briskly, almost jogging. But it was when he glanced over his shoulder nervously that she knew she had her guy. She recognized him from the photos in his office. It was Mark Rawls.

As she broke into a sprint, she voice texted Ryan: *Rawls is headed for second floor stairwell on opposite side; older, pudgy, gray hair, blue sports coat.* She managed to catch up, get to the door before it closed, and yank it open. Rawls was just rounding the landing of the final set of stairs leading to the first floor. She took the steps three at a time and caught up to him just as he was reaching for the door to the lobby.

She slammed him against the door, knocking it closed again, then swung him against the adjacent wall by the back of his jacket so that he was facing her. She got her first good look at him. He was in his early sixties. His face was flushed, exacerbating the cragginess of his many wrinkles. His gray hair was just starting to thin. His brown eyes were wide with terror.

"Mark Rawls, I presume?" she asked.

He nodded nervously.

"I've got to tell you, running from the cops is rarely a good look, especially on a supposedly respectable dean of a university department."

He looked like he wanted to respond but was still too winded. Just then, the lobby stairwell door flew open and Ryan barreled through. He almost started up the stairs before he saw Jessie and Rawls against the wall in the corner.

"That's an unexpected sight," he said between heavy puffs.

"I thought someone was robbing my office," Rawls protested as he gasped for air. "I was running for my own safety."

Jessie looked over at Ryan in disbelief that the dean would try to sell this line of crap. Her fiancé gave her a nod, indicating that she should run with it.

"Mr. Rawls," she said, releasing him and taking a step back, "that's not the way to go. You overheard us talking in your office. You obviously know who I am, since you've been trying to get rid of me. To suggest you thought you were being robbed is a level of lame deception I wouldn't have expected from someone in your position. It's almost enough to make an investigator suspect you of something untoward, especially after looking at the binder you've compiled on Professor Tobias."

Rawls's expression was filled with panic.

"You think I killed him?" he asked, aghast.

"It makes sense," Jessie said calmly. "Based on what I saw in your binder, you knew what he was up to. Maybe you decided he was too big a liability to the department and that this was the best way to get out of a potential P.R. nightmare."

"That's not true," Rawls insisted.

"Then tell us what *is* true," Ryan demanded. "And dispense with any attempts to cover up what Tobias was doing. We already know so you might as well come clean."

Rawls looked back and forth between them, clearly trying to come up with some verbal escape plan.

"Can we do this somewhere else?" he pleaded.

"No," Jessie said bluntly. "We're certainly not going to sit on a bench out in that courtyard and I'm not in the mood to go back to your office. So unless you want to talk down at the station, this is it. After all, we could book you right now for evasion. So which do you prefer?"

"Here is fine," Rawls muttered.

"So explain," Ryan instructed.

The man sighed, giving himself one last reprieve before everything changed.

"I'd suspected for some time that Roman was engaged in inappropriate behavior with students. There were rumors circulating for a few years but he was careful enough that nothing was ever definitive. So I began to gather supporting materials that I hoped would prove sufficient to get him removed, even without a smoking gun. I feared that at some point it would all blow up and we'd be faced with lawsuits, not to mention the terrible publicity."

Jessie silently noted that his concerns didn't seem to include the emotional well-being of Tobias's victims but held her tongue for now. The man was finally talking and she didn't want to interfere with that.

"I hoped that if I had enough on him, I could present it to him directly and convince him to leave quietly, saving the school from any ugliness. But I kept collecting everything I could because I knew I would probably only have one chance to resolve this without a mess. I could feel tensions rising in the department. Other professors resented him because the rules didn't apply to him."

"What do you mean?" Ryan asked.

"He was only one with an office in another building and it was big. He skipped department meetings and even entire classes if he had a TV interview. He would cancel speeches and publicized campus lectures at the last minute. He put inappropriate pressure on the admissions staff to get his preferred students into the school. He treated everyone in the department, including myself, like his peons. And all that is independent of his liaisons, many with his own students, girls whose work he was evaluating, some of whom I believe were underage."

He stopped and took a deep breath, apparently relieved at having gotten everything off his chest.

"Why did you try to get me kicked off the case?" Jessie asked.

Rawls looked reluctant to answer but seemed to sense that he had no choice.

"Once Roman was killed, I thought our problem had resolved itself. If he wasn't around anymore, there was no longer any brewing scandal to hide. But when you started poking about, I feared it would all come out anyway. I thought that your removal might prevent that."

"But getting rid of me wouldn't have stopped the investigation," she pointed out. "Detective Hernandez would still be working the case, along with others."

"In retrospect, I see that," Rawls conceded. "But in the moment, I was worried about you. Everywhere you go, media attention follows. I thought it might dissipate without you around. And because you teach here, I worried you'd have particular insight that might elude complete outsiders. It was foolish, I admit."

"Okay," Ryan said, "But the fact remains, with Tobias dead, you don't have to push him out and face potential blowback. That's what we cops sometimes call a motive. So we've got to ask—where were you between 10:00 and 10:30 yesterday morning."

For the first time since they'd caught him, Rawls seemed to relax slightly.

"I was at a lecture that entire time," he said. "I sat right up front. Many people saw me. In fact, Roman gave the introductory remarks.

I thought he was there that whole time too until another professor told me he skipped out as soon as the lights went down—typical."

For what felt like the hundredth time, Jessie and Ryan exchanged the same look. If Rawls's alibi was verified, they had reached another dead end.

"We're going to need all your files," Ryan told Rawls.

"Of course," he said, "But could we please take the elevator back up?"

"Fine," Ryan said, sounding reluctant though Jessie knew there was no way he wanted to deal with the stairs again either.

As they left the stairwell and crossed Palm Court, Jessie tried not let despair set in. They'd uncovered so many secrets but, so far, none had led them to the killer. Meanwhile, they were hours closer to Laird forcing her off the case entirely. She needed to find another angle to come at the case. And she needed to find it quick. That meant going back to the beginning.

CHAPTER TWENTY FIVE

Hannah tried not to get despondent.

It was hard, considering that the morning was bleeding away, and she was down to her last lead. There was only one female patient Dr. Tam had in his notebook that she hadn't talked to. But it was a challenge to corner her somewhere that Dr. Tam wouldn't see them together. After his visit last evening, she was particularly careful to conduct her investigation beyond the prying eyes of cameras and loose-lipped aides.

When she finally caught up to the patient—while "coincidentally" going to the bathroom at the same time—it turned out to be for naught. The girl, a surly twenty-something named Jenny Nunn, didn't like Tam, but it was mainly because he didn't seem all that interested in her problems, not because he took *too* strong a personal interest.

With the final patient crossed off her list, Hannah walked slowly back to her room. Her morning group therapy session was over. She wasn't meeting with Dr. Lemmon until later. And because she spent all night worrying about a secret visit from Dr. Tam that never came, she was exhausted. A nap sounded perfect.

She was just passing the hall where Merry's room had been, where she'd found her dead body, when she had an idea. Jessie had said that when her leads dried up, she went back to the beginning, where it had all started, to see if she had missed anything. In this case, the place it had all started was Merry's room.

Hannah hadn't been back there since that awful night six days ago. As unpleasant as the thought was, it was time to return. If she was going to find something that might help her understand what happened to Merry, that room might be the best place to look.

Despite her uneasiness, she walked slowly down the hall she'd carefully avoided until now. She moved past the spot where she'd sat on the floor, slumped over and numb, as she listened to staffers in the room confirm Merry's death.

She reached the door. Police had officially cleared the scene days ago but the door was still locked. It made sense. The staff knew it would be a while before they could use the bedroom for a resident but they also didn't want anyone sneaking in out of morbid curiosity. That didn't stop her. She removed a paper clip that she always kept in her pocket and used a technique that her future brother-in-law, Ryan, had taught her to pick the lock. She was inside the room within seconds.

After re-locking the door, she turned around. The room was bare. The bed was stripped of sheets and all Merry's personal touches—family photos, her pieces from art therapy, her books and posters—were gone.

Though she doubted she'd have much luck finding anything the cops had missed, Hannah searched the room. She looked in the closet, feeling along the shelf that ran its length at eye level. She re-checked the chest of drawers but found nothing other than one dull pencil in the top one.

Moving over to the bed, she lifted the mattress and checked underneath. Unsurprisingly, she found nothing. If anything had been there, it would have been discovered when they changed out the old mattress, which was soaked in blood, for this one.

She sat down on the edge of the bed, imagining what Jessie would do in this situation. It wasn't hard to guess. Her sister would try to put herself in Merry's shoes, to imagine what she was thinking that night in the moments before her death.

I need to do what she did, be where she was.

Though it made her feel ghoulish, Hannah lay back on the bed, resting her head where Merry's had been as she took her last breaths. She closed her eyes, picturing how Merry's hands were always moving, smoothing out wrinkles in her pants, running her fingers along whatever surface was nearby.

Hannah did the same, letting her fingers dance along the plastic mattress top, before reaching back to the headboard and sliding her fingertips along the flat, smooth wood until they encountered a rough spot before becoming even again. She traced her finger back the other way over the irregular section, picturing Merry doing the same thing to soothe herself as she drifted off to sleep.

Hannah felt herself starting to float a little when something occurred to her. One of the rough grooves her finger was running along was shaped a lot like a letter. She popped upright and looked at the headboard. It was hard to be sure because the scratches were so shallow but it looked like they might form a word. Merry must have used her fingernails, scratching the same spot over and over, night after night.

Hannah remembered the dull pencil in the top drawer and dashed across the room to grab it. Quickly, she rubbed the pencil over the headboard like it was an ancient engraving. When she was done she saw that it spelled out a single word: GRAND.

In a flash she knew what the word meant. It was a clue left by Merry from the grave. And if Hannah was right, it pointed directly to the person responsible for her death. She knew who did this. And she knew who she had to tell first.

CHAPTER TWENTY SIX

Jessie tried to clear her head. She needed to get rid of the sticky spider web tendrils of false leads, dashed hopes, and nightmare-induced fatigue in order to get back on track.

So while Ryan went to the UCLA police station to check in with Lieutenant Schrader on the off chance that they'd uncovered something new, she wandered the campus, allowing the crisp, mid-March morning air to wipe her mental slate clean. As students rushed past her, hurrying to get to their next classes, she ambled through the Murphy Sculpture Garden, letting the curves of the delicately carved figures guide her thoughts.

She decided it was time put her own advice into effect, and go back to the beginning, where it all started, to see what she might have missed the first time around. In this case, that was Roman Tobias's office.

She didn't need to actually physically revisit it, and had no intention to, now that the media had returned and was camped out in front of Haines Hall. No, she needed to understand what had led Tobias back to that office, when he should have been elsewhere, essentially hurrying to the place of his eventual death.

She sat down on a bench and closed her eyes, hoping it wasn't too disrespectful to the sculpture in front of her called *The Bather*. Letting her body relax, she tried to piece together the timeline from yesterday morning.

At 9:45, Tobias had given introductory remarks for a lecture that ran until 11 and which etiquette suggested he should have stayed for. But he had scheduled a "meeting" with Phoebe Lewis for 10:30, right in the middle of the lecture. Why do that?

Part of it made sense. If he snuck out unnoticed, then he could use the lecture as an alibi if things went poorly with Phoebe and she made some kind of accusation against him. Assuming no one saw him leave, he could claim that he wasn't even in his office when Phoebe alleged he'd behaved badly.

But the killer couldn't have known about Tobias's plan. If they were tracking his schedule, they would have seen that he was supposed to be in Royce Hall for the lecture. So how had they managed to be there when he returned to his office? Was it just luck?

But there was something else to consider. Tobias hadn't snuck out of the lecture at 10:20 to get back for his 10:30 appointment with Phoebe. According to Monica Littleton, he left the hall before 10. Why go back so early when he wasn't meeting with Phoebe for another half hour—just to catch up on paperwork? That didn't strike Jessie as a Roman Tobias move. The answer seemed clear. He had another appointment, one scheduled for 10 a.m. in his office, one that was off the books, and that, like Phoebe's, he didn't want anyone else to know about.

And almost certainly, the person he was meeting for that secret appointment was the same person who killed him. The timing made sense. Sometime between 10 and 10:30 a.m., Roman Tobias was murdered. Then the killer left the door unlocked and escaped, possibly just minutes before Phoebe Lewis arrived.

But who was it? Could Tobias have been so bold as to schedule a liaison with one girl for 10 when he had another coming at 10:30? That seemed reckless, even for him. If not, then what other kind of meeting would necessitate such secrecy?

She didn't know but decided it was time to loop in someone who could help find out. Standing up and heading back toward the library, she started to text Ryan when her phone rang. It was him.

"We've got something," he said.

"What?" Jessie asked, holding back her revelation for now.

"An anonymous caller left a voicemail on the university police tip line late last night. It was just logged. The caller, who was female, said she saw a man she didn't recognize walking down the hallway from the direction of Tobias's office around 10:10 a.m. yesterday morning. She said she wasn't paying close attention and that the possible significance didn't register for her until later, when she heard he'd been murdered."

"Did she give a description?" Jessie asked.

"Yes," Ryan confirmed, "but it's pretty basic: male, darkish hair, looked to be older than a student but she never really saw his face. And she didn't actually see him leave Tobias's office, just coming from that direction."

"Still," Jessie countered, "the timeline fits."

"It made me wonder if maybe we've been too traditional in our thinking," Ryan mused. "What if it *was* a student, or even a colleague, that Tobias was involved with. Maybe he was bisexual?"

It was unwise to eliminate any theory too early but Jessie was dubious.

"Anything's possible, I suppose," she conceded "but I have my doubts. We've done a lot of legwork and pored over Rawls's files as well. So far, we haven't found any evidence to support the idea that he was involved with men. Besides, having some tryst with anyone, regardless of gender, when he knew Phoebe was on her way over, feels like a tough sell."

Ryan was quiet for a second. When he responded, he sounded especially curious.

"Why do I get the feeling that you have another theory?"

"Because I kind of do," she said. "I think he may have been meeting with someone, but because of a different secret."

She proceeded to tell him about her suspicion that Tobias had another meeting on the books at 10 a.m., one he had to leave the lecture early to get to.

"So you don't think it was related to an affair at all?"

Something about the way Ryan phrased that jogged her memory. She had a flash of something she'd read but dismissed in Rawls's files, then immediately stood up.

"Maybe it wasn't an affair," she told him, "But it might have been affair-adjacent."

"What does that mean?" he asked.

"Can you pick me up? I'll explain on the way."

CHAPTER TWENTY SEVEN

They pulled up in front of the modest house on Herbert Street in Mar Vista, only seven miles from UCLA but a world away.

Unlike the mansions and fancy condo buildings that encircled the campus, this neighborhood was aggressively upper middle-class, with giant apartment complexes next to cottage-sized homes that probably still cost three quarters of a million dollars. In the cottage home they'd parked beside was the suspect they planned to question.

"It was when you mentioned an affair that I recalled Rawls's files," Jessie had explained as they made the short drive over to the house. "There was a passing reference to another possible source of scandal for the department—an affair that Rawls suspected Tobias was having with a professor in the history department."

"With whom?" Ryan had asked.

"Rawls suspected a professor of early constitutional history named Daphne Hinton," Jessie had explained. "There were some telltale signs, including suspicious receipts from conferences they both attended and a level of physical intimacy in casual environments that he found unusual."

"That's it?" Ryan had asked skeptically.

"I don't remember all the details," Jessie had told him, "But there were a lot. To be honest, at a certain point I moved on because I dismissed her as a suspect."

"Why?"

"Because she's been gone all week," Jessie had said. "She's at a conference in Philadelphia, something on the Constitutional Convention and the Federalist Papers. She won't be back until Sunday."

"So then why are we headed to her house?" Ryan had wondered.

"Because she's married," Jessie had said, "and if Rawls suspected something, then maybe her husband did too. And he's been home all week."

Now they were here, walking up to the front door of the small house, which boasted a drought-resistant garden in the front, along with a white trellis, metal roof, and a small porch with a two-person

130

swing. From somewhere inside, they could hear what sounded like an electric saw.

"Are you sure he's home?" Ryan asked as they climbed the steps.

"According to Jamil, Daryl Hinton works from home. He's a wood sculptor."

They knocked on the door and waited. The sound they'd heard stopped, replaced by approaching footsteps. When the door opened, they were greeted by a wiry-looking man in his mid-forties with dark hair and brown eyes that were hidden behind protective goggles. He wore blue jeans and a long, flannel shirt, both under a large apron covered in wood shavings.

"You're not the pizza delivery guy," he said, disappointed.

Jessie noted that he seemed awfully relaxed for a man who may have murdered someone barely twenty-four hours earlier.

"Afraid not," Ryan said, flashing his ID. "I'm Detective Hernandez with the LAPD. This is Jessie Hunt, a consultant for the department. We'd like to ask you a few questions."

Hinton's expression immediately changed to concern.

"What's wrong?" he demanded. "Did something happen to Daphne? Is she okay?"

"To the best of our knowledge, she's fine," Jessie said quickly. "This is about another matter. May we come in?"

A wave of relief crossed over Hinton's face.

"Sure, I guess," he said opening the door for them. Jessie noticed his eyes dart back behind him to a closed door before he returned his attention to them. She pretended not to notice.

They stepped inside to find themselves in a small living room separated from the kitchen by a half-wall. A short hallway led to what Jessie assumed were the bedrooms. Dozens of packing boxes filled both rooms and lined the hallway, piled three high anywhere there was space.

"Should we talk in here?" Hinton asked.

"That's fine," Ryan said, then pointed to the goggles. "Do you still need those?"

"Oh, no, sorry," Hinton said, pulling them off. "Sometimes I forget I'm even wearing them."

They sat down on the small loveseat in the living room and he took the rocking chair opposite them.

"Moving?" Jessie asked, nodding at all the boxes.

"Just some spring cleaning," Hinton replied unconvincingly before asking, "What is this about?"

Jessie looked over at Ryan. In the car, they'd agreed that he should take the lead to suss out how much the man knew. He planned to take the direct approach.

"Do you know Professor Roman Tobias?" he asked.

Hinton nodded gravely.

"Of course," he said. "He was in the same department as my wife. I saw him at lots of university functions. A terrible shame what happened."

"So you only knew him through school functions?" Ryan pressed.

Hinton shrugged.

"We'd see him out and about occasionally. Despite its size, the history department has an incestuous quality to it."

"Did you like him?" Jessie asked, joining in the questioning for the first time.

"He was all right," Hinton said, shrugging again.

"That wasn't entirely convincing," Jessie noted.

Hinton sighed.

"I don't want to speak ill of someone who just died, but he was a bit of a pretentious prick. Charming for sure, but not as much as he thought."

Ryan looked at over at Jessie and she knew he was wondering whether they should pursue the affair angle. But she didn't want to play that card just yet, and gave him a subtle shake of her head. He picked up on it and followed a different line.

"Let me get to the point, Mr. Hinton," he said. "We're talking to everyone Roman Tobias knew, even tangentially, and asking where they were yesterday morning between ten and 10:30. So what were you doing?"

Hinton leaned back in the rocking chair, seeming to search his memory.

"I'm pretty sure I was right here, working on a piece," he said. "I'm a sculptor. Most mornings, I'm at it by 7 a.m. and I don't take more than five-minute breaks until around noon. I don't think yesterday was any different."

"Can anyone verify that?" Ryan asked. "Did someone stop by? Did you speak to anyone on the phone?"

"I always have lunch delivered just after noon. That's why I thought you might be the pizza guy arriving a little early. Yesterday was sushi. And I don't usually make or receive calls when I'm working."

"So no one can verify your whereabouts, then?" Ryan confirmed.

"I mean, I guess not," Hinton said uncomfortably.

"Where's your restroom?" Jessie asked suddenly, deciding that now, while he was in a nervous, compliant state, was the best time to ask for a favor that would allow her to snoop.

"It's actually through my studio," Hinton said, pointing back at the door he'd involuntarily glanced at when they'd first arrived. "Sorry about that but it's a small house with a weird design and just one bathroom."

"That's okay," Jessie said. "Maybe I'll take a peek at a piece or two while I'm back there."

"Feel free," he said, incorrectly hoping that his hospitality would win him points.

Jessie left him to fend his way through the minefield of Ryan's questions, which were actually intended primarily to keep him busy while she looked around for anything that could tie him to Tobias's death.

She opened the door to Hinton's studio, which she realized was actually just a converted garage. It was packed with countless wood-carved sculptures, some as small as ashtrays, others the size of grown adults. Closing the door behind her and weaving her way among them, she went to the bathroom and turned on the light and the fan, hoping the noise would reassure their host that nothing was amiss. Then she walked around the space, looking for anything that seemed suspicious or out of place.

There were no blood-soaked aprons or crossed-out photos of Tobias. None of his sculptures showed a professor in physical agony. That would be too easy.

She moved to his small desk in the corner of the garage and began rifling through anything that was visible on the table. The majority of the papers were receipts for work materials. Some were contracts for shows at various galleries.

In the back she saw a small notebook that looked like a journal. She grabbed it and leafed through it. Most pages were filled with rough drawings for potential projects with scribbled notes off to the side. She was just about to put it back down when she noticed one page that had writing but no drawing. As she read it her mouth dropped open. The entry was short and to the point.

Go when it's busy. Draws less attention. Dress like a professor. Keep saw in satchel. Remember to charge before use. Use key behind bust. Knock him out right away. Stuff gag in mouth. When he wakes up, start with fingertips, one at a time. Work your way down. Then finish with the throat. Make him pay.

Jessie felt a surge of excitement and bit her lip to stay quiet. She tried not to overreact, though what she'd read was hard to misinterpret. While Tobias was never specifically mentioned, the key behind the bust was. That, combined with the reference to dressing like a professor and the strong possibility that his wife was having an illicit affair with the man, was enough to justify making their conversation with Hinton more formal.

She pulled an evidence bag from her jacket pocket and placed the notebook inside. Then she turned off the bathroom light and fan. As she steered her way through the sculptures, she made sure to stay even-keeled so as not to reveal anything when she walked out of the garage. She passed an electric saw, and just to be sure, checked it for signs of blood, skin, or bone. Maybe her assumption was wrong. Maybe Hinton was after someone else and had already killed his intended victim. But the only thing on the saw was wood dust.

"Everything cool?" Ryan asked when she returned to the living room.

Hinton turned around too so she nodded amiably, making sure to hide the evidence bag with the journal behind her back. Only when the sculptor turned around to face Ryan did she hold up the bag and motion for her partner and fiancé to remove his gun.

Though it was clear that he didn't understand the significance of the bag's contents, it seemed he didn't need to. Jessie making the request was enough for him. With stunning speed, he pulled out his gun, though he didn't point it at Hinton.

"I'm going to need you to raise your hands above your head, sir," he said calmly.

"What the hell?" Hinton demanded, though he did what he was told.

"Ms. Hunt will explain," Ryan told him, mostly because he couldn't.

Jessie walked around to where the sculptor could see her and held up the bag with the notebook.

"I found what you wrote in your journal," she said, "about your plan involving the electric saw and fingertip removal, among other things."

"What? No. That isn't what you think."

"I think it's a pretty vivid description of what you intended," she countered. "'Make him pay,' Mr. Hinton?"

"I know this looks bad," he started to reply before Jessie cut him off.

"Better arrest him and read him his rights before he says anything else, Detective," Jessie suggested. "We don't want this to fall apart because of a technicality."

Ryan nodded and pulled out his handcuffs as he began talking.

"You have the right to remain silent…"

CHAPTER TWENTY EIGHT

They never would have made it downtown.

It became clear to Jessie within sixty seconds of putting Daryl Hinton in the back seat of the car that he wasn't going to make it to the station while staying silent until they could set up a formal interrogation. So they went to the UCLA police station instead.

"Hold on," Ryan ordered as Hinton again tried to explain himself. "Wait until we get into the interview room. Then we can talk."

Hinton nodded, although it looked like he might explode at any moment. Lieutenant Schrader, whom they had called on the way, had everything set up when they arrived.

"Already recording," he muttered to them as Hinton stepped inside the room.

They followed and told him to take a seat. He did and started to open his mouth again.

"Mr. Hinton," Ryan said before he could get a word out. "This conversation is being recorded. Can you confirm that I have already read you your Miranda rights?"

"Yes," Hinton blurted out, squirming in the chair.

Jessie had rarely seen a suspect so intent on talking, despite repeated warnings that his statements could be used against him. He was either about to make his situation much better or irretrievably worse.

"Are you now saying that you are willing to speak to us without a lawyer present?" Ryan asked slowly, refusing to be rushed.

"Yes," Hinton said. "I've been trying to talk this whole time. Can I do that now?"

"Why do you have a notebook describing killing Roman Tobias with an electric saw?" Ryan demanded, not letting Hinton dictate the direction of the interrogation.

"It was just a cathartic fantasy," he nearly shouted, now that he was finally able to talk. "I would never have actually done that."

"Why did you fantasize about killing him?" Jessie pressed.

Hinton froze. It was odd to see him so still and quiet after the last fifteen minutes of human frenzy. Then the ice cracked.

"Listen, I think you already know. Otherwise why would you have come to see me in the first place? He was having an affair with my wife."

"And you wanted to make him pay for that?" Jessie wondered, again quoting his journal entry.

"Yes, I did want to," he conceded, "but I didn't actually do it. I mean, was Roman killed with a saw?"

"That's hardly a defense, Mr. Hinton," Ryan noted. "Just because a saw wasn't used doesn't mean you couldn't find another tool to get the job done."

"But I didn't do it," the man insisted, as if those words alone should set him free.

"You knew about the hidden key behind the bust in the hallway," Jessie reminded him.

Hinton nodded, looking sheepish.

"That's true," he admitted. "But I didn't use it. I only saw it at all because I came to surprise Daphne at work one night and saw her walking out of Bunche Hall with him. I was about to call out to her but something about how close they were to each other made me stop."

"What *did* you do?" Ryan asked.

"I followed them to his building, up the stairs to his floor. I hid behind the staircase banister at the end of the hall and saw him pull out the key and open the door. As she walked in ahead of him, he took off her coat and ran his finger along her shoulder."

"That must have been upsetting," Jessie noted sympathetically.

"Incredibly," he replied. "But not as upsetting as what I heard when I got close to his door. It was clear what was going on."

"But you didn't break the door down?" Ryan asked.

Hinton shook his head.

"No. I was stunned. I didn't know what to do. So I left. I went home to compose my thoughts. Daphne got home about an hour later. That's when I confronted her."

"When did all this happen?" Ryan asked.

"Four days ago, on Monday night."

"What did she say when you confronted her?" Jessie asked, continuing to keep the sympathetic tone in her voice, hoping he might view her as someone he could confide his deepest, darkest secrets to.

"She didn't try to deny it," he said, with less venom than she would have expected. "She told me that it was good that I found out, that she wanted a divorce. She was catching a flight the next morning to Philadelphia for a conference and said she planned to spend the rest of the night here at a hotel. She told me that she wanted me moved out by the time she got back, which is this Sunday."

"I'm surprised you didn't tell *her* to move out," Ryan said, clearly trying to show he was on Hinton's side, but the man surprised both of them with his response.

"No. It was me confronting her that set her off in the first place. If I'm going to have any chance at salvaging this marriage, I couldn't do that. It would blow everything up forever."

Jessie thought the thing was already pretty well blown up but didn't say that. She doubted it would endear her to him and she needed him compliant. Ryan went a different way.

"So your wife's out of town, off discussing her work, and enjoying late night drinks with friends while you're left in your studio, simmering with rage over what this man has done to you. I mean, he was getting to enjoy Daphne in ways you never would again."

"She'll come back to me," Hinton said pathetically.

"Maybe," Jessie offered. "But in the meantime, she's gone. That gave you the chance to eliminate your competition. It would be the perfect murder. If she returns to town to find that her lover is dead, there's a chance she comes back to you, right? It had to occur to you."

"It did occur to me," he surprised her by saying. "Right before I wrote that journal entry. But I didn't act on it. First of all, Tobias dying wasn't going to send Daphne back into my arms. Hell, she probably would have accused me of doing it, just like you are. No, I need to win her back the right way, by making her love me again, not by eliminating the competition. Also, I'm not a psycho! I'm not going to chop him up or kill him any other kind of way. Can't you look me up? I've never committed an act of violence in my life."

"That's true of lots of people," Ryan replied, "right up until it isn't. I'm sorry, Mr. Hinton, but the facts are that you have a motive to commit this crime, you knew where Tobias's key was, you have no alibi, and you wrote about murdering him. We're going to have to book you."

Daryl Hinton's face turned scarlet and he looked like he was about to scream, but before anything came out, his eyes got cloudy and he fell out of his chair. He had passed out.

CHAPTER TWENTY NINE

Jessie was restless.

After Hinton woke up and they made sure he was stable enough to move, she waited in the car while Ryan coordinated the details of the man's transfer downtown. They'd agreed not to tell anyone, even Decker, about this turn of events until they had it completely locked down.

That meant having Jamil check Hinton's cell phone GPS data to confirm that he was at Tobias's office yesterday morning. He might have left his phone at home as cover but if they could show hard proof that he was at Haines Hall between ten and 10:30, their case would be bulletproof. Ryan had agreed to the delay, even though, in his words, "this case is already bulletproof."

It was hard to dispute that, and yet something was eating at Jessie, frustratingly nibbling at the corner of her brain without revealing itself. Part of her unease was because of the journal. If Hinton had killed Tobias, would he really have kept that entry, which described his plan in dramatic detail? It's not like he would have forgotten about it after writing it down only days earlier. Why didn't he toss it?

But it wasn't just that. Hinton had to know that if anyone else was aware of the affair, they would view him a suspect and potentially report him to the authorities. In fact, as he said himself, Daphne might have called it in. But neither the journal nor his near-certain status as a person of interest in the case was what really bugged her.

She glanced at the Rawls file, sitting in a tote bag on the floor at her feet, and grabbed it, hoping it might clear the expanding cloud of irritation and weariness in her head. She flipped to the section with Rawls's notes on his suspicions about the affair between Tobias and Daphne Hinton and re-read them. But nothing jumped out at her. Still, she felt she was on the right track.

She switched to the section labeled "general complaints" and reviewed them. Just as the last time she'd read them, she found them frustratingly vague. There were multiple references to self-aggrandizing behavior, rudeness to students, preferential treatment for others, influencing admissions staff, conduct unbecoming, and unwillingness to adhere to departmental norms. But none of that was cause to initiate an effort to terminate a popular, famous, tenured professor. They weren't even enough to put into the formal record. They barely deserved to be in his "dirt" file. No wonder Rawls had felt so hamstrung.

She was about to close the file when she noticed the initials next to one of the complaints. Some were anonymous but a few had initials beside them. The one about "conduct unbecoming a faculty member" was noted with the initials D.H. Jessie could immediately think of two people with those initials. Daphne Hinton didn't seem to have much cause to complain about Tobias but her husband Daryl certainly did.

The complaint was not dated but it was the most recent one listed. It stood to reason that Hinton had gone to Mark Rawls with his concerns earlier this week after seeing them together. That would explain why the dean knew about the affair and also why he noted the complaint in a separate section. It gave him plausible deniability if Tobias ever came at him for compiling dirt on him. A "conduct unbecoming" allegation and a set of initials were fuzzy enough to protect Rawls from blowback.

But Jessie was less interested in Rawls's decision to obscurely notate the complaint than in Hinton's decision to make it in the first place. If he'd gone to the dean, then he clearly hoped that doing so might lead to Tobias's firing, maybe even his public downfall. Why would he kill him before getting a chance to see how everything played out? It didn't make sense.

Just then, she saw two uniformed officers escort Hinton outside and usher him quickly into a squad car. Ryan was right behind them. She got out of her car and jogged over. She arrived just as the car was starting to pull out and waved for them to stop. The driver looked nervous but the passenger whispered something that seemed to calm him. She suspected that he recognized her. He rolled down the window.

"Can we help you, Ms. Hunt?" he asked amiably.

"Yes, I have one quick question for Mr. Hinton. Do you mind?"

The cop in the passenger seat got out and opened the back door where the man sat forlornly. She knelt down so that she was at eye level with him. To her left, she noticed Ryan looking on curiously.

"Mr. Hinton, why didn't you tell us about the 'conduct unbecoming' complaint against Tobias you made with Dean Rawls?"

Hinton looked momentarily taken aback that she knew about it. But when he answered, it was with a sense of resignation.

"There was no point," he said. "I already told you what he did. Why would you care that I also mentioned it to Rawls? You already have me pegged as his killer. This wouldn't change that. Besides, when I went to Rawls, he told me that he was compiling a comprehensive list of potential infractions involving Roman. I didn't want to taint his investigation by revealing that one of the complaints had come from a guy now accused of murdering him. I guess I was hoping that, despite Roman's death, Rawls would still release his findings and that Daphne would see what a scumbag he was and come back to me. Not the most realistic plan, I admit."

"When did you see Rawls?" Jessie asked.

"On Tuesday, the day after Daphne left town."

"Okay," she said, "thank you Mr. Hinton."

He looked like he had a question of his own for her, but then seemed to change his mind and faced forward. She shut the door and told the officers they could leave. As they pulled out of the parking lot, Ryan came over to her.

"What was that all about?"

Jessie turned to face him.

"If you were going to murder someone, would you go to see his boss two days earlier to say you were pissed that the guy was having an affair with your wife? Wouldn't you want to see if your complaint did any good before taking such drastic measures? And wouldn't you worry that you'd just put a target on yourself?"

"I don't know," Ryan said, clearly not as perturbed as she was. "Maybe he figured that two days was long enough. Maybe his rage overwhelmed his good sense. What I know for sure is that the guy wrote a detailed description of killing a man who was murdered days later. I think we can defend this arrest."

Jessie couldn't argue the point. Killers didn't necessarily think rationally, especially if the murder they committed was a crime of passion. And yet, she still felt on edge.

"Fair enough," she said, as they walked back to the car. "But will you at least humor me?"

Ryan sighed deeply.

"I have a feeling I'm going to regret this. What do you want to do?"

"It's still only 1:15," she reminded him. "At this hour, with midday traffic, it'll take an hour to drive Hinton to the station. When he's arrived, we'll get a call from Decker. Let's use that time to explore other angles. That way, when Decker starts peppering us with questions, we'll have buttoned everything up and I won't have any remaining reservations."

Ryan smiled wearily as they got in the car.

"I get the sense that you already have another 'angle' in mind," he said. "Do you want to spill the beans?"

"When I was reviewing Rawls's files," she said, immediately launching in, "he made reference to Tobias pressuring the admissions staff to consider his preferred students."

"Right," Ryan said. "He also mentioned it to us when we questioned him in the stairwell. So what are you thinking?"

"What if an admissions officer resented Tobias's pressure enough to lash out? Remember that whole scandal involving payment for admission into competitive schools a few years back? It wasn't just places like Yale and Stanford. Some of the charges involved local schools, including my alma mater, USC, along with the place we're at right now. Those admissions people took a lot of heat for that. They're trying to re-establish the school's integrity. I could see one of them going to extremes to make sure this place doesn't get caught up in another incident and permanently ruining the school's reputation."

Ryan shrugged.

"It strikes me as a long shot," he said. "But if that's how you want to spend the next hour, I'm game. Did you have anyone particular in mind to talk to?"

"I did," Jessie said, grabbing Rawls's file and flipping to the appropriate page.

"According to this, he suspected that Tobias had inappropriately pressured the staff. But when he talked to the director of admissions, the guy vehemently denied it. It's clear that Rawls didn't believe him but couldn't do anything about it. He hit a brick wall and had to let it go."

"But *we* don't have to let it go," Ryan said, starting to warm to the idea as he turned on the car.

"No we don't," Jessie agreed. "So I guess you'll be wanting directions to the admissions office?"

CHAPTER THIRTY

No matter what Ryan said, the admissions office receptionist kept insisting that they make an appointment.

Jessie watched as Ryan tried to control his annoyance. If they weren't so pressed for time, she would have been amused. Watching her "all-business, no B.S." fiancé attempt to stay cool as he dealt with the officious receptionist was its own kind of entertainment.

The admissions office was in the same building as the chancellor's office, Murphy Hall, though it wasn't as fancy. But that didn't stop the woman at the reception window, whose nameplate read "Matilda Maynard" from bringing her own brand of formality to the proceedings. Likely approaching seventy, with gray hair and a relentlessly prim bearing, nothing seemed to bother her, not even having a police detective flash his badge at her.

"This is an urgent matter," Ryan reiterated to the receptionist, trying and mostly failing to keep his frustration from boiling over. "We need to speak to the director of admissions immediately. What's his name again?"

"Arthur Pelphrey," Jessie offered helpfully.

"Yeah, that guy," Ryan said.

"As I said, Detective, he is in an all-hands staff meeting," the receptionist said. "They are reviewing potential applicants for the fall semester. It's a complicated, time-sensitive process. There is usually a break at 2 p.m. I can touch base with him then to see if he can fit you in. Otherwise, I can pencil you in for a 4 p.m. appointment once the meeting is completed. Which do you prefer?"

Ryan could no longer control the bubbling aggravation.

"Here's what I prefer," he said, his voice low and tight. "You can get up and walk us to the location of that meeting or I can start opening doors and shouting his name, which I will begin doing in about five seconds. Now which do you prefer?"

After a resentfully long pause, the receptionist stood up huffily, buzzed them in, and led them down the hall to a room with large oak doors. Then she knocked softly and poked her head in. She said something quietly, to which they heard a muffled reply. The receptionist looked back at them.

"If you would please wait just a moment," she requested before stepping into the room and pushing the door closed enough so they couldn't see inside.

Ryan didn't honor her request. Instead he shoved the door open and entered the room. Jessie followed him. They were greeted by a large, ornate space that looked more appropriate for cocktail parties than admissions staff meetings. There were detailed carvings in the walls, and a giant chandelier hanging low over a long, rectangular table that could have accommodated thirty people but was currently seating a dozen.

At least half of the people at the table looked like they had only just graduated from college themselves. But one who didn't was the man seated at the head of the table, currently listening to the receptionist whispering in his ear.

Jessie gathered that it was Arthur Pelphrey. He looked much as she imagined he would. Bald and wearing a suit and bowtie, he appeared to be in his late fifties. He wore thin glasses and had a mug of tea on the table next to his paperwork.

The receptionist wasn't done whispering but Ryan had enough. Just as they heard the muttered words "…detective insists on seeing you now…," Ryan piped in.

"That's right," he said loudly, startling the receptionist, who hadn't seen them come in and jumped slightly, "we do need to see you now."

The woman turned around with a stern expression and replied tartly, "I believe I asked you to wait outside."

Ryan was readying his reply when Pelphrey interjected.

"That's all right, Matilda," he said crisply. "I think we can accommodate the detective. We'll just take our afternoon break a little early today. Everyone!"

The last word seemed to indicate to the others at the table that they should leave the room. They began to stand, but that wasn't what Jessie wanted. Mark Rawls had struck out in his private conversation with Pelphrey and she doubted they'd fare much better unless they changed the dynamic. Ryan clearly felt the same way.

"Actually, we'd like everyone to stick around for a minute," he said in a tone that indicated the instruction was non-negotiable.

"That's most unusual," Pelphrey said uncomfortably, "but we're happy to accommodate you."

"May I go at least?" Matilda asked sarcastically. "Someone needs to watch the front entrance should a visitor arrive."

"Go right ahead," Ryan said sharply, obviously pleased to be done with her. Once the door closed again, he moved further into the room so they could all better see him and continued. "I'm Detective Hernandez with the Los Angeles Police Department. This is Jessie Hunt, who consults for us. We're here investigating the death of Professor Roman Tobias and we need your help."

With that, he motioned to Jessie, indicating that she should join him. Of course what he secretly meant was that this was her "angle" and it was time for her to pursue it.

"Thank you, Detective Hernandez," she said, stepping forward. "I understand this is a sensitive issue, but it's one we need to address as part of our investigation. We've received credible reports that Professor Tobias improperly used his stature and influence in order to help get prospective students admitted. We need to get to the bottom of that."

Arthur Pelphrey swiveled his chair to face her and spoke in a harsh tone at odds with his earlier, mannerly comments.

"I have heard this assertion in the past," he said, his voice, now cutting through the air like glass, "and I can assure you that there is no merit to it. I don't know how many times I have to repeat that in order for it to sink in."

"Thank you for that, Mr. Pelphrey," Jessie replied sweetly, before turning her attention back to the others and going on as if he'd said nothing at all. "We get that validating such an accusation about someone who has died might feel inappropriate or secondary in light of his passing. But let me assure you that it's not. It could be crucial to resolving this case. That's why I'm giving you all my number and Detective Hernandez's."

As she walked over to a giant whiteboard against one of the walls, she noticed a younger guy in slacks and a button-down shirt with long, dirty blond hair that swept across his forehead and rested on one side, like a singer fronting a 1980s new wave band. He was shifting uncomfortably in his chair and avoiding eye contact. She made a mental note as she found an empty spot on the board amid the names of multiple students and scribbled their numbers.

"That's quite unnecessary," Pelphrey insisted.

"I'm afraid it is, sir," she said, turning around and squaring up to face the group. "A man was murdered on this campus just over twenty-four hours ago and the killer is still at large. Anyone who has information that could be helpful and doesn't share it is aiding and abetting that killer. I don't have to tell you the legal ramifications for such a thing."

Jessie didn't have to because she couldn't. The truth was that unless the person withholding information was the killer, there wasn't a lot the legal system could do if these folks kept quiet. Even if she and Ryan discovered that someone *was* holding back, it would be hard to bring a charge, and it certainly wouldn't be anything as intimidating as what she'd suggested. But the people around that table didn't need to know that.

"Is that all?" Pephrey asked, seemingly irked that his authority was being undermined.

"We expect you to do the right thing," she said, eyeing everyone in the room in turn, finally ending with her gaze squarely on the new wave hair guy. "We'll do our best to keep anything you share confidential. Now you all are free to take that afternoon break."

She and Ryan left as everyone got up for real this time, just as she'd hoped. She didn't have much faith that anyone would call, but if she could corner her prey in person here and now, while everything was still so intense, maybe she could get something worthwhile.

"I think we should both visit the restrooms as well," she told Ryan quietly as they walked back down the hall. "Keep your eyes out for the young guy with the Duran Duran hairdo. He's hiding something and he looks like he's about to physically burst, so he'll probably show up in there any minute."

Ryan nodded and headed for the men's restroom. Jessie went to the women's but didn't go inside. After a minute, the new wave guy walked into the men's room, only to pop out three seconds later. Jessie gathered that he must have seen Ryan. He made a beeline for the nearest exit. He had just left when Ryan came out. Jessie pointed at the exit, then darted to one closer to her.

Once outside, she debated pulling out her gun as a precaution, but the young guy hadn't been armed, so it felt like overkill. Of course, she had to consider that he might be hiding a knife in his pocket. Just then, she got a text that said simply: *headed your way.*

Jessie felt her breaths get quicker and shallower and forced herself to slow them down. She could hear rapid footsteps approaching and squared up in the direction she expected him to come from. She bent her knees slightly, ready for anything.

CHAPTER THIRTY ONE

Sure enough, the young guy hurriedly rounded the corner a few seconds later, almost running right into her.

"How's it going?" she asked, smiling broadly as he nearly stumbled—empty-handed—to the ground to avoid a collision. "If I was a more sensitive gal, I'd think you were trying to avoid me."

"I...I was just stepping outside for a smoke," he stammered.

"Go ahead, don't let me stop you," she replied, inhaling deeply and smelling no cigarette odor emanating from him.

He felt around lamely for a few seconds before saying, "I must have left them inside."

He turned to go back the way he came but Ryan had just rounded the corner, stopping him in his tracks. He turned back to face Jessie.

In that moment, she had twin thoughts. First, this kid clearly had something valuable to offer, something that could advance their investigation. But her instincts told her that he wasn't involved in what happened to Roman Tobias. His nervousness wasn't that of a guy afraid he was about to be busted for murder. His energy was more like that of a student who had cheated on a test and was afraid he might get caught. Instinct alone didn't make or break a case. But more often than not, she found that hers was right on.

"What's your name?" she asked him.

"Justin Carper," he answered timidly.

"Well, here's the thing, Justin," she said, keeping her tone light even though her words were not, "you're a terrible liar. You definitely don't smoke. And based on how you were acting in that room when I talked about people with information coming forward, it's obvious that you have something worth sharing."

"I don't," he insisted, less convincing now than when he'd claimed to be a smoker.

"If you say so, Justin," she replied, still keeping the chipper tone as she laid down the hammer. "But just to make sure, we'll probably want to take you back to Central Police Station—that's the downtown station where we work—and have a more comprehensive chat. Unfortunately, that means everyone on campus, including students, staff, the press, and of course your co-workers, will see us escorting you to our vehicle. They'll probably have some questions for you. It might get a little messy."

"Listen to her," Ryan volunteered. "She's been through that media ringer. She's an expert on how it usually goes down."

"I know," Justin squeaked. "I've seen you on TV a lot."

"Then you know how unpleasant it can get, Justin," she told him. "Of course, right now, it's just you, me and Detective Hernandez standing behind a building, not having a smoke together. No one has seen us. No one thinks it's weird that you're not around. But I'm guessing that when your afternoon break ends and you're not in that room, people are going to notice and start asking uncomfortable questions. How long are your breaks, Justin?"

"Fifteen minutes."

"And I bet Pelphrey's a real stickler about that," Jessie said mildly, looking at her watch. "That leaves us about eleven minutes before you're missed. Now if you were willing to tell us what had you squirming in your chair earlier like there were ants in your pants, and if we found what you said worthwhile, it's entirely possible that you could make it back inside with time to spare. So would you rather go with that option or the 'escort you to the police station in public view of everyone' route?"

"The first one please," Justin said without hesitation.

Jessie smiled.

"I think you made the right choice," she told him, "so let's get started. Did Professor Tobias ever pressure you or anyone else to admit a student?"

"Yes," he said, cringing at his own words.

"We're going to need more than that, Justin," Jessie warned. "Don't make this like pulling teeth."

"Right, okay," Justin said, looking down at the ground aggressively. "I graduated two years ago with a history major. I took this job to help pay for my masters, which I deferred to next school year so I could build up a nest egg. I took several of Professor Tobias's classes as an undergrad. I think that's why he came to me. He knew that I needed him on my side if I wanted the program to go well. He also knew that it was a financial struggle for me to stay here. So he paid me under the table to help him."

Jessie had expected Justin to reveal someone else's wrongdoing. Instead he had seemingly just admitted to a crime. She remained pokerfaced, not wanting to give him any hint that he'd said something incriminating or any reason to stop talking.

"To help him with what?" she asked, unsure where this was going.

"To advocate for a couple of students he wanted to gain admission last fall."

"How much did he pay you?" Ryan wanted to know.

"For the first student, this kid named Arlo Kemper, he gave me $10,000—half up front and the other half if he was accepted."

"Was he?" Jessie asked.

"Yes," Justin said. "But he didn't end up coming here. He got into Cal Berkeley too and decided to go there."

"Did Tobias say why he wanted Kemper to get in?" Ryan pressed.

"Just that it was a favor for a friend. But Kemper's mother is a congresswoman from Orange County so it wasn't that hard to figure out."

"But Kemper didn't end up coming," Jessie reconfirmed. "Did Tobias appear upset about that?"

"No. he seemed satisfied, like he'd done what was asked of him, regardless of how it turned out."

"Okay, Jessie continued. "You said there were two students. Who was the other one?"

"Her name is Amanda Bratton," Justin said. "She was a lot harder. That's why the professor paid me double."

"$20,000?" Ryan exclaimed.

"Right," Justin answered. "It was the same deal as before—half up front and half if she got in."

"Did she?" Jessie asked.

"Yes, but like I said, it wasn't easy. She was a mediocre student, C+ average, coasted along on her looks, I think. Other than cheerleading, she didn't have many extra-curricular activities. I had to work with her to fudge the application, and then massage it once it came in. Even then, it was close."

"Why did he want her to get in so badly?" Jessie asked, afraid she already knew the answer.

"He never said," Justin admitted, "but I doubt it was out of the kindness of his heart. When I was helping her with her application, she told me how she visited some late night show when he was one of the guests. He invited her and her folks backstage. They got to talking and he suggested he might be able to help get her in here. Amanda's pretty dense but I got the sense that her folks agreed to some kind of payment in return."

"Who else in the admissions office knows about this?" Ryan asked.

"No one," Justin said emphatically. "After what happened with the previous scandal, everyone around here is on high alert. Plus, no one liked Tobias because he was always informally 'recommending' potential students despite a prohibition on that. That's why he only went through me. He knew I needed the money and that I'd keep quiet."

"Well, that's about to end, Justin," Jessie told him. "I need Amanda's admission application. Can you send it to me?"

Justin nodded vigorously, clearly excited for any scenario that allowed him to return to his life.

"If you let me go now, I could probably send it to you before the meeting starts."

"Do that," Jessie told him. "But this isn't the end of our communication. If we call, you pick up right away. No avoiding us. No backtracking. No refusing to answer our questions. Are we clear?"

"Yes," Justin said, nodding so hard that his blond hair started flopping wildly.

"Then get back in there, Justin," she instructed. "We'll be waiting to hear from you."

As Justin scurried off, Ryan muttered, "I don't think he understands that he just confessed to a felony."

"Nope," Jessie agreed. "I almost feel bad for him."

"Let's wait to see if this pans out before shedding any tears," Ryan countered. "Also, this Amanda Bratton doesn't sound like Tobias's type. He didn't seem to go for the conventionally pretty cheerleader sort."

"True," Jessie conceded. "But maybe he made an exception in her case. If he did, he might have gotten a surprise."

"What do you mean?" Ryan asked.

"Amanda Bratton doesn't strike me as the shrinking violet type. What if he tried to make a move and she decided to fight back?"

CHAPTER THIRTY TWO

Hannah had to stop walking and lean against the wall.

She wasn't used to this. She so infrequently felt strong emotions that when one hit her this hard, it was almost overwhelming. She knew what it was—a flight of nervous butterflies in her stomach. But since it was so rare for her, it was hard to know what to do with the feeling.

At least she understood why it was happening. She was about to tell the administrative director of the Seasons Wellness Center that Merry had been murdered and that she knew who did it. She had no idea how it would go. Once she came clean, the situation would be out of her control. But that was the only way to get justice for Merry. So she would have to push through this unfamiliar feeling and hope for the best.

She walked into his outer office and waited for his secretary to look up. It took a while, so long that Hannah started to wonder if the woman, whose nameplate said "Gina, executive assistant," was keeping her waiting on purpose. Finally Gina looked up and offered a fake smile. She had lipstick on her teeth and wore too much eye makeup. Even though she was clearly in her thirties, she'd made herself look a decade older.

"How can I help you, dear?" she asked insincerely.

"I need to speak to Director Goodman," Hannah said simply.

"Certainly," Gina replied, "let's see when we can set up an appointment for you. I know he's fully booked through the middle of next week."

"No, I need to speak to him right now."

Gina offered her a pitying look.

"I'm afraid that's not possible, dear," she told her. "Director Goodman has a packed schedule. No one, not even one of our valued residents, can just come and meet with him right away."

"Tell him it's about Meredith Bartlett," Hannah said loudly. "Trust me—he'll want to hear what I have to say."

154

Gina's eyes widened briefly before she regained control. Hannah watched her trying to calculate the consequences of sending her away versus letting her in. It didn't take long to make her choice.

"Hold on a moment," she said, picking up her phone and pushing a button. After Goodman picked up, she whispered quietly. "I have a resident at my desk who insists on speaking with you about the Bartlett girl."

Goodman said something Hannah couldn't hear.

"I don't know," Gina replied, then looked up at Hannah.

"What's your name?" she asked.

"Hannah Dorsey."

Gina repeated that into the phone, waited as Goodman said something, and then hung up.

"He'll see you," she said, standing up and escorting Hannah to the door. She opened it but didn't enter herself. Once Hannah was inside, Gina closed the door without a word. Goodman was at his desk with his head down, scribbling something.

"Just give me one second, Hannah," he said without looking up. "I'm just finishing up."

"Okay," she said, doing her best not to let the butterflies fly up into her throat. She awkwardly shoved her hands deep in her pockets, squeezing a ball of tissues in one of them and fiddling with the phone in the other.

While she waited, she looked around his office, hoping it might give her a better sense of the person she was about to speak with. The walls were covered with various diplomas and certificates of commendation, too many to read. She noticed one from the Malibu Chamber of Commerce, another from the local sheriff's office, and a third from some nearby conservancy.

She wasn't sure if the man truly deserved all the honors, or if he was just fishing for stuff to put on his wall. The Seasons at Sea speech yesterday morning certainly suggested that he liked being in the limelight, but she was counting on there being more beneath the man's shiny surface. Otherwise coming here was likely a waste of time.

"I'm sorry to have kept you waiting," he said, putting down his pen, taking off his glasses, and looking up. His gray hair wasn't as tidy as at yesterday's speech and Hannah noted that while he wore a different tie and shirt, he had on the same suit jacket as yesterday. "Gina said you wanted to talk about Meredith Bartlett, correct?"

155

"Yes, sir."

"Mr. Goodman is fine," he told her, motioning for her to sit on the loveseat against the wall by the door. "Please, go ahead. What about Meredith?"

This is it—all the sneaking around, all the questions, just to present my suspicions to this guy, without any idea if it will do a bit of good.

Goodman stared at her, pretending to be patient. She shook off her apprehensions. If she was going to make a compelling case to Goodman, she had to *sound* compelling.

"I have important information about her death," she said, the words tumbling out more quickly than she liked. "We need to get the authorities to re-open the case."

Goodman looked at her quizzically and folded his hands on his desk, like a one-room schoolteacher preparing to deal with an unruly student.

"Why?" he asked. "My understanding is that she committed suicide. Do you have reason to doubt that?"

"I do, sir…Mr. Goodman. But I worry that no one will take me seriously."

Goodman sighed softly, apparently deciding how best to handle such a touchy situation.

"Why wouldn't you be taken seriously?" he asked.

"Look at me, Mr. Goodman," she replied. "I'm an underage resident in a psychiatric facility. That doesn't scream credibility."

"That shouldn't be disqualifying, Hannah," he said kindly. "Have you told someone about your concerns and had them dismissed?"

"No. I haven't told anyone else yet," she answered. "I was worried that if I went through—what do you call it—the chain of command, that what I had to say would never get to someone in a position to actually do something. That's why I came straight to you."

"Well," he said, his face now grave, "normally I don't approve of skipping steps in the process, but considering the seriousness of the matter, I'll make an exception. This is a judgment-free environment. So tell me what has you so troubled and I promise that I'll do my best to help."

"Okay," she said, closing her eyes tight. There was no more delaying. This was the moment of truth. "I think someone murdered Merry and made it look like a suicide."

She opened her eyes to find Goodman staring back at her, stunned. He tried to speak, then stopped himself, and tried again.

"I see why you hesitated in sharing this," he said quietly. "That's hard to accept. I say that not because I doubt your sincerity, but because the police investigated this. I saw their report. It was quite definitive. Now that doesn't mean you're wrong, of course. But I need to know why you feel differently than the authorities, the people who do this for a living."

"I know it sounds crazy, Mr. Goodman," Hannah said plaintively, "but I think the person who did this was afraid that Merry was about to reveal something about them and had to shut her up before she could."

Goodman leaned in closer, seemingly having trouble wrapping his head around what she was saying.

"What do you think she was going to reveal?" he asked.

Hannah opened her mouth, and then closed it, shaking her head.

"I can't say it," she whispered.

"Hannah," he said slightly sternly. "You've bravely come here. I know that can't have been easy for you. But you chose to come to me with this for a reason. Now I need you to put your trust in me. If you have some information that could change the nature of this case, you need to share that. I'll help get it to the people who need to have it and let them evaluate it fairly. But you can't come all this way and then, for lack of a better phrase, chicken out. Tell me."

Hannah nodded and looked at the floor as she answered.

"I think she was going to reveal that this person was sexually abusing her."

The room was silent for a long time. Hannah looked up to see Mr. Goodman staring blankly past her, his jaw open. Finally he swallowed hard and spoke.

"If this is true, then that means we have a potential predator on our campus," he said, his voice becoming more commanding with each new word. "Of course, we'll alert the authorities. But before we do that, I need to call security in for the rest of this conversation. I know it might not be easy for you to repeat this, but we need to have our people on high alert until we can get to the bottom of it. Hold on a moment."

He got up from behind his desk, hurried over to the door, and opened it wide.

"Gina," he said urgently but quietly, "I need you to go directly to the security office and ask Chief Gluck to come here immediately. Don't use the phone or speak to any intermediaries. Only talk to him. Tell him I have a situation that requires his assistance. Do you understand?"

"Yes, Mr. Goodman," Hannah heard Gina say. "I'll have him here as fast as I can."

"Thank you," he replied, "we'll be here waiting."

He closed the door and sighed heavily. This time, instead of returning to his desk, he took the chair opposite Hannah's loveseat. After wavering briefly, he appeared to have rediscovered his sense of authority.

"It's all going to be okay, Hannah," he said, putting his hands together as if praying for it to be so. "We'll have you tell Chief Gluck everything you told me. You can get into all the details at whatever pace you're comfortable with. But for now, I think you should at least tell me what kind of evidence you have. It's not that I doubt you, but the chief is going to ask the same question, so you should get used to talking about it."

"That makes sense," Hannah said. "Okay. I was in Merry's room earlier today—I know I shouldn't have gone in without permission—but I was looking for anything that could support my suspicions. And I found something—a single word carved into her headboard. It was faint, like she'd used her fingernails to scratch over the same area repeatedly."

"What was the word?"

Hannah gulped hard before answering. This was her one real piece of evidence. She needed it to be as impactful for him as it was for her.

"GRAND," she said loud and clear.

Goodman looked perplexed.

"I'm sorry, Hannah," he said, "maybe I'm missing something but I don't get the significance of the word."

"It was a clue," she explained. "Merry couldn't say who did this to her out loud so she wrote it down, or more accurately, scratched it down. Maybe she was hoping it would be discovered so that someone could rescue her. Maybe she was building up the courage to say the word out loud. Either way, the word points to the person who killed her, the one person who uses that word all the time."

Goodman's confused look slowly melted away, replaced by something she couldn't quite identify. But at this moment, Hannah wasn't worried about that. She took a deep breath and went for it.

"Have you figured it out yet, Mr. Goodman?" she asked, her voice rising in anger, "Because you should have. After all, you're the only person around here who says that word on a regular basis. In fact, I remember you using it a couple of times just yesterday in your Seasons at Sea speech. Maybe you've gotten so used to it that you don't even realize that you're saying it. But Merry did. Clearly, it was burned in her mind. Maybe scratching it into her headboard was her way of trying to exorcise it—and you—from her nightmares."

Goodman stood up, looking aghast.

"Are you actually accusing me of harming one of our residents? And all based on a single word scratched into a bed?" he demanded. "Why would you do such a thing? I think I should call Dr. Lemmon in here right now. Maybe she can talk some sense into you."

Hannah felt a flicker of panic. This wasn't the reaction she had anticipated. Had she guessed that wrong? Was it possible that Merry had just scratched the word into the headboard out of boredom? Could the resident in the room prior to her have done it? Her mind was swimming with uncertainty.

Goodman turned toward his desk, but instead of walking over to the phone, he stopped. With his back to her, he lifted his right hand up to his face and did something that she couldn't see.

Hannah stood up, her whole body tense, waiting to see what he would do next. When he turned around, there were deep, bloody scratches down the right side of his face. He had used his own nails to rake away the flesh. His mouth was twisted into a grotesque grimace.

She wanted to scream and opened her lips, but discovered that her voice wouldn't cooperate.

Her whole body had frozen up.

CHAPTER THIRTY THREE

Hannah gulped hard, willing herself to speak.

"What the…?" she started to whisper.

"Why would you do this to me?' he demanded, his voice echoing all around her.

"What is wrong with you?" she asked, finding her voice again as she took a side step toward the door. "Why would you scratch your own face like that?"

"I didn't do this, Hannah," he said, eerily composed. "You did. You came at me in a crazed frenzy, screaming that you had to get out of this place. I tried to calm you down but you wouldn't stop. I had to defend myself so I pushed you away. That's when you slammed your head on my desk. You died right there. I was horrified."

Hannah didn't need to hear anything else. She spun around and grabbed the office door, turning the knob, even though she was fairly certain it was locked. Sure enough, it was. She flashed back to Goodman telling Gina to get security and closing the door as he sighed heavily. He must have locked it then, using the sigh to cover the sound of the locking door, already knowing what he would do next.

She was about to smash the frosted glass of the door when he grabbed her by the wrist, yanking her backward. She stumbled, trying to keep her balance. With one hand on her wrist, he used the other to grab the back of her head. He cupped it like a melon and squeezed hard as he forced her over to his desk. Then he grasped a chunk of her hair and jerked her head back, before clutching the back of her skull again.

She could feel him shifting his weight so he could slam her forehead down onto the edge of his desk, when there was loud, sudden rap on his door. Goodman froze. Hannah didn't. She twisted around and reached up, clawing at the unmarked half of his face, ripping down as hard as she could.

160

Goodman screamed and let go. Hannah, off balance, dove away from him, in the direction of the door, landing on the floor a few feet from the locked doorknob.

"Help," Goodman yelled. "She's attacking me."

She saw a body moving quickly toward the frosted glass door and smash into it, sending it flying open. The glass shattered. Standing in the doorway was Brian, the tall, skinny, glasses-wearing psychiatric aide.

"Thank God you're here," Goodman bellowed. "She just came at me. Look what she did. I thought she was going to kill me. She kept saying 'First Merry, now you.'"

Brian nodded at his boss's words, almost like they were expected.

"Don't worry, Mr. Goodman," he said without even questioning the story. "We'll take care of her."

Hannah's heart sank. After all this, was her plan going to fall apart because of one of Goodman's lackeys? And how was he going to "take care of her?"

"That's not true—," Hannah began to object but Goodman shouted her down.

"She's gone crazy," he barked. "She was having paranoid delusions. I think she needs to go straight to the Assistance Wing. Once she's medicated, we can help her."

Brian grabbed Hannah by the forearms and pulled her up. She struggled to break free but his grip was too strong.

"I'll move her somewhere secure right away, Mr. Goodman," Brian promised, "but I think I know someone who might be better able to diagnose her."

"Who?" Goodman asked, not loving the idea.

"Me," Dr. Janice Lemmon said, stepping through the door with her cane in hand, her shoes crunching the glass on the carpet.

"Stand behind me," Brian whispered in Hannah's ear, letting go of her forearms.

She looked at him, confused for a second before a wave of understanding came over her. Brian wasn't Goodman's right hand man. He was Dr. Lemmon's.

"Thank goodness you're here, Janice," Goodman said. "Look at what this girl did to me. She's lost it."

"Is that true, Hannah? Have you lost it?" Dr. Lemmon asked.

"No."

"Oh dear," Lemmon said, seemingly troubled. "If only there was some way to definitively determine who was telling the truth."

Hannah reached into her pocket and pulled out the phone she'd been using to record everything that had happened since she stepped into Goodman's office.

"Maybe this will help," she replied.

Goodman looked at the phone. Hannah watched in real time as he began to comprehend how he'd been played. His face again contorted into the same grimace from when he'd raked at it with his fingernails. Without a word, he lunged at her, reaching out for the phone.

Before he got to her, Brian stepped forward, throwing a shoulder into the older man's chest. Goodman toppled backward, slamming into the floor. He'd barely hit the ground before Brian was zip-tying his wrists together, and then his ankles.

Dr. Lemmon stepped over to Hannah.

"Sorry for the delay in getting here," she said. "But I was on the phone with the sheriff, who's on his way here right now by the way. Our exchange took longer than I expected, which is why I sent Brian to check on you and make sure you were safe."

"You should have walked a little faster, Brian," Hannah said sharply.

"I'm sorry," he said. "I got caught in the hall by Goodman's assistant, who seemed panicky. I worried that if I just ignored her and ran this way, she'd get suspicious and warn Goodman."

"Please don't be too hard on him, Hannah," Lemmon said. "He had a lot to do this week, what with his normal job and watching out for you in my absence."

Hannah looked at Brian, who gave her a sheepish grin.

"Is that why you gave me all those weird looks this week?" she asked. "The way you were acting, I thought you might have killed Merry."

"I guess I'm not the best secret agent ever," he conceded.

"And that's why you came over when I was having lunch with Silvio earlier this week and threatened to put him in the Assistance Wing."

"He started yelling at you," Brian said. "I wasn't sure how far he'd take it. Dr. Lemmon instructed me to keep you safe, so I had to err on the side of caution."

162

"I get it," she said. "But he was just upset. Losing Merry was a big deal for him. He blamed himself, thinking he should have seen signs that she was considering suicide. If nothing else, this will ease him of that burden."

She sensed Dr. Lemmon's eyes on her and looked over.

"What?" she asked.

Lemmon smiled at her.

"I'm just impressed," she said. "I'm gone for a week and you make more progress than the entire time I was working with you."

"What do you mean?"

Lemmon took her by the arm and stepped out into the outer office where Brian and Goodman couldn't hear them.

"When you came into my office earlier today," she said quietly, "it wasn't to discuss your urges or your sister or how sick you were of being here. It was out of concern for someone else. Not a loved one, but a girl you barely knew who you believed deserved justice. Then you put yourself in harm's way to get her that justice. And just now, you expressed genuine concern a for a young man's emotional well-being. You did these things, not because they advantaged you in some way, but because you felt for these people."

"I didn't think about it that way," Hannah protested.

"Nonetheless, it's an enormous sign of growth, Hannah," Dr. Lemmon told her. "I believe that you always had the capacity for empathy. The flame was inside you the whole time. It was almost snuffed out of you by a series of traumas that would undo anyone. Your mother was murdered when you were a baby by your serial killer father. Then he returned years later and slaughtered your adoptive parents in front of you. You've been kidnapped and tortured and almost killed on multiple occasions. That would shut anyone down emotionally. But that flame still flickered, somewhere deep within you. And now it's started to grow. You just need to nurture it, to remember how good it feels to care about other people, especially when you don't expect to get anything in return. I know you got addicted to the thrill of danger, but isn't this better? You can get the high without the risk or the crash, and it's all natural."

Hannah didn't respond. She knew if she tried to speak that she would cry—something she hadn't allowed herself to do in years. Instead she just nodded. Dr. Lemmon didn't seem to expect an answer. Instead she simply pulled Hannah close, wrapping her arms around her and squeezing.

163

Despite her best efforts, Hannah started to cry anyway. And it felt good.

CHAPTER THIRTY FOUR

Jessie looked at her watch and frowned.

It was 2:02 p.m. They had less than fifteen minutes before Daryl Hinton would arrive at Central Station and they'd get a call from Captain Decker demanding answers. She tried not to worry about that as they pulled up in front of Amanda Bratton's house.

To cover their bases, they'd first gone to her dorm room to talk to her, but her roommate said she'd already gone home for the weekend. Luckily for them, her home was just a ten-minute drive to Santa Monica.

The house matched what she imagined was possible for a family that was willing and able to secretly shell out big money to get their daughter into a school she wasn't qualified for. A large, Tudor-style mansion, it sat on a street only five blocks from the ocean, along a stretch with similarly sized homes.

"Nice digs. I guess that's what you can get when mom is a cosmetics company executive and dad is a corporate banker," Ryan noted, referencing biographical information they'd gotten from Jamil. "If Tobias was paying Justin Carper twenty grand, I can only imagine how much he was getting from the Brattons."

"Unfortunately, he may have gotten something extra from Amanda," Jessie reminded him. "Shall we go in?"

Ryan nodded, chastened.

As they walked up the path to the house, Jessie felt the lack of sleep from last night really hit her. Her legs seemed heavy and her eyes ached. She tried to ignore all of it and focus on the task at hand. Ryan looked at his phone, reviewing the college admission application file on Amanda Bratton that Justin Carper had sent them.

"Based on the info in this file, and especially the photos," he said, "Amanda definitely doesn't seem like Tobias's type. She's tall, blonde, and curvy, without any interest in his area of expertise, or academics in general. She's way more of a social butterfly than I would expect him to go for."

"She may not have the look he gravitates toward," Jessie agreed. "But she's still his type in the crucial ways. She's emotionally vulnerable and open to manipulation. With those other girls, it was all about the internal—playing on their deep-seated self-consciousness about themselves. With Amanda it would have been more external pressure—emphasizing how embarrassing it would be to get kicked out of school after her parents bribed people to get in. She wouldn't want to look bad in front of her friends. Tobias would have exploited that."

They arrived at the door and Ryan rang the bell. The chime lasted for a good ten seconds and had just finished playing when the door opened. They were greeted by a large, barrel-chested, pink-cheeked guy in his mid-forties, with a shock of thick, blonde hair and brown eyes with deep crinkles at the corners. He was wearing casual slacks and a golf shirt with sweat stains at the armpits and near his rounded stomach.

"Can I help you?" he asked, with a big smile and a boisterous voice.

"Just wrap up eighteen holes?" Ryan asked, looking at the man's attire.

"Actually, yes," he replied amiably. "Was it the shirt or the sweat that gave me away?"

"It was the shirt," Ryan told him, "along with the pants, the sweat, the cap-matted hair, and the red cheeks that come from four hours on the course."

"You have me at a loss," the man said, laughing. "I'm Jason Bratton. Who are you, Sherlock Holmes? And is this your Watson?"

"Close," Ryan said, showing Bratton his badge. "I'm Detective Hernandez with the LAPD. This is our consultant, Jessie Hunt. I'd say that she's closer to Sherlock Holmes. Is your daughter, Amanda, here, Mr. Bratton?"

The man's wide grin faded instantly.

"No," he said, much more seriously now as he glanced behind him. "She's at an afternoon movie with her mother. Why? Is something wrong?"

"We hope not," Jessie told him, wondering if he was telling the truth about his daughter's whereabouts. "May we come in? We can explain what's going on but it's a bit of a sensitive matter."

"I suppose," Bratton said reluctantly, opening the door.

"Thanks," she said, stepping inside and holding up her phone. "You don't mind if we record this conversation, do you?"

"Why?"

"It protects both you and us," she said, hitting the record button. "What we need to discuss with you is difficult and not everybody reacts well. It's on now. Where should we talk?"

"The den, I guess," he said, leading them down a long hallway festooned with photos of the Bratton family.

"Where's your son?" she asked, pointing out a sullen-looking teenage boy in many of the pictures.

"He's at school," Bratton said as they entered the den, a massive room with vaulted ceilings and a TV at one end that Jessie guessed was 120 inches. "He's got a baseball game in an hour. I was about to head over there after I showered up."

"Is he any good?" Ryan asked as they took seats on a giant couch opposite his lounge chair.

"Very good," Bratton replied, his pride shining through despite his discomfort. "He made honorable mention all-area last year as a sophomore. He's already getting scholarship offers."

"Congratulations," Ryan said in a tone that Jessie recognized. He was about to get down to business.

"Thank you," Bratton replied.

"Speaking of college, that's why we're here," Ryan said bluntly. "There's no easy way to say this, Mr. Bratton, but we know that you paid Roman Tobias a large sum of money to get Amanda admitted to UCLA."

Bratton's look of paternal pride was immediately replaced by shock.

"Wait, what?" he asked. But to Jessie, his response seemed to be less a refutation and more simply astonishment at having this secret be called out so directly.

"There's no point in denying it, Mr. Bratton," Jessie replied, intent on keeping him off balance. "But that's not why we're here. I'm sure you've heard that Professor Tobias was murdered yesterday morning."

"Yes, of course," he answered, his eyes still wide. "It was all over the news, but what does that—?"

"We believe that Tobias was blackmailing Amanda," she interrupted, and then, after a long, uncomfortable pause, added the part she most dreaded telling a father about his daughter, "and forcing her to have sex with him in exchange for his silence about the payments you made."

Jason Bratton's face fell and the frantic energy seemed to drain out of his body. But it wasn't the reaction of a man getting shocking news. Instead, he had the bearing of a man forced to face a truth he'd tried to put out of his head.

"I get the sense that what I'm telling you isn't a surprise," she said quietly.

He was silent for a moment before taking a deep breath.

"No," he acknowledged. "She finally told me this week. She didn't know anything about the payments so she didn't believe him at first. But he showed her how there was no way she could have gotten in on her own. He told her that she wouldn't make it through four years there unless she 'did her part.'"

"Had she already done her part by the time she told you about the blackmail?" Ryan asked.

His lowered head and silence was all the answer they needed.

"So then you know why we're here," Jessie pressed. "It's not a stretch to imagine that in one of those private moments when Tobias was getting...reimbursed by Amanda, that it all became too much for her, and in a moment of blind fury, she lashed out and killed him."

Bratton looked up suddenly, horrified.

"There's no way she would do that," he asserted with a passion and certainty that took Jessie aback.

That's when all her doubts fell away. She still remembered the anonymous call from last night mentioning seeing a possible adult man leaving Tobias's office around 10:10 yesterday morning. From the moment Bratton conceded that he knew about what Tobias was making his daughter do, Jessie considered him a credible suspect.

"No," she said slowly. "Amanda didn't have to do anything because you did it for her."

He immediately shook his head but his eyes were less convincing.

"No, that not true," he said weakly.

"Let me stop you there, Mr. Bratton," Jessie said. "Detective Hernandez is going to read you your rights. If you still want to tell us why it's not true after that, feel free."

She waited as Ryan walked the man through the process. When he was done, he concluded by asking if Bratton was willing to speak with them. At first he didn't answer.

168

"That's fine," Jessie said preemptively. "If you don't want to talk, maybe Amanda will. Perhaps I'm wrong. After all, she's got just as strong a motive as you."

"No," Bratton exclaimed. "I'll talk. Leave her alone."

"Okay then," she said, not waiting for him to change his mind. "How much money did you pay Tobias?"

"$200,000," he said blankly. "Half up front and half once she was accepted."

"But that wasn't then end of it, was it?" she coaxed.

"No," he admitted. "Once the last quarter started, he came back at us and said that Amanda was struggling. He said he could surreptitiously tweak her grades but that it would require a twenty percent kicker. I told him no way. It was a one-time payment and we weren't going to be shaken down for another forty grand. That's when he went to Amanda. He told her that if she didn't do what he wanted, he'd reveal the secret payments. He said she'd be kicked out of school and that her parents would lose their jobs and be prosecuted. He demanded she pay him with…her body. Unfortunately, in that moment it didn't occur to Amanda that if it came out, he would be ruined too. So she did what he said."

"How did you find out about it?" Jessie asked gently.

"She came to me this week," he said, his voice clenching up in anger. "She said she would have kept doing it to protect us but that he made her do things that…she wouldn't get specific, but she showed me bruises. And her eyes had this hollow look to them. It was like he'd broken her."

Jessie nodded. She pictured Jason Bratton getting this information from his only daughter and another realization hit her. Tobias hadn't scheduled that secret 10 a.m. meeting. Bratton had.

"Let me guess," she said, "once you found out what was happening, you called Tobias and told him that you'd changed your mind, that you were open to paying him the $40,000 but that you needed to see him in person."

"That's right," Bratton said quietly. "I told him I wanted to look him in the eye and get his word that this would be the last payment. Of course, I knew his word meant nothing. It was just a way to get in a room with him."

Ryan spoke up.

"And you knew he'd be just as careful as you were to make sure the meeting would be secret."

"Yes," Bratton said. "He told me to wait by Royce Hall at 9:45 a.m. and that he'd call me on a burner phone with a time and location to meet. I got a call just before 10 to meet right away in his office. He was already there with the door open when I arrived. He actually patted me down and took my phone to make sure I wasn't recording him."

"But you weren't planning on recording what happened next, were you?" Jessie guessed.

Bratton shook his head.

"I didn't plan for it to happen that way," he insisted. "I walked in there thinking I would rough him up, maybe give him a pop or two in the mouth, and tell him never to go near my daughter again. I was going to remind him that this works two ways. If our little deal got out, he'd lose everything and go to prison too. But we never got that far."

"What do you mean?" Jessie asked.

"He was so arrogant," Bratton replied. "Before I even got to any of that, he started talking about me coming to my senses, but that now it was going to cost twenty-five percent. Then he offered me another option: to keep the payment at twenty percent and have Amanda pay off the rest in 'personal services.' He actually used that term. That's when I snapped."

"What did you do?" Ryan pressed.

"I saw that award on his shelf, the one with the scroll on it and I thought how heavy it must be. I grabbed it. His back was to me but he must have heard me pick it up. He turned around."

He stopped talking for a moment and Jessie thought he might be done, but then he continued. Tears were streaming down his face as he spoke.

"The only thing I regret is that he only had about half a second to process how badly he'd miscalculated before the thing crushed his skull in. I would have liked for him to have suffered a little more."

No one said anything for several seconds. Jessie recalled how upset she would have been if she'd had to bring in one of Tobias's young victims for his murder. This was almost as bad. Some part of her couldn't blame Bratton for what he had done. If Hannah had been victimized in the same way, would she have acted any differently? She wasn't sure she could say no. Finally, Ryan stood up, returning her to the moment.

"You know we have to take you into custody now, Mr. Bratton," he said quietly. "We can call your wife on the way downtown. She'll probably want to pick up your son before this breaks in the news."

Bratton nodded and stood up, holding out his hands.

"I assume you need to handcuff me," he said.

"I'm afraid so," Ryan told him, as he unhooked them from his belt. "It's a bit of a drive, maybe an hour at this time of day, so if you want to go to the bathroom, now would be the time."

"I'd appreciate that, thanks," Bratton said, somehow maintaining his good manners despite being arrested for murder. "All of a sudden, I really need to go."

Jessie stood up too and turned off the recorder on her phone. They had all they needed.

"That's fine," Ryan said. "But I'll have to go with you. No offense, but there are a lot of potential weapons in bathrooms and you've lost the benefit of the doubt."

"I understand," Bratton said, pausing for a moment to think. "In that case, there's one right over there in the corner, next to the stairs."

As they walked over, a thought came to Jessie.

"Those UCLA officers are probably close to arriving at the station with Daryl Hinton," she told Ryan. "I'll call Decker and let him know not to make any announcements regarding the case just yet. We can give him more details on the way in."

"Sounds good," Ryan said as Bratton led the way to the bathroom and Jessie started dialing.

Bratton was about to open the door when Ryan stopped him. "I need to check it out first," he said.

"Of course," Bratton said, stepping to the side.

Ryan opened the door to the darkened room and was just reaching in to turn on the light when, without warning, Bratton lunged at him and slammed his shoulder into his back. Ryan disappeared from sight.

CHAPTER THIRTY FIVE

Jessie got a sickening pit in her stomach as she heard a repeated thudding sound like Ryan was tumbling down a flight of stairs.

Before she could react, Jason Bratton slammed the door shut, grabbed a small, heavy-looking lamp from a table by the door and smashed it against the doorknob, knocking it off completely. Then he turned to face Jessie, holding a thick, pointed, porcelain shard from the destroyed lamp in his hand.

"I'm so sorry," he said, before darting through an adjoining door and out of sight.

"Hello," she heard Decker say on the phone. She had completely forgotten that she'd just called him. His voice sounded muffled and distant. "Hunt, is that you?"

Her body was frozen in shock at what she'd just seen. Had Bratton just killed Ryan right in front of her? The horror of that thought threatened to overwhelm her as she felt her knees buckle.

"Hunt, answer me!" Decker barked from a million miles away.

She reached out for the arm of the couch to steady herself as the world started to spin around her, a world without the man she loved.

And then a voice in her head shouted silently at her: *Stop this! You are in danger. Get control of yourself. Deal with the situation. Mourn later.*

She stood upright, shook her head forcefully, and pulled out her gun as she moved carefully toward the door.

"Captain Decker, send multiple units to 837 ½ Fifth Street in Santa Monica. Detective Hernandez is down. A suspect is unsecured and armed inside the house. Suspect's name is Jason Bratton."

"Repeat that, Hunt," Decker ordered. "Did you say Hernandez is down? Is he injured or dead?"

"I don't know," she whispered as she inched closer to the door. "Gotta go."

"Hunt!" Decker bellowed just before she hung up on him, never taking her eyes off the open space where Bratton had gone.

"Ryan!" she yelled as she peered around the corner into the room, which looked to be the kitchen. "Ryan, answer me. Are you okay?"

There was no response. She wanted to keep calling out to him or find another way to open the door but that wasn't the smart move. She had to eliminate the threat first.

Forcing herself to be quiet and focus, she stepped through the doorway into the kitchen. Her eyes darted everywhere, looking for any possible hiding place. There was an island in the middle of the room, which she edged around slowly. She glanced at the knife block on the counter and saw that nothing was missing from its slots. That offered her a moment of relief until she remembered that the porcelain lamp piece Bratton had been holding could do just as much damage as any knife.

She moved past the island and found no one there. The sliding door to the backyard was locked, which meant that Bratton was still inside. She kept her back to the door as she shuffled over to the pantry, keeping her eye on the only other doorway to the kitchen, next to the fridge on the opposite wall. The pantry door was closed but that didn't mean he wasn't inside. She turned the handle quickly and kicked the door open, then leapt over to get a clear view. It was empty.

She turned back around immediately. Now she had a clear view of both kitchen entry doors. She moved toward the one by the fridge, looking for any sign of movement, any hint of a shadow that might indicate Bratton was waiting there. She saw nothing.

Taking a deep breath, she prepared to dive into the hallway, when she heard a loud bang come from the den. She immediately ran that way, and rolled out of the kitchen into the room she'd just left. There was another bang. It was coming from the door Bratton had pushed Ryan through.

"Ryan?" she yelled, moving toward the door. "Ryan, can you hear me?"

She put her ear to the door and strained to hear a voice. But before she could detect anything on the other side, she heard a rustling sound from off to her right, just like the legs of a pair of casual slacks as someone ran in them.

She turned that way just in time to see Bratton flying at her from around the corner near the stairs. His arm was raised high above his head and he was gripping the porcelain shard from the lamp in his hand. There was no way she could raise her gun and shoot him before he plunged the thing into her.

So she did the only thing she could—lunge right back at him. She could only hope that by closing the space between them before he could bring the shard down, he would over-swing and miss her entirely.

Their bodies collided hard and she could hear him grunt as her shoulder slammed into his ribs. But her advantage was temporary as the force of his weight sent a shudder through her body and she felt herself toppling backward. She released her gun and threw her arms back, hoping to break her fall.

Her elbows hit the carpeted floor first and offered enough resistance to prevent the back of her head from slamming too hard. But a fraction of a second later, the full force of Bratton's body collapsed on her, knocking the wind out of her.

She lay there on her back, trying to gasp for air, as all 230 pounds of her attacker crushed her into the carpet. After a few eternal seconds, she managed to gulp down some air. As she did, she realized that Bratton was doing the same thing. He must have lost his breath in the fall as well.

She knew she didn't have long before he recovered, so she shoved her right hand against his ribs, hoping to roll him off her. The move seemed to shake him out of his inaction. He sucked in a greedy glug of air and looked down at her.

"Let me up!" she gasped.

He looked around and saw the same thing as she did. To his right, only a few feet away, was the porcelain shard, still intact, still a good four inches long.

"I'm sorry," he wheezed. "I can't. I still have time to get my family, maybe make it to Mexico. But not if you're alive."

He leaned over, straining to grab the shard. She clutched at him with her left hand, trying to prevent him from getting to it. Suddenly another slam from the locked door rattled the room, along with both of them.

"Jessie!"

It's Ryan! He's alive!

She looked at the door, hoping it would pop open. There was another slam but nothing happened. Heartened by that, Bratton reached for the shard again. Jessie clutched at him once more but her eyes were focused elsewhere. When she'd looked at the door, she

174

had seen something else: her gun, lying on the floor, just out of reach.

But maybe not. If she released her grip on Bratton, he would have to lift off her slightly to reach the shard. That might allow her enough space to grab the gun. It was just a matter of who would get to their weapon first.

She ignored the rattling door and fixed her eyes on her gun. Without another thought, she released her grip on Bratton's side. He wasn't expecting it and slumped to his right harder than anticipated, slightly off balance.

Jessie used her improved freedom of movement to thrust her body rightward, grabbing the gun handle just as she felt Bratton regroup on top of her. She didn't look to see if he had the shard in his hand. Instead, she gripped the gun and slammed its butt hard into his left temple.

He looked momentarily stunned, hovering over her like a tree that had been cut but had yet to fall. She didn't wait to see if he would, rearing back and smashing the butt of the gun into the same spot as before. She felt his body slacken—not completely, but enough for her to shove him off her.

He toppled to his right, woozy but not unconscious. He was lying on his side, holding the shard in his hand, though he didn't seem to realize it.

Jessie rolled to her right and scrambled to her knees, pointing the gun at him.

"Drop the shard," she ordered over the constant slamming of the nearby door, her voice still raspy from lack of air.

Bratton looked down at his hand, only then comprehending that he was still holding a weapon.

"I can't," he said. "Either I kill you and escape with my family or you kill me and they can start over."

"Those aren't your only options, Jason," she said, using his first name in the hopes it might help reach him. "Your family loves you. Your kids need you. They would rather have you in their lives somehow than not at all. Trust me. I speak from experience."

He started to respond when they heard another loud bang. The locked door suddenly sprang open and Ryan shot through, collapsing onto the floor between them. Bratton turned to look at him in confusion. Jessie didn't.

Instead, she switched the gun to her left hand, pulled out her taser, and turned it on as she dove at Bratton. He looked back at her just as she shoved it against the exposed skin on his neck. A garbled sound, part scream and part groan, exploded from his throat just before he tumbled to the ground, twitching.

She flicked the shard of porcelain away from his now empty hand, rolled him onto his stomach, holstered her gun and taser, pulled out her handcuffs, and slapped them on his wrists. A few feet away from her, Ryan pushed himself off the ground and maneuvered himself into a seated position on the floor.

"Are you okay?" she asked, climbing off Bratton and crawling over to him.

"I think so," he said uncertainly. "Everything seems to be in working order. But I guess I'm not back at full 'smash through the door' strength."

"Well, you *were* shoved down a flight of stairs," she pointed out. "Give yourself a minute."

"Yeah," he replied. "I wasn't expecting a basement in a house in Santa Monica. It took me by surprise."

"Me too," Jessie said, fighting off a sudden lump in her throat. "I thought I'd lost you."

He gave her a kiss and then pulled back with a wry grin on his face.

"No way," he said sarcastically. "I had to stick around to rescue you."

They both surveyed the wreckage in the room, the handcuffed man on the floor, and Ryan's minimal involvement in all of it. Jessie smiled back.

"My hero."

CHAPTER THIRTY SIX

They were halfway to Central Station when the idea came to Jessie.

She couldn't say anything right away because they were in the middle of talking to Decker. Jessie was driving because Ryan still felt a little shaky after his tumble. Soreness and exhaustion were taking their toll on her too, but she kept that to herself.

"So I guess we're releasing this Hinton guy," the captain said.

"Yes, sir," she replied. "Even if we didn't have Jason Bratton's confession, I just got word from Jamil that Hinton's GPS data shows him at home. He's in the clear."

"He'll be happy," Decker said wryly. "He's only been in lockup for about ten minutes and he's already begging for his wife."

"I think he's hoping this is what will get her to come back to him, "Ryan said. "He shouldn't hold his breath."

"All right," Decker said. "I'll give him the good news. What about that admissions officer, Justin Carper? When are you charging him for taking those payoffs?"

Jessie knew that was coming but sighed anyway.

"I was hoping that we could explore getting him immunity if he helps make a case against the Orange County congresswoman who paid to get her son admitted," she said. "He was a victim of Tobias too. If we can nail a corrupt politician and avoid ruining this guy's life, I'd like to try."

"Talk to the D.A. to see if they'll get on board," Decker said. "In the meantime, when is the squad car with Bratton getting here?"

"It'll be there before us," Jessie said. "We wanted to stop by the UCLA station first to thank Lieutenant Schrader for his help. I'm also coordinating with their campus CARE program to set up a meeting with all of Tobias's victims together. I'm hoping to coordinate a support group where they can try to make sense of what happened to them. They're going to need each other."

"Okay," Decker said. "I'll see you soon. Good work, you two. I look forward to throwing this back in Chief Laird's face, though that's off the record."

He hung up before Jessie could thank him for that. They came to a red light, where Jessie stopped, pulled out her phone, and quickly sent a text. Then she turned to Ryan.

"You still doing okay?" she asked.

"I'll survive," he told her, "but I may need to lie in a bath of liquid Advil for a few hours tonight."

"I'm not sure that's how that works," she cracked as her phone buzzed. She read the message, and then added, "but I might have another idea that might ease your pain a little."

"I'm all ears, "Ryan said, settling into his seat as the light turned green and they started up again.

"I was thinking," she continued, her eyes focused on the road. "Almost losing you today *again* really crystallized things for me. I think we should get married."

Ryan laughed.

"I thought we were already doing that."

"No," she said, "I mean soon, like before the end of the month."

Ryan popped up in his seat.

"Are you serious?" he asked. "The end of this month is in two weeks!"

"I know but I don't want to wait," she said. "I was thinking, those folks down at the Peninsula resort in Palos Verdes might help us out on short notice. We did solve a murder in their spa and save them from a ton of bad publicity. I think they'd be willing to accommodate a tiny wedding party. All told, we're probably talking a dozen people."

Ryan had a goofy grin on his face, as if he was on the first drop of a massive rollercoaster.

"I think it might be slightly bigger than that, Jessie," he said. "I know we're keeping it small, but there are going to be more than a dozen people who will show up, whether you invite them or not. Regardless, we should definitely ask."

Jessie tried and failed to stifle a giggle.

"What?" he demanded.

"I already did," she said, holding up her phone. "I just texted Hugo, our friendly neighborhood head of security at Peninsula. He says they'd be honored to have us and that they'd give us a discounted rate of $0. He suggested the 26th, pending your approval. Do you approve?"

"Do I approve? If you weren't driving a vehicle in L.A. traffic, I'd kiss you right now."

"Before or after your Advil bath?" she teased.

Before he could answer, her phone rang. Reluctantly, she glanced at it.

"It's Kat," she said. "I better take it."

She'd barely hit "accept" before Kat started speaking.

"You guys okay?" she asked. "I heard over the scanner that you had an incident in Santa Monica."

"It was touch and go there for a while, but we're okay now," Jessie replied. "Ryan decided to jump down a flight of stairs."

"Not even close to accurate," he noted drily.

"Well, it sounds like you're in good moods, so I hate to bring things down," Kat said, "but I have bad news."

"Go ahead," Jessie replied, trying to keep the apprehension out of her voice.

"I've spent the last two days trying to find some proof that Andy Robinson was involved with either the Livia Bucco or Eden Roth attacks. I couldn't."

"You don't think she was?" Jessie asked, taken by surprise.

"No, I absolutely do. It's just that she's covered her tracks so well that they're invisible. I even went to see her, hoping to shake something loose."

Jessie suddenly felt a sense of dread.

"I wish you hadn't done that," she said. "Now you're on her radar. You don't want that."

"Jessie Hunt," Kat countered, mildly offended, "you know I can take care of myself. Anyway, it was a last-ditch effort to rattle her."

"Did she talk to you?" Ryan asked.

"Yes, for a while actually," she answered. "She walked me through her connections to both Livia and Eden. I could tell she was lying. She didn't really even try to hide it. But she didn't make any slip-ups. Her story was airtight, even if it was a total fabrication. All this is to say I don't have any new ammunition we can use for her hearing, which is still on for 3:30 today."

"Well, it was worth a shot," Jessie told her, attempting to hide her disappointment.

"There is one last option," Kat said. "You could show up and make a personal plea to the parole board. Remind them what she did to Victoria Missinger, how she coldly murdered her and framed an innocent woman for it. Describe how she laced your drink with peanut oil when she realized you were going to figure it out, knowing you were deathly allergic. Maybe it will be harder for them to let her go free if they have to look you in the eyes. It might not work but it can't hurt."

Jessie looked over at Ryan, who shrugged.

"It's 3:07 now and we're headed that way anyway," he said. "We could probably just make it in time. If you're up for it, we can have Decker keep Jason Bratton on ice for a little longer."

Jessie nodded.

"I think they've already made their decision," she replied, "but I may as well try. I don't want to look back on this and think I could have done something and didn't."

"Good," Kat said. "If you want, I'll start a protest in front of the building."

"That's okay," Jessie laughed. "I think you already gone above and beyond. Thanks for trying, Kat. You're a good friend."

"I'm just sorry I couldn't do more," Kat said.

After she hung up, they drove in silence, bummed at how their giddiness from a few minutes ago had been unceremoniously snuffed out.

"Still want to marry me?" Jessie finally asked, hoping to lighten the mood. "I tend to attract the crazy."

"How do you think you snagged me?" he countered with a grin.

"Are you kidding? You're the least crazy person I know."

The phone rang again. Jessie looked at the caller ID. It was Dr. Lemmon. She answered on the first ring.

"Is Hannah okay?"

"She's fine," Lemmon answered immediately. "But there's been a situation. I wanted to call earlier but I was stuck talking to the sheriff."

"The sheriff? Why? What happened?"

"Calm down, Jessie," the doctor said slowly. "Everything is okay now. It's hard to explain what happened. But the gist is that your sister solved a murder that was committed here at Seasons."

"I'm sorry—what?"

"I'll get to all of that," Lemmon promised, "but more importantly, she's asking for you. I think she really needs you. Can you come out here now?"

Ryan glanced over at her and Jessie knew what he was thinking: this almost certainly meant that, without her voice in opposition, Andy Robinson would walk free. But there wasn't really a choice. He said nothing as she pulled off the freeway at the approaching exit.

"We'll be there right away," she said.

CHAPTER THIRTY SEVEN

By the time they arrived, they already knew everything.

On the drive over, Dr. Lemmon told them about Hannah's suspicions regarding Merry's death, her dogged investigation into it, her discovery of the scratched word in the dead girl's bedroom, and her plan to entrap Marshall Goodman, which Lemmon helped put into action.

Jessie held her tongue on that last matter for now, though she had a bone to pick with the therapist over letting Hannah put herself at risk. Mostly she was overwhelmed.

"I'm not sure whether to be proud, angry, or both," she told Ryan as they hurried through the facility to meet Hannah in Dr. Lemmon's office.

"Maybe stick with the first option for now," he suggested.

"You're right," Jessie agreed. "Mostly, I'm just happy that she's okay."

They rounded the corner and Lemmon's office came into view. Jessie could see multiple people inside, including the tiny doctor, who was leaning on a cane, the sheriff, and two men she didn't recognize—one in a lab coat and another, a tall skinny blonde guy with glasses. Then she saw Hannah. She broke into a run.

Hannah heard the footsteps echoing in the hall and turned around. Suddenly she was running too. They reached each other just outside the office, both throwing their arms around the other sister and squeezing tight. Jessie could feel Hannah's chest heaving and knew she was crying. She did too. Neither spoke for a long time. When they finally released each other, Jessie looked in her little sister's wet eyes.

"I'm glad you're safe," she whispered.

"I'm glad you're here," Hannah whispered back.

Ryan stood awkwardly off to the side until the younger sister pulled him in for a group hug.

"I hear you've had a busy day," he cracked when they all separated.

"She has," Dr. Lemmon said, joining them in the hall along with the man in the lab coat, which had the name "Dr. Kenneth Tam" written on it. "If not for her, we'd have no idea what really happened."

"Your sister really is an incredible young woman," Dr. Tam volunteered, "even if she did kind of break into my office."

Jessie looked over at Hannah, who turned slightly pink.

"I'm sorry," she said. "I got so invested in figuring this out that I went a little overboard. I guess I misjudged you."

"Don't worry," he replied with a smile. "I'm not pressing charges or anything. You were looking out for someone who needed it. I was actually trying to do the same thing. I suspected that Meredith might be suffering some kind of abuse as well. I had been trying to get her to open up. That's why I didn't take any notes during our sessions. I hoped to gain her trust by letting her know I would just listen and not write anything down. I felt like we were getting close to a breakthrough."

"Unfortunately," Dr. Lemmon explained to Jessie and Ryan, "apparently so did Goodman. He must have sensed that Merry was on the verge of revealing what he was doing to her to Dr. Tam. So he killed her and made it look like a suicide. With his access to all the patient rooms, along with his knowledge of staff schedules and camera placement, it wouldn't have been difficult for him to get in and out of her room without being seen."

"I only wish I could have gotten her to open up in time," Dr. Tam muttered, his head down.

"It shouldn't have come to that," Dr. Lemmon said. "We were supposed to be a safe haven for our residents and we failed to meet that responsibility. We're going to conduct a thorough internal audit of our procedures. I've also asked the sheriff's department to do their own investigation. This happened right under our noses and it's not acceptable."

"I'd like to be with you when you tell her family," Hannah said quietly. "I don't want them to just hear about the awful things that happened to her. I want them to know how Merry brightened lives around here, including mine."

"Of course," Dr. Lemmon said.

"Dr. Tam," the sheriff called out from Lemmon's office. "I have a few more questions for you if you don't mind."

"Excuse me," Tam said and returned to the office.

183

"He seems like a decent guy," Ryan said once he was gone.

"Actually, he's an arrogant, condescending jerk who is overly reliant on medication as a cure-all," Hannah said. "But he's not a killer and he seems to care, so there's that."

"A topic for another time," Dr. Lemmon said, stifling a smile. "For now, we have a more pressing matter."

"What's that?" Jessie asked.

"Well, for the time being at least," Lemmon told her, "I don't think Seasons can offer the standard of care that Hannah deserves. And while I'm not convinced that we've reached all of our therapeutic goals, I've seen incredible progress of late."

"How so?" Jessie asked.

"She has begun to cultivate a real sense of empathy for others," Dr. Lemmon said, "something I wasn't sure we could easily unearth two weeks ago. In addition, she has worked hard on techniques to redirect her urges to recapture the ecstasy she felt after the…passing of the Night Hunter."

Jessie was impressed with how Dr. Lemmon managed to cryptically refer to the fact that Hannah got a high from killing a man and, until recently, was actively looking for other potential opportunities.

"She still has work to do in terms of seeking out less dangerous ways of finding thrills," Lemmon continued, "but at least now she's started directing that inclination toward helping others rather than just pursuing that intensity merely for the sake of it."

"I still have a long way to go," Hannah conceded.

"That's true," Lemmon agreed, "but I might argue that in your pursuit of living passionately, you're not all that different from people with jobs that help the public while providing an adrenaline rush, like for example, firefighters, police officers, and criminal profilers."

She raised her eyebrows as she uttered that last line. Out of the corner of her eye, Jessie could see Hannah trying not to giggle.

"So where are you suggesting she go, Dr. Lemmon?" she asked, skipping over the comparison being drawn.

Lemmon smiled pleasantly, seeming to enjoy Jessie's sudden discomfort.

"I'm suggesting that, while we get a longer term solution sorted out, Hannah return home for now. She would need to continue to have daily therapy sessions with me, either in person or in a telehealth situation. She would also need to stay vigilant with her meds. Finally, she would have to agree to constant check-ins with you, as well as a limit on extra-curricular activities outside of school, including friend hangouts or solo outings. We can slowly re-integrate those based on her ability to meet prescribed goals. How would that arrangement work for everyone?"

Jessie looked at Hannah, who spoke first.

"I'd like that very much," she said. "How about you guys?"

Jessie exchanged looks with Ryan.

"I'll do whatever you two want," he said, "but it sounds reasonable to me."

Jessie was torn. She desperately wanted for her sister to be able to finish her senior year at an actual high school instead of in a psychiatric facility. She also wanted to recreate those family dinners, where Hannah whipped up delicious meals while she and Ryan watched in amazement. She wanted to sit on the couch together and watch bad TV. Mostly she just wanted a return to normalcy.

But she feared that once Hannah was back in her old environment, her old habits would return too: the emotional shutdowns, the self-destructive need to take crazy risks, the terrifying bloodlust.

Plus there were the external concerns. Would Hannah be able to handle the stress of the upcoming wedding? How would she adapt to Jessie's impending change from college instructor and sometime LAPD consultant to full-time profiler who worked at all hours? And what would happen if Andy Robinson was released and decided to inject herself into their lives?

But as she looked at her little sister, Jessie made a choice—to let hope trump fear. Her sister deserved a second chance. It was time she got one. She gave Dr. Lemmon her answer.

"Let's do it."

EPILOGUE

Andy couldn't hide her disappointment.

She'd waited patiently, sitting in her blue shirt and gray pants in the parole hearing room, waiting for Jessie Hunt to burst in, call this whole process a travesty of justice, and appeal to the board members' better nature. But she never came.

Just like Jessie never came to meet with her at the PDC, sending her new BFF in her place. Maybe she had just moved on. Maybe she didn't care about Andy's ability to "help" track down unstable women intent on committing heinous crimes. Maybe she was more focused on her friend and her fiancé and her little sister.

That would have to change. Andy knew what it would take. She'd have to make herself invaluable, so that Jessie had no choice but to ask for her help, or be instructed to accept it, whether she wanted to or not. There were ways to do that. She still had several cards to play— including additional acolytes like Zoe and Corinne, ready to her bidding, just waiting for her coded authorization to wreak havoc on the city and its unsuspecting citizens.

And if that didn't bring Jessie back to her, she'd have to take more drastic measures, hit closer to home. That would be a lot easier now.

She stepped out of the Western Regional Women's Psychiatric Detention Center, wearing street clothes for the first time in two years, and strode confidently to the waiting cab. It was good to breathe fresh air. It was good to decide when and where she would go next. It was good to be free.

*

Zoe Bradway watched the evening news with bated breath.

The Principal only spoke to the press briefly after her parole hearing but Zoe parsed every word. Andy apologized for her past actions, thanked the board for their mercy, and promised to do all she could to help keep Los Angeles safe.

186

But she never used the words Zoe was waiting for. She never spoke the code phrase authorizing her to activate the plan she'd spent five months working on.

Zoe was disappointed but she understood. The time wasn't right. It wasn't her place to question the Principal's decisions. Her only task was to be ready to act when she was called upon, whether that was in a day, a week, or a year.

She knew the time would come. And when it did, she would complete her task, filling Andy's heart with pride and everyone else's with terror.

NOW AVAILABLE!

THE PERFECT HUSBAND
(A Jessie Hunt Psychological Suspense Thriller—Book Twenty-Two)

Wealthy Beverly Hills couples are being found dead, with seemingly nothing to connect them other than their troubled marriages. Jessie senses a pattern, and knows this killer will strike again. But can she outwit him in time?

"A masterpiece of thriller and mystery."
—Books and Movie Reviews, Roberto Mattos (re Once Gone)

THE PERFECT HUSBAND is book #22 in a new psychological suspense series by bestselling author Blake Pierce, which begins with *The Perfect Wife*, a #1 bestseller (and free download) with over 5,000 five-star ratings and 1,000 five-star reviews.

Jessie encounters a wall as she pries into the private lives and marriages of the rich. But beneath the seemingly perfect façade, she senses a dark undercurrent—one that lead to all of these couples' deaths.

But can she enter this killer's mind fast enough to solve the thread that connects them before he strikes again?

A fast-paced psychological suspense thriller with unforgettable characters and heart-pounding suspense, the JESSIE HUNT series is a riveting new series that will leave you turning pages late into the night.

Books #23 and #24 in the series—THE PERFECT SCANDAL and THE PERFECT MASK—are now also available.

"An edge of your seat thriller in a new series that keeps you turning pages! ...So many twists, turns and red herrings... I can't wait to see what happens next."
—Reader review (Her Last Wish)

"A strong, complex story about two FBI agents trying to stop a serial killer. If you want an author to capture your attention and have you guessing, yet trying to put the pieces together, Pierce is your author!"
—Reader review (Her Last Wish)

"A typical Blake Pierce twisting, turning, roller coaster ride suspense thriller. Will have you turning the pages to the last sentence of the last chapter!!!"
—Reader review (City of Prey)

"Right from the start we have an unusual protagonist that I haven't seen done in this genre before. The action is nonstop... A very atmospheric novel that will keep you turning pages well into the wee hours."
—Reader review (City of Prey)

"Everything that I look for in a book... a great plot, interesting characters, and grabs your interest right away. The book moves along at a breakneck pace and stays that way until the end. Now on go I to book two!"
—Reader review (Girl, Alone)

"Exciting, heart pounding, edge of your seat book... a must read for mystery and suspense readers!"
—Reader review (Girl, Alone)

Blake Pierce

Blake Pierce is the USA Today bestselling author of the RILEY PAGE mystery series, which includes seventeen books. Blake Pierce is also the author of the MACKENZIE WHITE mystery series, comprising fourteen books; of the AVERY BLACK mystery series, comprising six books; of the KERI LOCKE mystery series, comprising five books; of the MAKING OF RILEY PAIGE mystery series, comprising six books; of the KATE WISE mystery series, comprising seven books; of the CHLOE FINE psychological suspense mystery, comprising six books; of the JESSE HUNT psychological suspense thriller series, comprising twenty four books; of the AU PAIR psychological suspense thriller series, comprising three books; of the ZOE PRIME mystery series, comprising six books; of the ADELE SHARP mystery series, comprising fifteen books, of the EUROPEAN VOYAGE cozy mystery series, comprising four books; of the new LAURA FROST FBI suspense thriller, comprising nine books (and counting); of the new ELLA DARK FBI suspense thriller, comprising eleven books (and counting); of the A YEAR IN EUROPE cozy mystery series, comprising nine books, of the AVA GOLD mystery series, comprising six books (and counting); of the RACHEL GIFT mystery series, comprising six books (and counting); of the VALERIE LAW mystery series, comprising nine books (and counting); of the PAIGE KING mystery series, comprising six books (and counting); and of the MAY MOORE suspense thriller series, comprising six books (and counting).

An avid reader and lifelong fan of the mystery and thriller genres, Blake loves to hear from you, so please feel free to visit www.blakepierceauthor.com to learn more and stay in touch.

BOOKS BY BLAKE PIERCE

MAY MOORE SUSPENSE THRILLER
NEVER RUN (Book #1)
NEVER TELL (Book #2)
NEVER LIVE (Book #3)
NEVER HIDE (Book #4)
NEVER FORGIVE (Book #5)
NEVER AGAIN (Book #6)

PAIGE KING MYSTERY SERIES
THE GIRL HE PINED (Book #1)
THE GIRL HE CHOSE (Book #2)
THE GIRL HE TOOK (Book #3)
THE GIRL HE WISHED (Book #4)
THE GIRL HE CROWNED (Book #5)
THE GIRL HE WATCHED (Book #6)

VALERIE LAW MYSTERY SERIES
NO MERCY (Book #1)
NO PITY (Book #2)
NO FEAR (Book #3
NO SLEEP (Book #4)
NO QUARTER (Book #5)
NO CHANCE (Book #6)
NO REFUGE (Book #7)
NO GRACE (Book #8)
NO ESCAPE (Book #9)

RACHEL GIFT MYSTERY SERIES
HER LAST WISH (Book #1)
HER LAST CHANCE (Book #2)
HER LAST HOPE (Book #3)
HER LAST FEAR (Book #4)
HER LAST CHOICE (Book #5)
HER LAST BREATH (Book #6)

AVA GOLD MYSTERY SERIES
CITY OF PREY (Book #1)
CITY OF FEAR (Book #2)
CITY OF BONES (Book #3)
CITY OF GHOSTS (Book #4)
CITY OF DEATH (Book #5)
CITY OF VICE (Book #6)

A YEAR IN EUROPE
A MURDER IN PARIS (Book #1)
DEATH IN FLORENCE (Book #2)
VENGEANCE IN VIENNA (Book #3)
A FATALITY IN SPAIN (Book #4)

ELLA DARK FBI SUSPENSE THRILLER
GIRL, ALONE (Book #1)
GIRL, TAKEN (Book #2)
GIRL, HUNTED (Book #3)
GIRL, SILENCED (Book #4)
GIRL, VANISHED (Book 5)
GIRL ERASED (Book #6)
GIRL, FORSAKEN (Book #7)
GIRL, TRAPPED (Book #8)
GIRL, EXPENDABLE (Book #9)
GIRL, ESCAPED (Book #10)
GIRL, HIS (Book #11)

LAURA FROST FBI SUSPENSE THRILLER
ALREADY GONE (Book #1)
ALREADY SEEN (Book #2)
ALREADY TRAPPED (Book #3)
ALREADY MISSING (Book #4)
ALREADY DEAD (Book #5)
ALREADY TAKEN (Book #6)
ALREADY CHOSEN (Book #7)
ALREADY LOST (Book #8)
ALREADY HIS (Book #9)

EUROPEAN VOYAGE COZY MYSTERY SERIES
MURDER (AND BAKLAVA) (Book #1)

DEATH (AND APPLE STRUDEL) (Book #2)
CRIME (AND LAGER) (Book #3)
MISFORTUNE (AND GOUDA) (Book #4)
CALAMITY (AND A DANISH) (Book #5)
MAYHEM (AND HERRING) (Book #6)

ADELE SHARP MYSTERY SERIES
LEFT TO DIE (Book #1)
LEFT TO RUN (Book #2)
LEFT TO HIDE (Book #3)
LEFT TO KILL (Book #4)
LEFT TO MURDER (Book #5)
LEFT TO ENVY (Book #6)
LEFT TO LAPSE (Book #7)
LEFT TO VANISH (Book #8)
LEFT TO HUNT (Book #9)
LEFT TO FEAR (Book #10)
LEFT TO PREY (Book #11)
LEFT TO LURE (Book #12)
LEFT TO CRAVE (Book #13)
LEFT TO LOATHE (Book #14)
LEFT TO HARM (Book #15)

THE AU PAIR SERIES
ALMOST GONE (Book#1)
ALMOST LOST (Book #2)
ALMOST DEAD (Book #3)

ZOE PRIME MYSTERY SERIES
FACE OF DEATH (Book#1)
FACE OF MURDER (Book #2)
FACE OF FEAR (Book #3)
FACE OF MADNESS (Book #4)
FACE OF FURY (Book #5)
FACE OF DARKNESS (Book #6)

A JESSIE HUNT PSYCHOLOGICAL SUSPENSE SERIES
THE PERFECT WIFE (Book #1)
THE PERFECT BLOCK (Book #2)
THE PERFECT HOUSE (Book #3)

THE PERFECT SMILE (Book #4)
THE PERFECT LIE (Book #5)
THE PERFECT LOOK (Book #6)
THE PERFECT AFFAIR (Book #7)
THE PERFECT ALIBI (Book #8)
THE PERFECT NEIGHBOR (Book #9)
THE PERFECT DISGUISE (Book #10)
THE PERFECT SECRET (Book #11)
THE PERFECT FAÇADE (Book #12)
THE PERFECT IMPRESSION (Book #13)
THE PERFECT DECEIT (Book #14)
THE PERFECT MISTRESS (Book #15)
THE PERFECT IMAGE (Book #16)
THE PERFECT VEIL (Book #17)
THE PERFECT INDISCRETION (Book #18)
THE PERFECT RUMOR (Book #19)
THE PERFECT COUPLE (Book #20)
THE PERFECT MURDER (Book #21)
THE PERFECT HUSBAND (Book #22)
THE PERFECT SCANDAL (Book #23)
THE PERFECT MASK (Book #24)

CHLOE FINE PSYCHOLOGICAL SUSPENSE SERIES
NEXT DOOR (Book #1)
A NEIGHBOR'S LIE (Book #2)
CUL DE SAC (Book #3)
SILENT NEIGHBOR (Book #4)
HOMECOMING (Book #5)
TINTED WINDOWS (Book #6)

KATE WISE MYSTERY SERIES
IF SHE KNEW (Book #1)
IF SHE SAW (Book #2)
IF SHE RAN (Book #3)
IF SHE HID (Book #4)
IF SHE FLED (Book #5)
IF SHE FEARED (Book #6)
IF SHE HEARD (Book #7)

THE MAKING OF RILEY PAIGE SERIES
WATCHING (Book #1)
WAITING (Book #2)
LURING (Book #3)
TAKING (Book #4)
STALKING (Book #5)
KILLING (Book #6)

RILEY PAIGE MYSTERY SERIES
ONCE GONE (Book #1)
ONCE TAKEN (Book #2)
ONCE CRAVED (Book #3)
ONCE LURED (Book #4)
ONCE HUNTED (Book #5)
ONCE PINED (Book #6)
ONCE FORSAKEN (Book #7)
ONCE COLD (Book #8)
ONCE STALKED (Book #9)
ONCE LOST (Book #10)
ONCE BURIED (Book #11)
ONCE BOUND (Book #12)
ONCE TRAPPED (Book #13)
ONCE DORMANT (Book #14)
ONCE SHUNNED (Book #15)
ONCE MISSED (Book #16)
ONCE CHOSEN (Book #17)

MACKENZIE WHITE MYSTERY SERIES
BEFORE HE KILLS (Book #1)
BEFORE HE SEES (Book #2)
BEFORE HE COVETS (Book #3)
BEFORE HE TAKES (Book #4)
BEFORE HE NEEDS (Book #5)
BEFORE HE FEELS (Book #6)
BEFORE HE SINS (Book #7)
BEFORE HE HUNTS (Book #8)
BEFORE HE PREYS (Book #9)
BEFORE HE LONGS (Book #10)
BEFORE HE LAPSES (Book #11)
BEFORE HE ENVIES (Book #12)

BEFORE HE STALKS (Book #13)
BEFORE HE HARMS (Book #14)

AVERY BLACK MYSTERY SERIES
CAUSE TO KILL (Book #1)
CAUSE TO RUN (Book #2)
CAUSE TO HIDE (Book #3)
CAUSE TO FEAR (Book #4)
CAUSE TO SAVE (Book #5)
CAUSE TO DREAD (Book #6)

KERI LOCKE MYSTERY SERIES
A TRACE OF DEATH (Book #1)
A TRACE OF MURDER (Book #2)
A TRACE OF VICE (Book #3)
A TRACE OF CRIME (Book #4)
A TRACE OF HOPE (Book #5)